DIVIDED WARRIORS

INTERGALACTIC ENOSIS: THE PYXIS SYSTEM

AURORA WELKIN

ALSO BY AURORA WELKIN

DIVIDED WARRIORS

INTERGALACTIC ENOSIS: THE PYXIS SYSTEM

BOOK 3

AURORA WELKIN

ISBN: 978-0-6489774-5-2

Cover design: Kasmit Designs

Editor: Stephanie Pretorius, Clause for Effect

❀ Created with Vellum

This book is dedicated to all my lovely readers.
You guys are the best, and I appreciate every single one of you!

THE ROYALS OF SABER

Kali

I should have been dreaming, yet sleep evaded.

Snuggled as I was between Rorc, who was lying on his stomach, and Mes, who had his arm draped over me, I should have been able to rest.

Instead, I lay wet, dissatisfied, and aching. Deep and fervent longing filled me as I traced my mates' naked bodies in our reflection in the mirrored ceiling.

All of them had loved this feature when we'd stayed at the Wravukian palace, so Arana had warriors install them in our palatial chambers too.

It had its advantages...I loved to watch their muscles ripple and their faces strain while they did everything in their power to make me orgasm as many times as possible before they reached their peaks.

I trailed my fingers along Mes's forearm.

He didn't even stir.

Argh, I swear they do it on purpose.

Let's punish them. Then they'll realize they've been neglecting your needs, Dawn—my occasionally bloodthirsty sabertooth, and willing conspirator—said.

A sigh escaped my lips. Unfortunately, drawing orgasms from me wasn't something they did anymore. As my pregnancy progressed and my belly grew, they became more distant.

Oh, they were still doting on me, the perfect mates really... unless it came to sex. Then they turned into guardians, like I was a fragile being about to break if they touched me intimately.

It frustrated me to no end. My mood had soured, and my patience was wearing thin.

I freely admitted that the first trimester hadn't been easy.

Morning sickness should be named differently because it didn't just occur during mornings, but all freaking day long. Trying to keep food down had proved to be a challenge, and I'd ended up vomiting at least twice a day. I still did.

My hormones were all over the place, and my sex drive, the same one that had been non-existent until recently, had skyrocketed.

I was just going through what many women on Earth experienced while pregnant. My symptoms were nothing out of the ordinary.

Was it fun? Definitely not.

Was it scary? A little bit.

I was certain, though, all first-time mothers felt similarly. Unfortunately, it drove my mates' protective instincts through the roof. Especially since there'd never been another one like me, and they had no information on Humans.

Telling my mates that what was happening was normal was not enough for Mes—who wanted scientific evidence. And until he got it, he'd decreed that we wouldn't be mating, lest they hurt me or the babies.

Well, if I have to lie awake, they should too.

Having decided on their punishment for now, I was about to wake them up when suddenly an acute pain zinged through my lower abdomen and I felt liquid gush out of me. My eyes were still glued to the mirror, and I watched the color drain from my face and stain the sheet underneath my thighs. The room spun and became blurry.

Dawn leaped to the surface. Her claws sprang through my fingers, but it was too late. Everything turned black.

Mes

Kali's panic brought us out of our slumber. Was she having another nightmare?

Rorc turned sideways and raised his head. "Wake up, little one. It's just a dream."

A metallic scent permeated the air, and Arana gasped, "Kali."

Pain seared through my forearm—Dawn's claws had burst from Kali's hand and raked me.

What had me ignoring the pain, and all of us scrambling to our feet, though, was the red circle widening under her body.

Our bond radiated with fear.

"Mes, what's happening?" Rorc's first instinct was to act, yet he refrained from doing so because he trusted I'd do everything to help our mate, to fix whatever was wrong.

Arana pushed him out of the way and was about to lift Kali's body when a growl from Savage—my sabertooth—stopped him. "She's still bleeding. I need to stop it before we move her to the Healer's Hall," I explained.

Images of his mother's last moments blinded me for a moment, and his fear that the same virus was now claiming our mate had me in its grips.

"Arana, look at Kali. What happened to your females isn't being repeated." I did my best to reassure him before I called forth my healing light and placed one palm over our mate's heart and the other over her lower abdomen. Closing my eyes, I let everything else but our female disappear.

Her heart rate kept increasing, and her breathing was loud and labored.

Time was running out.

I concentrated on her lower half. Her body transformed into a map of muscle, tissue, veins, bones and organs inside my mind. I saw our babies and heard their fast-beating hearts. They were aware something was wrong with their mother, but they were nestled safely in her uterus. I released the breath I'd been holding when I found the blood was coming from Kali's cervix. I could temporarily fix that.

Carefully targeting the problematic area with my healing light, I stopped the flow and repaired the damage. But our mate wasn't out of danger yet.

Picking her up in my arms, I secured her close to my chest

so as not to jostle her, and raced to the Healers' Hall where the med-pod was.

"She needs a transfusion, immediately," I informed my Pair-bonds, who trailed behind us.

Both of them remained silent while I laid her down, retrieved neutral blood and plasma units, inserted them in the med-pod's transfusion portal, and activated the machine that would help her recover.

Its adaptable protective capsule soon enfolded Kali. It stretched all over her, then shrank to mold around her body.

Our offspring moved inside her swollen belly, and I clenched my fingers where I was holding on to the control panel, then closed my eyes and hung my head. My entire body shivered as the reality of how close we'd been to losing her—and them—sunk in. "She has a fucking fragment embedded in her cervix." The sudden lump in my throat made speaking difficult. "I can't remove it alone, and my Healers aren't familiar with her physiology...we need to bring a Human Healer here."

Desperation filled me because it'd been a close call, and I wasn't willing to risk her. The darkness in me reared its ugly head, and Savage fought for control over our body. He wanted to expel its energy before it overpowered us and we ended up hurting those we loved.

My Pair-bonds sensed my inner turmoil and placed their hands on my back, lending me their strength, allowing me to rein in my dark side once again. But I couldn't stand still, so I started pacing.

"How are we going to get the Earthling to come here?" Arana asked.

Unbelievable. He was putting another's life over our female's. I exploded. "I. Don't. Care."

Let's challenge him. It's time we took the reins. Savage snarled in my mind, equally furious.

Maybe my sabertooth was right. I advanced on Arana. "No one is more important than Kali. We'll do whatever the fuck it takes."

Rorc laughed out loud, and we zeroed in on him.

"I'm really enjoying the role reversal we've got going on." Grinning like a fool, he added, "Usually I'm the hot-headed Pair-bond."

Noticing the death stare I was giving him, he raised his arms up in surrender. He'd only been trying to lighten my mood to keep me from spiraling.

"Of course Kali takes precedence over everyone else, Mes," Arana interjected. "But our warriors need Human females. We can't mess this up. Our request needs to go through the Intergalactic Enosis first."

"We can't spare that much time—"

The door opened and Grim—Urien's sabertooth—burst in, followed by many sabertooths.

Having my Pair-bonds with me usually lessened the impact others' emotions had on me, but they caught us by surprise, and without Kali's shield that kept external feelings at bay, their panic hit me all at once. A thousand needles pierced my skull—the pain blinded me and muddled my thoughts. It would have brought me to my knees, if it weren't for Savage's strength.

Arana, experiencing my feelings through our Sacred Bond and needing to protect me, ordered them to shift at the same time with a furious Rorc.

The combined command blasted through the warriors, whose pained groans from the forced change echoed in the hall and around us.

Urien, like those behind him, kneeled on the floor in front of us, panting. All of their faces were etched with worry. "Is the Queen all right? We all felt her terror," he asked while scanning the chamber.

We knew he saw her when he swiftly sucked in a deep breath and staggered to his feet, trying to go to her.

"What do you mean you all felt her?" Arana asked, taken aback by the new development.

The tension in his body had both me and Rorc paying our undivided attention to their discussion.

"Her terror...it woke us up." He was shaken. "The same way she spoke in our minds at the Queen's Fight."

"I'd hoped that was a one-time thing." My Pair-bond rubbed his bottom lip with his thumb, lost in thought. "Did Dawn make those?" He pointed to the four angry pink lines decorating my forearm. The edges of where the skin melded together, jagged and bumpy.

"Yes."

"She shouldn't have been able to shift partially yet. It takes many rotations to achieve such a feat. Her powers are growing," Arana commented.

An ominous cloud settled over us. We didn't know whether there would be any repercussions to her gifts. Many were easy to control, but the stronger they were, the heavier the toll on the individual.

Protect our mate. Savage paced within the confines of my

mind, every few paces pushing against my boundaries, trying to take our body over, but we didn't need his aggression. We needed a level head and a plan.

"Is our Queen all right?" The pain was clear in Urien's voice, who was standing next to the med-pod.

"She will be. We'll allow no other outcome," I declared, and stared pointedly at Arana.

"Is she stable now?" he asked, and I nodded. The Saberian then turned toward the crowd and ordered, "Gwyr, stay with Kali. If anything changes, inform us immediately. Urien, come with us. Let's move to the Communications Chamber."

"I want Zoltor to stay as well," the Saberian Healer asked, and I accepted his request. The more looking after our mate, the better.

A commotion had Rorc running outside, Urien, Dag, and Aux right on his heels.

I chuckled when I heard him cursing under his breath. Having others shadowing him annoyed my Pair-bond to no end. He was used to being the one doing the protecting, but he was now the Third King of Saber, and he had no choice but to allow the warriors to do their duty.

After checking the updated report on the med-pod and making sure Kali was safe and comfortable, I joined the others outside.

"Return to your posts, warriors," the King ordered, and the crowd started dispersing. "Admiral," Rorc turned to Thora, "put your weapon away. No one will hurt the females here."

The Admiral's emotions were like an angry volcano erupting—its spewing lava swallowing everything it came into contact with. The hatred and distrust emanating from him burned me with their intensity, but his expression revealed nothing. His hand holding the blaster steadied as he lowered it to his side.

"Kings," he acknowledged and briefly bowed his head. "I came to deliver the Mardonians per your Queen's request."

One circle ago, my father had insisted on shipping the females back to their planet, but our stubborn mate would hear none of that. She had proclaimed them citizens of Saber and had demanded they'd be brought here immediately. I hadn't expected him to accept. The last time I'd seen the King of Wravuk acquiesce so easily was when my mother was still alive.

Kali's uncanny ability to wrap those she met around her little finger kept surprising me. She was extraordinary.

The older female was shifting from one foot to the other, and there were scratches across her forearm where the youngling was clutching her.

"Of course, they are welcome to stay here." Arana was quick to say, wanting to put the fidgeting females at ease. "Tris, Kas," he addressed the mother and then the daughter, "Ewen will accompany you to the guest chamber, and once Kali is up, we'll find you a permanent dwelling."

"Thank you, my Kings." If her verbal acknowledgment of our authority hadn't been proof enough of where she stood, tilting her head to the side, declaring her submission, made it very clear before the females followed the Royal Guard, leaving my Pair-bonds and me alone with Thora and Urien, who'd stayed even though everyone was ordered to return to their positions.

A rumble vibrated in Rorc's chest, sounding loud in the

quiet of the night. Brute didn't like disobedience any more than his biped counterpart did.

The leader of the Main Territory revealed his neck. "I need to help." His tone was demanding, insistent.

Arana's eyes snapped the warrior's way. A subconscious current of worry zinged from him through to our bond, alerting both me and Rorc that there was something we were unaware of. In the short time I'd known the Saberians, I came to care for them, to claim them as mine—Kali was solely to blame for that. So I let my walls fall, wanting to get a feel for Urien's emotions and see if there was any way I could help him.

What I sensed shook me, and abruptly, I turned away from everyone.

Arana's brother—in all ways but blood—was hanging on by a thread. Grim's blood-thirst was almost out of control. The warrior's sheer will seemed to be the only thing controlling the dangerous sabertooth.

Lethe, the bane of every unmated Saberian's existence, would claim him soon and end his life, unless he found his mate.

I shared what I discovered with my Pair-bonds, and it was as if I could see the gears turning in Rorc's mind, already forming a plan.

"First, we contact the Enosis," Arana reiterated.

"Yes, but we need a contingency plan, and I happen to have found the perfect one," Rorc said, arms crossed and a look of superiority adorning his face.

I doubted these two would stop antagonizing each other, no matter how much time passed.

"I'll leave you to it, then," Thora interjected. "I'm just asking for permission to stay on the surface tonight, so my crew can rest."

"You aren't dismissed, Admiral," Rorc replied, and since my father hadn't stripped him of his rank yet—a hybrid in a position of power was a first—the Wravukian had to obey his superior. "Your assistance will be needed."

"Let's take this meeting to the War Chamber. Urien, you're coming too," Arana said, turning on his heels to head to our destination with us behind him.

EXCITEMENT FOR THE HUNT
URIEN

It was a fifty-fifty chance when I demanded to help that one of my Kings would tear my head off, but despite the dire situation with our Queen in danger, I'd been lucky. So I trailed after them, ignoring Grim's attempts to take over our body and attack the Wravukian trailing behind us. My sabertooth hated placing ourselves in vulnerable positions. And usually I agreed, but I couldn't let him influence me now. We were safe, and Kali needed all the assistance we could provide. So I followed them, ready to volunteer for whatever the males I'd give my life for had planned.

Once we were all seated at the round table, Arana initiated the virtual call.

All the species participating in the Intergalactic Enosis appointed a Senator to represent them and take part in the Committees responsible for different matters and for creating laws and procedures the Enosis members abided by.

Every ten rotations, the Senators would elect sixteen

beings who would act as Ambassadors—usually in charge of everything the Committees couldn't handle. The Ambassador with the most votes was appointed the title of Cardinal Prime and had the final say in all escalated issues.

I didn't know how crazy my Royals' plan was, but I was in nonetheless. No matter what the Enosis would decree.

The Delegates from the Preliminary Committee would be the ones answering Arana's call and cataloging the request, but it would be at least a couple of circles before our issue was escalated, and we heard back from the Core Committee— who handled the affairs regarding primitive planets—about whether we were allowed to proceed or not.

Slowly, a figure taller than me, with a strong broad back dressed in partial armor, appeared through the holo-projector in the middle of the table, and my mouth fell open. "King Arana." The helmet covering this being's face didn't muffle his deep voice. "What a pleasant surprise. Have you reconsidered my proposition?"

Fuck. The situation must have been worse than I assumed because my warrior brother bypassed the Intergalactic Enosis' established procedure and called the Cardinal Prime —Lord Mo'dta.

"I wish I could say the same." Arana's grim tone had the imposing being straightening his shoulders. "This isn't a social call. I'm here to collect one of the favors you owe me."

Everyone held their breath. My King's move was bold.

The head of the Intergalactic Enosis lifted his clawed fingers and took off his helmet. He retracted the white membrane that covered his narrowed eyes and locked his bright-orange gaze on Arana. "What is this about?"

Mine widened, partly because I was surprised and partly because the sight was terrifying. I'd never seen a Shartja, commonly known as Apex Hunters, without his armor's mask. Even though our physiques were similarly built, his head with the horns where brows should have been, the protective membrane over his big round eyes, the lack of lips over his rows of sharp teeth, and the three mandibles on each side—like the ones our arachnids had—made for a dread-inducing sight.

Arana didn't seem disturbed at all, so I schooled my features and paid attention to their discussion.

"We ask for permission to access a primitive planet and acquire one of their Healers." My brother wasn't in a mood to beat around the bush.

Mo'dta crossed his arms, waiting, appraising my King silently. When he divulged no more information, the Cardinal Prime heaved a sigh. "Why would you need one from a primitive world? My Healers are at your disposal, you know that."

"My mate," Arana started, but a loud growl—coming from Rorc—reverberated in the room, interrupting him and making Admiral Thora tense. "Our mate," he corrected, "is in danger."

The image of the holo-projector went completely still, and I wondered whether it was a glitch or if the Head of the Enosis was just speechless. "Our?" he asked as his mandibles went slack and his jaw dropped.

Ha. He was stunned.

I grinned.

Arana's hand hovered above the holo-projector before tapping a key that allowed the whole chamber to be viewed through the projection. "Mo'dta, allow me to introduce my Pair-bonds—Second and Third King of Saber—Mes and Rorc."

The Hunter's head jerked back. "Your female evoked an interspecies Sacred Union?" he asked, but before my brother could speak, he continued in a rush, "Which planet?"

"Earth. We need to acquire one of their Healers as soon as possible," Arana reiterated, drawing his mouth into a straight line, unease leaking through the connection we all had with our King.

He wasn't amused by the fact that the Cardinal Prime had ignored the introduction to his Pair-bonds, both of which had gone rigid while he'd focused on the Queen.

I didn't like it either. We'd never warred against the Shartja, but if the Apex Hunter got any funny ideas in his big head regarding our most prized female, he had another thing coming. Every single Saberian warrior would protect her until his last breath.

Mo'dta leaned forward, his eyes practically glowing orange. "Earth…" he trailed off, his gaze turning inward for a moment before he caught himself and continued, "I allow you to request one of their Healers to assist you. You will offer your protection with no strings attached, and return him unharmed once his knowledge is no longer required."

"Of course," Arana promised, in a rush to wrap up their meeting.

"Expect my presence on Saber in a cycle's time. I'm looking forward to making the acquaintance of your female," he said, and it was like a dark cloud entered our chamber, lowering the temperature and causing chills to erupt on our skin. "Kings." He nodded and his image disappeared as the connection was terminated.

"That went well..." I let my voice trail off in a failed attempt to lighten the mood.

Foolish male, Grim—who'd remained silent thus far—told me. *How does lightening the mood help? Our Queen needs our help, let's go pick up the Healer.*

Arana finding his mates was an event almost all Saberians rejoiced in. I was truly happy for my brother, but at the same time, the joyful event dredged up a deep pain I thought I'd put to rest.

It had been more than a hundred rotations since all the male warriors had left to defend the Zirgnoln, but I remembered the events as if it were yesterday because earlier that day I'd found my mate.

She'd come to the Main Territory from the South to protect Queen Aenthear and Caeleah while all the males were off-planet. I was so certain that she'd be there the moment we returned that I'd barely spoken to her. Wanting to remain focused on the upcoming battle, I didn't allow the bond to strengthen when I knew we'd be apart for a while and the distance would have only brought us pain.

Little did I know that Yenoctonia—the day we lost all our females—would rob me of the opportunity to get to know her...to cherish her...to create a family with her.

I was devastated, but since the bond hadn't been established, I could still function. Helping Arana rebuild our society had further softened the loss. Being needed by so many others had taken my mind off my own troubles until at some point the pain faded completely.

From the moment Arana had found his mates, Grim's mood had gradually but steadily deteriorated. I had chalked it up to the new reality we had to get used to. He was still our brother, but he now had two Pair-bonds who were there to assist him, so he no longer needed our help.

Hope we'd still be useful had bloomed when I'd seen the size of the Human female. Then we'd fought the Queen's Fight and lost. Kali had demonstrated how strong she was, not only by establishing a mind-link with every Saberian alive, but by asserting her dominance over everyone but her mates.

She definitely didn't need us. She was powerful, and she'd proved just how much when she stopped the Southern and Western Territories' rebellion...the one we, the Royal Guards, and the Elite warriors had failed to prevent.

Observing the Sacred Mates together was like rubbing salt in wounds I thought had been healed. I was wrong, and my sabertooth started slipping slowly down the path to Lethe, and I didn't know how to stop him. The Creator had blessed us with a Sacred Mate, but we'd lost her. There was nothing on the horizon for us, and it fucking tore me apart.

So Grim suggesting to help now was a big deal. It meant he hadn't given up completely, and maybe we'd escape Lethe —the madness that would end us both—for a little while longer.

The sound of Mes's fist connecting with the table pulled me back to the present. "We have the Intergalactic Enosis' permission. We need to act now," the usually calm Arch-healer said.

Arana turned to his other Pair-bond. "Rorc, what's the plan?" he asked.

"We'll lure a Healer to us." The Second King started pacing around the chamber, breathing evenly and exuding tranquility as he shared his idea. "We'll need to be near Earth's orbit, but we'll advertise that a hefty payment will be given to the Earthling who is willing to travel to an unknown destination to assist with a Queen's difficult pregnancy." He stopped as if considering what he had just proposed, then continued, "Yes, and we won't divulge any other information until the Human has arrived on Saber for privacy reasons."

"I'll go fetch the Earthling," Thora volunteered.

Why would he want to help us? A Wravukian Admiral with his own fleet was the last person I'd expect to step forward for such a mission.

"No need. I'll bring the Healer here," I declared.

"And how familiar are you with intergalactic travel, Saber-ian?" His condescending tone grated my nerves.

I opened my mouth to tell him exactly what I thought when Rorc said, "It's not a one-male job. Both of you will go, and you'll be rewarded upon your return."

The mistrust was a knife slicing me deeply. "Arana, I will not fail my Queen," I appealed. "I don't require a reward, and there's no reason to involve an outsider."

Something passed between the Sacred Mates that I couldn't decipher.

"You'll both go," my brother decreed, and I could not deny him. I nodded my assent.

"I do not require a material reward either, but I wish for

something in return," the Wravukian said, and locked gazes with Rorc.

"What is it you want, Admiral?" Arana asked.

When he remained silent, Rorc nudged him. "It's not my story to tell. Go on, Thora. This might be the only chance you'll ever get."

These two had a history, and it made me curious. What was so important that the Wravukian would give up a financial reward for?

The older male squared his shoulders and planted his feet wide apart. "I demand Ivar Al-Jurjani be punished for his crime." He clenched and unclenched his fists before continuing in a tart tone, "He killed my Chosen Mate."

Curling my upper lip at him, I let the snarl brewing in my chest out. Simultaneously, I stepped back, putting more distance between us because I wanted to punch him for accusing a Saberian warrior of such a serious crime.

"That old male has no tact," Rorc mumbled under his breath, but thanks to our enhanced senses, I heard him just fine.

And maybe in any other instance, I'd have found his comment funny, but not now.

"Do you have proof?" Arana asked.

Thora furrowed his brows and ground his teeth. "I don't. But I was the one who cost him his right eye." Volunteering no more details, he simply waited for the Saberian King's reaction.

Arana let the silence stretch, measuring the Wravukian, and I could tell by the tightness on Thora's face that he expected his request to be declined. "Your accusation is of a despicable crime. Before we pass judgment, we will set up a hearing with both of you present, Admiral," my brother said.

"That is acceptable, thank you." The Wravukian bowed respectfully, then added, "I'm also to inform you of what we found during the prisoner's interrogation."

"Go on," Rorc ordered.

"A new group that calls themselves the Order of the Prime hired the Crootan. Their orders were to capture a Saberian male and deliver him to them—in one piece or many, it didn't matter. They want to finish the job they started so many rotations ago when they had your females killed."

My guttural roar joined Arana's and drowned all other noises. The desire for vengeance, the need to hurt those responsible, to see their blood spill was amplified by my King's emotions, and overpowered my other senses. "Do you have their location?" I growled, my voice less intelligible than normal due to Grim rising to the surface.

"No. He was more afraid of betraying this Order than he was of our interrogator," Thora said.

I stomped to him, ready to grab him by the collar and demand he take me to the prisoner, when Arana stopped me.

"Urien, stand down," he said, then addressed the Admiral, "Where is the pirate?"

"He was murdered in his cell."

Rorc's lips pulled back in disgust. "That means there's a fucking traitor high in the Wravukian ranks."

Thora's posture was stiff, his jaw set. "An investigation is being conducted according to King Nathraichean's orders." His clipped words indicated he wasn't willing to discuss the matter further.

Arana clapped Rorc's shoulder in camaraderie. "We'll contact him, to let him know he has our support if he needs it."

The Second King of Saber nodded, then told Thora, "As soon as the sun rises on the horizon, Urien will come get you, so make the needed arrangements for your departure. You'll travel with the S-970, as time is of the essence and that's the fastest ship at our disposal." Then he turned to me. "Inform Mok to add Thora's biometrics to the navigational system before you depart."

I agreed, and when no one had anything else to add, the Third King of Saber said, "That is all for now. We'll be in constant communication for anything else that may come up," wrapping up our meeting.

And for the first time in a while, lightness replaced the hollowness that had been dragging my chest down as excitement for the hunt filled both me and Grim.

IT WAS TIME FOR A CHANGE
RIVER

Meanwhile on Earth.

Why did I agree to come to Dark Angel on a Friday night? Having the weekend off was a rarity for me. I could have been snuggling under my new duvet that made me feel like I was surrounded by heavenly clouds, instead of sitting on an uncomfortable stool at the overcrowded bar.

It was all my best friend's fault, that's why.

I was one of the most respected ob-gyns in the country, and one of the best in the field because the motivation driving me was solid. I'd taken a vow to try my hardest to not let another woman lose her baby.

Helplessly watching my loving mother slowly wither away after the fourth time she'd lost a child had solidified the course of my future. And soon after she passed away, my dad followed—he'd slept with her pillow that still smelled like her and never woke up.

Their love had been so strong that not even death could keep them apart for long. Science didn't acknowledge soul mates as having a perfectly matched individual who was your other half, but I'd seen proof of such a bond—my parents.

Their relationship had been imperfectly perfect, and I wanted what they'd had. I'd witnessed the real thing—true love—and I couldn't accept anything less than that.

Unfortunately, that led to me being in my early thirties, newly single, and a virgin. And it was not for lack of having men ogle me. According to some, I was quite attractive. My skin remained sun-kissed no matter the season, and I had an hourglass figure that men seemed to love lately.

Yet I didn't see what others saw. To me, what was within mattered more than the outer shell. Because we did grow old and we did lose what youth offered, and what we were left with was our souls.

Yeah, I had set the bar too high.

My best friend said I'd set it to fail.

Others said it was an old-fashioned notion to wait for Mr. Right and that I should let it go.

But I knew that person was out there. I'd thought I'd found him in William, but I'd been proven wrong, and now I didn't have the slightest idea where my soul mate might be in the world.

"Where are you, doc?" Serina's voice brought me out of my reverie, and I focused on her, but she didn't give me a chance to explain. "When your eyes go dreamy like that, I know you are either thinking of your parents or your mythical creature.

The elusive Mr. One. But I hope you're not wasting any brain cells on Dr. Asshat William."

She knew me all too well. In another life, we would have been sisters.

"It amazes me that you can get lost inside your head in a place like this!" She huffed as she slowly swirled the liquid in the glass she was holding before lifting the cocktail and taking a sip—her eyes scanning the bar. "You could definitely find a rebound. Do you want me to be your wingwoman?" she teased.

Dark Angel attracted a certain clientele like blood drew sharks. It was full of people in suits—full of ambitious men and women eager to climb the corporate ladder, and entrepreneurs of all ages. This place seemed to cater to the upper crust, despite its less-than-glamorous location.

I didn't belong in that world, and the music was a tad too loud for my liking, but it was one of Serina's favorite places to grab a drink.

Letting my gaze roam the dimly lit pub, I noticed there were quite a few men in various states of inebriation blatantly looking at her.

My best friend, who could have easily become a model, was striking. Her blonde hair and electric-blue eyes turned every man she met into putty in her hands. Her lithe body was what every man wished he had under him. But what nobody knew at first glance was that she was one of the smartest people in the world. Her IQ was off the charts and she had a job many coveted. She was a director in a prestigious investment firm.

"It's easy. I am a doctor." I stuck my tongue out at her, and her melodious laughter attracted more stares from those near us. "If I hadn't found a way to block out distractions, I'd never have graduated med school," I said, ignoring the rebound part.

Serina lifted her nose in the air, all hoity-toity, and pinned me with her stare. "River Claire Margeaux, are you calling me a distraction?"

Now it was my turn to giggle at her silliness. "Of course not, Miss Younc. I'd never commit such an atrocity."

She tapped my arm with the back of her hand. "Liar," she accused playfully, and my smile grew wider.

Two guys that had been staring at us for the last hour seemed to have found the courage to approach because they got up and started walking our way.

This was the part I hated because I wasn't interested in what these men wanted ninety-nine percent of the time.

"Hello, ladies. Can we buy you a drink?" the bolder of the two asked.

Dark-chocolate hair, light-blue eyes, and a dark-gray pressed suit. He was good-looking and he knew it. He exuded arrogance. He was definitely the one-night-stand type, and he had set his sights on Serina.

His friend, equally handsome with boyish looks and a dimpled chin, moved next to me and slid his hand inconspicuously behind me.

Serina did not miss my flinch. She knew how I felt about this type of man, and although she had no problem having one-night stands, when we were out together, she always declined any offers. That was one more reason why I loved her. She was considerate of other people's feelings.

The one who had talked had the nerve to touch her hair and tuck it behind her ear.

Her eyes grew cold at the liberties they took. "We can buy our own drinks. Thank you." Her austere tone made our mood clear.

Not that it deterred them.

"Aw! Don't be like that, honey. Let us show you a good time," the guy ogling Serina insisted, not taking the hint. His whiskey-scented breath hit her in the face, making her pucker her lips in disdain.

She crossed her arms in front of her and the action lifted her breasts. His eyes immediately dropped to her bust. "Eyes up here, loverboy." Leveling her gaze on him like a Queen dealing with an annoying peasant, she continued, "We were already having a great time before you interrupted. Now do you want me to call Daemon to make it clear to you?"

We came here so often, we were on a first name basis with the staff.

"Daemon?" the second asked, not understanding who we were referring to.

Out of thin air, like we had somehow summoned Dark Angel's bouncer, he appeared next to Serina. His imposing height towered over the other two. He had the sleeves of his pristine white shirt folded over the elbows, and the bulging muscles of his broad chest—along with his rope-like arms—demonstrated that he was not someone they wanted to mess with.

"Serina, River," he growled in greeting, "are these men bothering you?" His eyebrows furrowed over his brooding eyes as he turned his attention to the two guys.

They instantly stepped backward. "No, man, we just wanted to say hi to the ladies," the light-haired one said and they both turned and walked away.

Daemon gave Serina a disapproving look and left without a word.

"Well...that was fun," Serina blurted out while her eyes tracked Daemon until he disappeared from our view.

"I think he likes you...but more importantly, I think you like him," I teased while feeling the truth in my statement.

"As if! The day Daemon likes me will be when hell freezes over." She huffed, but pink infused her cheeks. "Did you see the contempt in his eyes? What's his problem?"

I chuckled and was going to tease her about skipping over the fact that she liked him when she threw me a mischievous look that promised retribution. In a contest of wills with her, I'd end up losing, so I chose to let it go. After all, she had stood up for us, and torturing her wouldn't show my gratitude.

"Thank you for that," I told her sincerely.

"For what?" she asked, sobering just as fast as my mood changed.

"You know," I raised my hand in front of her and counted using my fingers, "one, for standing up to them, and two, for not saying anything to me for cockblocking you."

Her eyebrows nearly reached her hairline, and she pretended to be aghast at my words. "Did you just say...cock?" Then she touched her forehead with the back of her hand, as if she were about to faint. "What is the world coming to?"

Her antics cracked me up. "Oh shut up," I said with a smile.

Time flew by fast, and we soon found ourselves bumbling loudly outside my house.

"Shhhhh!" I lifted my finger in front of my mouth, almost dropping my keys and losing my balance.

Serina bent at the waist from laughing so hard and almost fell forward before she slapped her hand on the door to steady herself.

After a few tries, I managed to put the key in the right hole and turn it to the right direction. I opened the door without noticing my best friend had been using it as a way to stay upright.

She ended up sprawling across the floor and laughing even harder.

I could not keep my giggles in either. "Oh my God! Are you okay?"

Managing to close the door and help Serina to her feet took some serious effort.

Darn it, I'm drunk.

With my arm around her waist, I tried to move us to the living room to our left. She would not budge. I turned to look at her questioningly.

"You know I love you, right?" she blurted in a serious tone.

"Of course. I love you too. Are you going to get all sappy with me?" I half-jokingly replied.

But she didn't laugh. All mirth had been scraped off her face. "I prefer sleeping here, with you because you have a home." Her tone conveyed the importance of her message.

My buzz started wearing off, and I felt a headache coming on. I ignored it.

"You have a home too, silly!" I interjected, but she just shook her head.

"You remind me of Dorin," she said. "She was the only one who loved me and made me feel like I had a home for once in my life."

Dorin was one of the foster parents Serina had while growing up. She had a rough childhood, to say the least.

I made a snap decision. "Well, you know what? This is your house, too. I will add you to the deed and the title so that when I die, this is all yours."

Unexpectedly, she started tearing.

I'd only wanted to make her feel better. We'd met during the most difficult period of my life, and she'd stayed—not balking when I pushed her away because I was depressed and each day was too painful. She became the sister I never had, a sister of the heart, which to me was so much more important because I'd chosen her.

If only my parents had been open to adoption. Maybe then our paths would have crossed sooner. Maybe then we would have been real sisters. Maybe then they would have still been alive. That train of thought only held heartache for me, and I cut it off, immediately returning my focus to the present.

"Serina?"

"Don't ever say that," she chastised between sobs. "You will not die."

My inebriated mind came up with an idea, and I just blurted it, "All right. We will find a vampire and make him bite us. That way we'll live forever. How about that?"

My proposal was on the crazy side—even to my own ears, but it seemed to appease her, and her sobs soon turned to hiccups. Stumbling only four times, I led her to the guest bedroom, which was basically her room since she stayed so often at my place, and helped her settle. No sooner had I turned my back than she started snoring lightly.

Adorable. If I swung that way, I would definitely pursue her.

People thought her obnoxious and intimidating, but only because they didn't know her. They only saw the outer shell. The hard-core, professional, not-taking-anyone's-bullshit woman.

I knew better.

She had a big heart. Every chance she got, she spread love and always made time to help others.

Closing the door softly, I went to my bathroom and got in the shower.

A long bath would have been lovely, but it was just one of those nights where sleep was tugging at the edges of my consciousness.

Quickly cleaning the tobacco smell from my body and hair, I changed into the fluffiest bathrobe I owned and headed straight to my bed. I fell like a brick on the mattress.

I'd thought sleep would take me right away, but it was an hour later and I was still looking at the ceiling.

Good thing it's my day off tomorrow because no one likes Dr. Zombie, I thought to myself as I got up and opened the French balcony doors.

The slight breeze felt refreshing on my face.

I lifted my gaze to the sky. The jewels decorating it

seemed brighter than usual, and I was taken aback by their beauty.

How would it feel flying among them? Freeing, I bet.

From my periphery I saw a blazing star falling. I closed my eyes and made a wish. *Please, God, send my other half my way.*

A deep sigh escaped my lips. I should give up on this childish habit at some point. It was pointless, and with my track record, I had a better chance of winning the lottery than actually finding a man who'd see the real me and like her.

William was a psychologist working at the Psychiatric Institute of Washington. We'd met at a conference, and his courteous and cultivated manners had won me over. We'd started dating and I'd shared my desire to get to know each other first before our relationship evolved to a physical one.

He'd readily agreed, and it should have been my first warning, but like the romantic fool I was, I'd been overjoyed not skeptical.

Everything had been perfect...too perfect, until one of his female colleagues reached out to me and gave me the news that broke my heart. She was one of a string of women warming his bed. She'd recently found out and felt obligated to warn me.

I could still hear the candles flicker as they bathed our dinner table with soft light the night I confronted him. He'd taken me to a fancy restaurant to share some exciting news, but we never got to that point.

When I'd told him I found out he'd been cheating, his response had shocked me.

He'd assured me that the other women were meaningless

sex partners, not his girlfriend. He'd added that the title was mine alone and once we started having sex he'd stop.

Having had enough, I'd gotten up and left.

But by closing that chapter, I found myself back to square one.

It was time for a change. "Universe," I whispered, and chills raced up my arms. "I'm ready for my soul mate."

I wanted to return home after an exhausting day and be greeted by my husband. Have him ease the guilt of the times I would fail to help a woman, and rejoice with me when I would succeed. Was I asking too much? I was incapable of stopping my research or helping others—that was ingrained in who I was—but my family would be my top priority, and I'd make time for my man and our children.

The night sky carried a tranquility that slowly slipped into me as I gazed at all the constellations. "Please send him my way," I asked while trying to keep my heavy eyelids open. After a few minutes, though, I gave up and turned around to head to my bed, leaving the doors open. The night breeze provided a lovely caress, and as I closed my eyes I fantasized that my man's gentle touch would feel the same way.

I'D LIKE TO SEE YOU TRY
URIEN

My first stop was the Comms Chamber. I found Mok hunched over the main holo-board processor. Fibers and components, whose names I didn't know, were spread on the floor all around him as he tinkered with the cerebrum circuit.

"You can't sleep?"

He lifted his head and turned moss-green eyes—his saber-tooth's—toward me. "Nah. I'm too riddled with tension and... fear. Is Kali going to be all right? Is it the virus?" His voice broke on the last word. This new trial brought a long-buried pain back to the surface, and we all felt it anew.

"I think it's something different. They tasked me with bringing a Healer from our Queen's mother planet here."

For a few ticks, he just stared at me, mulling over what I'd said. "How can I help? Which ship are you taking? The S-970, right?"

One could always count on Mok. He had a quick mind and was loyal to a fault.

33

"Yes, but I won't be traveling alone...Thora will be the pilot." I swallowed Grim's growl the moment I mentioned the Wravukian's name. "You need to add the Admiral's biometrics to the ship's navigational system."

The corners of his mouth crinkled, and mirth colored his voice when he said, "Do you see a pattern here? What if the Healer is female?"

"No. That's your specialty," I deadpanned, not liking his train of thought. "Don't even dare utter such a thing where the Creator might hear you."

Laughing, he said, "Fine. But a Saberian, a Wravukian, and a Human traveling together...I'd say the odds won't be in your favor." Then he picked up the case with his tools—completely ignoring my loud snarl—and walked away, leaving me standing there.

"You cur," I swore at him, and his chuckles echoed in the corridor.

His words taunted me, and it seemed I enjoyed torturing myself because I couldn't get them out of my head.

But I'd already met and lost my mate. There was really no point in lingering in these kinds of thoughts.

After a while I managed to focus on the next task that needed to be completed, and I headed straight to my dwelling in the Main Territory's cave system to gather my exosuit and a few extra things I might need.

The Queen had talked about Humans wearing different garments than us. Hopefully, the matgen on the ship would be able to create them once Noymus—the S-970's AI—hacked Earth's grid, but even if it didn't, I wasn't worried. My Sirh uniform would protect me against their weapons, and it would also shift with me when I needed to camouflage my appearance according to the surrounding environment. I'd find a way to blend in either way.

Last stop was the communal armory. While on board, I couldn't rely on Grim to defend us in the case of any unpleasant surprises. Looking at the collection of blades, swords, and blasters, I debated which one to take.

What if the Wravukian had an accident that rendered him unfit to travel? My sabertooth's voice filled my mind.

Grim had been testing my patience lately. *When did you lose your honor?* Even though I knew it was Lethe's pull that was slowly poisoning his behavior, I couldn't keep the bitterness out of my tone.

Suddenly, I dropped to one knee, the agony of feeling ripped in two all-encompassing.

My sabertooth had lashed out at me even as he roared in pain—the same he'd inflicted.

Trapping him in the edges of my mind took effort, and no matter how much I hated the action, it needed to be done. Breathing deeply to center myself, I got up, grabbed two daggers, and left the armory.

As soon as my feet stepped on the moist soil, a plethora of wildflower scents invaded my nose and dew settled on my skin. The small sun's turquoise rays dappled through the leaves, creating flickering shadows on the ground. I closed my eyes and rejoiced at the short reprieve as tranquility slowly seeped into me. I'd miss this, and Grim would too, but we had an important mission.

A jarring note of something not belonging pierced the

harmonious rhythm of nature. The hairs on the back of my neck lifted, and my sabertooth stood at attention.

Frozen on the spot, I listened with all my senses.

Soft vibrations belonging to a biped male traveled through the ground. Although it could be another warrior, my gut was telling me otherwise.

Do you feel that, Grim?

He ignored my question, still angry at me for confining him, but as I raised my nose and inhaled deeply, his curiosity out won and he moved closer to the surface, making it easy to pick up the scent of the intruder.

I moved behind the trees across the sides of the path. My skin turned from the color of embers to brown, and my deep-green spots and stripes changed into lighter and darker patches resembling the ones on the barks around me. The camouflage allowed me to blend with my surroundings, making me nearly invisible. And thanks to our animal halves, we knew exactly where to step to remain quiet while traveling through the forest.

It only took us a few ticks to find him.

Once Grim was locked onto him, there was no way he could shake us, even if he knew we were following him. Which he didn't.

I told you the Wravukian is hiding something from us.

He will only find dwellings on this side of the caves, I replied. While I mostly agreed with Grim on this one, I wondered whether Thora was hiding something else, other than what he'd told Arana; or whether he was foolish enough to think he could take a Saberian warrior by surprise on his own turf.

I followed him, trudging sideways to the worn path, and I

stayed behind him while he traipsed over to trails he found interesting.

The fact that he hadn't lost his sense of direction and hadn't been turned around in the woods—when I knew he hadn't been here before—was surprising.

He didn't linger long near the caves where our dwellings were, but slowly sauntered toward our rendezvous point.

When he was nearing the S-970, I intentionally stepped on a dry branch.

The sound of the wood breaking had the Wravukian spinning on his heels, gun raised.

Doubting he'd shoot his traveling companion, I kept my smirk in place and waited until the realization that a silent predator had been stalking him the whole time hit him, then said, "Why are you sniffing around our dwellings, Admiral?"

"None of your business, Saberian," he spat, but the murderous stare he was giving me was comical.

If he'd thought pinning me with such a look would be effective, he was sorely mistaken; as a scare tactic, it failed miserably. He forgot I wasn't part of his fleet—one of his subordinates. I was a fearless warrior.

I bared my teeth at him in a grimace of a smile, and let a low snarl travel with the wind rustling through leaves his way. The birds and prey animals near us that had been chattering quieted in two heartbeats.

Let me shift, Grim demanded. *He wants to fight? I'll give him a fight.*

Steps from our right side heralded the coming of another Saberian.

"Warriors!" King Rorc admonished, not a single nuance

escaping him. "This is a very important assignment. Our mate is in trouble and we're counting on you to bring the best birthing Healer from Earth here. You will need to be quick and stealthy. The Earthlings must not know you are there. You aren't allowed to engage in battle. You'll infiltrate, grab the target, and return immediately," Rorc ordered, putting an end to our face-off.

"Affirmative," Thora grunted while none of the disdain emanating from him showed on his face.

Our sabertooths, though, allowed us a sensitivity other species didn't possess, and we could feel what he was hiding.

Rorc growled and took a menacing step toward him. "You will leave what happened where it belongs—in the past—until the hearing. Am I clear, Admiral?"

"Yes, sir!" Thora replied, rigidly saluting his superior.

"Then off you go, both of you. Travel safe and travel fast," my King said and continued on to his destination.

Thora placed his palm onto the biometric scanner next to the hatch, and it opened. Being the Admiral of the Third Fleet of Wravuk meant he was a skillful pilot—one of the best—and I had to follow his lead for the time being.

I saw him check the various instruments and typing commands. He was efficient and quick. In just a few ticks, I could feel the rumble of the engines as they came alive under his instructions.

"Strap in," he ordered.

I didn't like his tone, but I did as he said. It had been a while since the last time we'd traveled, and I felt Grim's agitation as he paced in the confines of my mind. We were land-bound creatures—not made to fly.

A soft growl rattled in my chest. The stronger the male, the stronger the sabertooth, and mine was making his feelings known.

The Admiral shifted his weight from one foot to the other. "Is your sabertooth going to be trouble?" he snapped.

I took offense to his question. Sometimes it took a lot to assert my control, but I had yet to fail, and I wasn't planning to do so now. "No," I said through clenched teeth.

"He better not be, unless he wants me to put him down," Thora warned, his tone low and menacing.

My answering snarl was equally threatening as the blazing inferno of anger consumed me from the inside. "I'd like to see you try."

Let's show him who'd put who down. Grim was furious too.

I unstrapped myself and left the bridge. My determination to keep my sabertooth from killing the Admiral was waning the more I stayed in his presence.

What was Thora's problem? I'd heard what he claimed about Ivar Al-Jurjani. Even though I was acquainted with the warrior, we weren't friends.

Whether he had committed a crime was yet to be seen. But one male's actions didn't represent the whole.

My and Thora's paths had never crossed before, so his behavior didn't make sense. And while our species had been enemies a few millennia ago, that had long been settled.

I wondered if he was one of the elitists who held grudges or considered themselves above all others as I headed to the quarters. Thankfully, there were two doors. I neared the first one and it whooshed open.

This ship was bigger than the S-950, and this chamber was

spacious, with a sofa and a table thrown in there, but only one big bed that could easily fit four Saberians.

Thora can have this one.

I stepped out and went to the second entrance that slid open as soon as Noymus—the ship's AI—detected my movement in front of it.

What the fuck? This wasn't a sleeping chamber but a Healer's chamber. There was a med-pod in the middle and various instruments Healers used were scattered around, but no bed.

What were we supposed to do? Did my Kings expect us to sleep together?

Well...he could have the bed. I'd sleep on the med-pod if that's what it took to stay away from him because I didn't entirely trust that Thora wouldn't try to kill me while I slept.

THE HEALER HAS BEEN FOUND
THORA

The nightmares had returned, but they had morphed from reliving Sharifah's—my Chosen Mate's—last few ticks of life that was cut short too soon, to Ivar—the Saberian who stole it —managing to escape me every single time.

And it was due to being in the presence of another one of those curs. They projected a different image—that of protectors—but I'd seen their true nature.

The ice-cold fury that was my constant companion since that fateful night unfurled inside me, nearly overshadowing every rational thought process. But the moment Urien left the bridge, I was able to breathe again. The muscles in my rigid body screamed to be released, and the edge of the control board of the ship squealed under the pressure of my tight grip.

One by one, I unclenched my fingers and shook my arms —the blood rushing in my veins felt like a swarm of insects crawling underneath my skin. I paced in the confined space until the pounding in my hearts eased and logic returned.

I had waited for a chance at revenge for too long to let the much younger warrior ruin my plans. I only had to put up with him for the duration of this trip. Then the filth that had escaped my wrath by hiding on his planet would die.

"Noymus, put the route you've mapped out on the viewscreen."

The AI responded instantly. He had us traveling through the Aquar System, then past the Centiru System, and through to the Intergalactic Enosis' borders, before we reached the Solar System.

"How long does this course take before we reach our destination?" I asked, a different path already revealing itself in my mind. One of my strongest gifts allowed me to visualize passages that hadn't been charted or tried by other Captains yet. I instinctively knew whether a wormhole was steady enough for a vessel to travel through. It was a very handy ability to have, when surprising an enemy meant winning the war.

"Three full circles, Admiral," it replied.

"Shift to manual control," I ordered as I settled in the Captain's chair.

Instantly, I felt an electric current run through my body. A lithe energy coursed through my veins, amping up my antici-pation to take control of this vessel. I could feel the ship take shape around me—the wires becoming an extension of my veins, the metal structure metamorphosing into a living, breathing cocoon. Every time I experienced such a connec-tion, the initial stage was disorienting and exhilarating. After everything settled, machine, AI, and male merged. The link was such that during battle, I didn't even need to check if we'd been hit or if we were out of weapons. I always knew. There had also been times that I'd felt other ships, and I'd successfully anticipated our enemies' moves.

The S-970 was designed for stealth and speed, which meant we had very few weapons at our disposal in case of an attack, but I was confident in my abilities to escape even the most dire circumstances if needed. Plus, my route would cut our travel time in half.

It was a win-win situation because that meant I'd only have to spend three circles in total in the Saberian's presence.

For the biggest part of our journey, we managed to avoid each other successfully. I remained on the bridge most of the time, and Urien in the Healer's Chamber.

Thanks to the cloaking tech on the ship, we'd passed undetected through both the friendly and unfriendly zones after exiting the wormholes, and we had less than half a circle left before we arrived at our destination.

Even though Urien's footfalls were silent, they still caused vibrations when his feet touched the floor, and those I felt in my bones—the floor an extension of myself. He was approaching. I could have commanded the entrance to stay locked, but I didn't, and the whoosh of the door indicated the Saberian had entered the bridge.

I scoffed, feeling him hover behind me. Why on Wravuk did Rorc think I could not manage this mission on my own?

I'd never understand. Humans were a primitive species. I was stronger, faster, cleverer, and the technology at my disposal was advanced compared to theirs. One Healer wouldn't cause trouble I couldn't handle.

When the Saberian remained silent behind me, a growl of frustration left my lips. The fucker chuckled.

"You know two is better than one, right?" His words were laced with innuendo, and instantly my thoughts turned sexual.

It had been a while since I'd indulged in the fairer sex, and even longer since I'd shared a female with another male. *What the fuck?* I shook my head, trying to dislodge the images he planted there and failing miserably. I jumped out of my chair and spun around. I desperately wanted to punch him, to erase the pretentious grin covering his face.

"Get the fuck out of my mind," I ordered.

"I am not in your head, Thora." His lighthearted comment vexed me even more.

"Get the fuck off my bridge then!" I was fuming. If he didn't make himself scarce, I doubted I'd keep my cool for much longer. He managed to ruffle my feathers just by being in the same room with me. An unbelievable feat since I was known for my cold exterior and endless restraint.

The Saberian snarled—balking at my order—and prowled toward me. Did he think I'd cower?

When we were chest to chest, he said, "I. Do. Not. Take. Orders. From. You." The nonchalant behavior he'd had in the beginning vanished.

His teeth seemed sharper than usual as he pulled his lips back.

"This is my ship—"

"No. This is our ship," he interrupted.

I pulled my arm back, fist clenched tight when the comms sounded. I dropped my arm, stepped backward, and pressed the key to receive the call.

His three Kings appeared on the viewscreen. Mes laughed, whereas Arana looked surprised. Rorc was the one who talked. "So, you did not kill each other."

"I was not aware we were allowed to," I replied—my tone cold, and Rorc burst into laughter.

Arana was the one who sobered first. "No, you are not. Just knowing both of your reputations...it was a gamble," he said, then added, "How close are you?"

"We will be there in five spires. Noymus has already breached their databases using their satellites, and is searching for the Healer," I reported, and at that exact moment the AI alerted us of its findings.

"The Healer has been found in DC. Her name is River Margeaux. She is the head of the Obstetricians Council in the US. She works at the Inova Fairfax Hospital and specializes in infertility and complicated births." Noymus kept listing all her achievements, and the list was long.

I was stuck on the fact that she was a female. Wravukians were a patriarchal species. Not that we didn't believe our females were clever or educated, but they weren't meant to be working. Their purpose was to take care of their families and to be treasured and protected by their mates.

What kind of world was this Earth? Where they put their most treasured beings to work and even allowed them to go to war, like Queen Kali had? My opinion of this planet was low to start with, but now it had reached the bottom.

"That's good. Don't waste time," he told us, then ordered the ship's AI to send the ad once it adjusted it to Human standards. "Warriors, retrieve her and come back at once," the Admiral of Wravuk and Third King of Saber said and terminated the connection.

"You'd better let me do all the talking when we find her, otherwise you might chase her away with your gruff disposition," Urien suggested, and although it irritated me, he had a point.

I was too old, too set in my ways, and too ragged. From what the AI was transmitting, the Earthlings were fragile beings, easily breakable. My appearance, and definitely my demeanor, would scare her. Maybe it'd be best to leave that part to Urien. I'd just make sure she came with us in the end. One way or another.

"Fine," I agreed, and we both set to work reading her file quietly. Her accomplishments were impressive, and her picture was breathtaking. But I still couldn't fathom that her father had allowed her to work. Humans had very short lifespans. Why was she without a mate at thirty-one rotations old? Something was probably wrong with her. There was no other explanation. My eyes strayed back to her photo, her light eyes capturing my attention. Her appearance was unusual, but it was the determination shining in the green orbs that was magnetizing.

"We are in orbit proximity. Landing will start soon," Noymus reported, and we both strapped in as I reclaimed manual control of the craft. AIs were great to have in a battle, but I never trusted anyone else to navigate my spaceship.

"Permission to update your translators?" the AI asked.

"Granted," we replied in tandem.

So many satellites littered the space around the blue and green sphere. No doubt some of them were used to track intruders, but our craft's stealth mode would ensure we remained undetected. We would invade their borders, land on the surface, acquire the Healer, return to Saber, and they'd be none the wiser.

I PROMISE
RIVER

It'd been a tough couple of days. Sitting on the cold steel lab stool, hunched over the microscope, I felt mentally and physically exhausted. And it was only Wednesday. My vertebrae cracked as I straightened and lifted my arms up to stretch. The hollow noise was too loud in the quiet room. I told myself three more days, and then I'd finally get the white cells to react the way my team and I had been working toward for the past six months.

A humorless laugh escaped my lips. *Another three days, and another three, and then another three.* When was the last time I had taken some time off for myself?

Life had become an endless cycle, and I was stuck on repeat.

Today had been especially bad—shifts in the ER usually were. I'd been called in three times so far, and twice I'd failed to save those women. The first one had been a victim of abuse, and the second had been stabbed three times in the abdomen. She'd been pregnant too.

Two more faces that would haunt me because I'd failed to keep them alive.

Black smudges decorated the once pristine paper I'd been holding, but I couldn't get my tears to stop flowing.

God, why was the world so cruel? These two women didn't deserve to die so young.

I should have tried harder.

When an unsolicited sob escaped my lips, I felt it again—a light touch on my shoulder. It filled me with tranquility, and my shoulders sagged, breaking the contact. This time, though, arms gently wrapped around me in a hug. Warmth enveloped my body. The tumultuous sea of emotions, with its crashing waves, calmed, and breathing became easier.

Arms...wait, what? I sprang up, knocking the stool to the floor, and turned around wildly.

No one was here, but I could have sworn I felt someone's arms holding me. I shivered, feeling eyes on me.

"Dr. Margeaux, to the ER. Dr. Margeaux, to the ER."

I yelped and pressed my palm to my chest, willing my frenzied heartbeat to slow down. But like a coward, I raced out of my lab. All week, among the hustle and bustle of the hospital, I'd felt eyes on me; every time, though, that I turned around and checked, I'd found no one.

But all those comforting touches...sometimes on my hair, other times on my cheek, couldn't have been a figment of my imagination, could they?

Maybe I was just too tired, and my mind was playing

tricks on me. I tried to compose myself before I reached the nurses' station.

"Hey, Debbi, you called me?" I asked the registered nurse on the ER floor.

When she raised her head and took in my appearance, her eyes softened. "It's not your fault, you know that, right?" she asked, ignoring my question.

The lump in my throat returned, and I had to swallow a few times to get my voice to work. "I know...doesn't make it any easier."

She covered my hand with hers and squeezed lightly. She was in her early sixties, with a warm heart and a kind soul even after thirty years of working at the hospital. I admired her.

"Dr. Orli wanted to speak to you—he's in the office." She smiled encouragingly before she picked up yet another phone call.

It was busy at the emergency admissions desk, and Debbi was a real trooper. I thanked her and headed toward the bays. The after-hours nurses ran around like busy bees, checking patients' saline bags, reading vitals, and distributing medicine as needed.

On my right, an alarm dinged, and I stopped to check the patient. An elderly woman was snoring softly, and her arm was hanging out of the bed. The heart rate monitor had fallen off her finger, so I put it back on and tucked her arm inside the blanket. The alarm stopped, and I checked her chart. She had just taken pain medication that was sure to knock her out for the rest of the night. She was in good hands, being monitored by Dr. Janshon, so I exited the bay.

Dr. Orli was one of the oldest doctors in this hospital and he seldom, if ever, asked for my opinion, so I was curious to hear what the matter was.

"Come in," he called when I knocked on the door.

"You asked for me, doctor?"

He gestured to the seat in front of his desk. So this wasn't a casual matter. *Curiouser and curiouser.* I sat down.

"Dr. Margeaux, there's a project that might be of interest to you. It will require traveling temporarily to another country for the foreseeable future. An agent contacted the hospital and asked for the best ob-gyn we had. I recommended you."

Was my jaw in its place or on the floor, I wondered by the time he'd finished speaking.

Dr. Orli, though a colleague, was technically my competitor. Plus, he was an excellent gynecologist, with multiple awards and vast experience under his belt. Why had he nominated me?

"Why didn't you accept the offer?" Usually, I was not that bold, but something felt off, and even in this room, I couldn't shake the feeling I was being watched. I felt a presence, yet this space was small, and we were alone. But why was my gut telling me to run, to hide? It made no sense.

I tried to focus again on what my colleague was saying, but I'd already missed a part.

"...watching you for a while now. You've got great potential as well as youth. You have a gentle heart and a stubborn streak a mile wide. You're more suitable for this job than me..." He hesitated for a second, and I'd thought he'd say more, but he didn't.

He was hiding something, but there was no point in trying to pry it out of him. If he wanted to share, he'd have done so already. Besides, he had seniority. If he wanted me to take this job, I'd have no choice but to accept. "How long is this project supposed to last, and what is it about?" I inquired.

"The details will be given to you after the contract has been signed," he said, and I realized he didn't know. Then he added, "But they mentioned in the email that the agreement is for at least a year, and that the doctor will be overseeing a pregnancy."

Wow...I wasn't aware the hospital catered to the elites. What did I know, though? I didn't work in administration. Maybe famous people did this all the time. "Okay. Can I meet the client first because what if I'm not the right obstetrician for her?"

Dr. Orli shifted in his chair, the base of the chair's mechanism squeaking loudly under his weight. He picked up a pen and cleared his throat.

Why is he acting like this?

He pulled a single piece of paper from one of his drawers and handed it to me, along with the pen. "They have sent the contract already and need our answer by tonight."

My eyes dropped on the sheet with the single paragraph in the middle. *Geez! Talk about secrecy.* It did not divulge any information at all, it had my name on the first line and then declared that if I signed, I'd agree to travel and stay within the palatial grounds for as long as the Queen needed my services.

I did a double take. *Palatial grounds? I'd help a queen give birth? Oh my goodness!* And it also mentioned that I would be personally compensated as well for the time there, and then I would safely be returned to America.

Darn it. I needed to brush up on my geography because no one came to mind when I tried to think of which countries had pregnant Queens still in power.

"Sign at the bottom," the senior doctor insisted.

Was he in a rush? Because if I accepted this, I'd be traveling abroad. Come to think of it, maybe it was time for me to try something else. A change of scenery was much needed. I was hoping for a vacation, whereas this was a job. So it wouldn't be a break exactly, but at least I'd be treating just one person. Although, having a queen for a patient was kind of intimidating. But maybe it was exactly what I needed. I could feel the burnout, and it scared me more than serving a Royal. Besides, I trusted my abilities.

What did I have to lose? My research project was working like a well-oiled machine, so nothing terrible would happen if my team took over the research for the next year.

"All right," I said and scribbled my signature in the designated spot. It wasn't like me to jump feet first and ask questions later, but I didn't hear any warning bells, and that was a good sign.

I placed the signed copy in Dr. Orli's outstretched hand, who then scanned it and sent the email back to whoever had contacted the hospital.

Goosebumps raced across my skin, and elation filled me. Either I had just made a mistake I'd deeply regret or this would end up being the best decision of my life. Only time would tell.

"As soon as they contact me again, I'll let you know. Meanwhile, it'd be wise to have your bags packed and ready."

"Of course. I'll be waiting," I murmured and left his office.

The rest of my shift was eerily calm, and by the end of my working hours I'd received an email from Dr. Orli saying a car would pick me up from my house at five-thirty in the morning. It also said that I should pack light, since clothing as well as anything else I happened to need would be provided.

Okey dokey. That would make everything much easier and give me time to have a drink with my bestie, so I texted Serina, **Hey, Freek! Drinks tonight?** Using the childish nickname I'd given her during a night in which we'd both drunk more than we should have was one of the ways I loved to tease her. She always played along.

Sure thing, Fraak! Are we celebrating? Was her instant reply.

She knew me so well. **Yes. Got some exciting news. Should I pick you up?**

No. Late meeting at the office. Dark Angel at nine?

It'd be louder than I would have liked, but it was her favorite spot. **Yes ^_^ Later alligator :D**

See you in a while crocodile 8========D

I snorted out loud as I sat in my car. I'd already parked it in my garage. I usually left it on the driveway, but I'd not be needing it for a while. I locked everything and entered my sanctuary, my home. Walking slowly toward the bedroom, I took everything in. This would be the first time I'd be away for so long. A pang of fear shot through me, but I squelched it immediately. Everything would be fine. It wasn't like no one would know where I'd be. The hospital knew, Serina would as well, and she'd raise hell if something bad happened to me.

I undressed and got straight in the shower. Turning the water to the hottest setting my skin could withstand, I let it wash away today's heartache. Wallowing in grief wouldn't bring those women back to life. Holding my head under the shower spray—eyes closed—I allowed the women's faces to enter my mind's eye for the last time, and after saying a little prayer, I pushed them behind the door that held all my failures.

When my skin became as wrinkled as a prune, I decided to turn the water off and dry myself. Then I picked my favorite little black dress and red heels and began getting ready. Black-winged liner, red lips, and my clutch completed my ensemble.

An hour later a cab dropped me outside Dark Angel, where I waited for Serina.

"Hi, Daemon," I greeted the bulky bouncer.

A grunt and a dip of his head was his reply, but I was fine with it. He seemed to be a man of few words, except when it came to Serina. Usually, he had something to say to her. I snickered, and he threw me a sideways glance.

There was no point in waiting in line since I knew he'd let us in. Plus, I felt safer waiting next to him because the feeling that I was being watched still plagued me. But it was silly. I looked around nervously and the only people here were those waiting in line to get in.

Daemon gave me another sideways glance. "Is everything all right?" The soft, deep timbre of his voice calmed me instantly.

Come to think of it, he was always there when we needed him to save us from insistent patrons. "Um...yes. Tough day," I said, as I didn't want him to worry for technically a stranger.

I guess I was more angsty than I thought if other people noticed it, even though he seemed to be the kind of guy who was protective of those weaker than him. He didn't say anything else, but he stepped closer to me. I didn't mind at all. He was big and emanated a dark vibe, terrifying enough that few men would choose to mess with him. Then I saw Serina walking toward me, looking like a million bucks and turning heads her way.

Daemon growled, and if I hadn't been standing right next to him, I would've missed it. *Interesting.* He was not as unaffected by her as he made us believe.

Serina hugged me tight, almost knocking me over. I wrapped my hands around her too.

"Hard day?"

"No shit," she trilled.

"Come on, let's go inside." We disengaged, and Daemon opened the door for us.

"Hello, D." Serina's voice was shy. If I was asked to describe how she was around men in a couple of words, I'd say a sexy vixen. She nailed that role, time and time again. Around this guy, though, it was like she turned into a clumsy, awkward sixteen-year-old.

"Behave," he replied, his demeanor having soured for some reason unknown to us.

That single word—or to be exact, order—was what he always told her when they spoke. And like all the other times she'd heard it, she just rolled her eyes at him.

I wondered when they would drop their walls and realize there was something there. It was amusing watching them, and I'd miss it.

The place was full already, and it was only nine o'clock. We squeezed through to the bar, ordered our usual, and sat there absorbing the energy of the place for a while. Both of us gathering our thoughts and letting some of the day's stress go.

"You want to talk about it?" I asked, since she seemed to be lost in thought.

"No, it's just my asshole boss. Same shit, different day," she said, "and I want to hear your exciting news."

We'd spent countless nights talking about the struggles we'd both had to face in the male-dominated professions we'd chosen. Sometimes a good whining session was needed to get over the backstabbings, but others took too much of a toll on us, making extra words unnecessary.

It seemed it was one of those days, so I did not push for details. Instead, I gave her something to take her mind off things. "I am going on a work trip."

"Oh my god! Work trip? Where? For how long?" Joy lifted her demeanor.

"The destination is a secret location that will be revealed tomorrow. I will be gone for almost a year! And guess who my patient is going to be?" I asked, but didn't give her a chance to answer, she'd never get it right. "A Queen...a freaking Queen. Can you believe that?" It was then I noticed her face had fallen, and she seemed upset.

I put my arm around her and squeezed lightly. "What is wrong, Seri?"

"You'll be gone for a year?" Her voice was barely audible

above the laughter and chatter around us. Her eyes broad-casting all the emotions running through her. She had a mean poker face, but she never hid anything from me.

I understood what she was asking without needing her to say the words. Since we became friends, we'd been insepara-ble. The longest we had gone without seeing each other had been a week.

"A year will pass in the blink of an eye, Seri; I'll be back before you know it." I tried to placate her, rubbing her back soothingly—like you would a small child.

"This feels different...what if they keep you there? What if you like it more and decide you don't want to come back?" One word ran into the other, anxiety rising her tone.

But I could see behind the words. I knew what she was really asking.

The trials and tribulations we'd gone through at a very young age had forged an unbreakable bond between us. "You are my sister, and I'd never leave you behind. I'll always come back to you." I made sure to look her in the eyes and infused strength and honesty in my voice. I meant what I said, and I wanted her to know it.

She dropped her eyes to the floor, and her shoulders sagged. I could hear her heavy breathing.

"Seri?"

She wrapped her arms around me and hugged me tight. We stayed like that for a minute or two until she composed herself again and released me.

"Okay. I'm happy for you. You work so hard, you deserve to be recognized for what you do." Her voice was soft and her smile timid.

"And…because I love you—and I'll miss you too—the first chance I get, I'll convince them to let you visit. I promise. And you know I don't do that lightly."

Her smile this time was wide and reached her eyes. I knew how she felt. I'd be all alone in an unfamiliar place, and she'd worry; but I needed to get away from the routine for a while.

BEING PATIENT SUCKED
URIEN

Shadowing the Healer for the past few circles while waiting for the hospital's reply to our request, I learned a lot. She listened carefully and didn't rush. She was respected, and her opinion was sought after. She was a fighter, and a damn good one, saving many Earthlings, but losing two. She didn't show weakness in front of others, but I'd witnessed the heavy toll the losses had on her.

I learned a couple of things about myself too. When I first laid eyes on the Healer, my world shrank until I only saw her. Her feline eyes were enthralling, and her golden skin reminded me of the sand dunes at home. I wanted to touch her to see if it was equally soft. She was magnificent, a goddess among Humans. When her scent had first reached me, the room spun, and I lost my balance. When her seductive voice had caressed my ears, my sabertooth almost erupted out of my skin. I'd barely been able to contain him—like I was a pubescent cub and not a weathered warrior. I had to leave her to get a grip on him, to regain control.

Mine. Mine. Mine! My sabertooth had yelled in my head as he kept pushing to take control of our body.

Even though a Sacred Line hadn't been formed upon hearing her voice, Grim had claimed her, which meant he'd never accept any other female, no matter what I did. Our chosen mate was magnificent, and she was the one coming with us of her own volition.

While I had been trailing her every move, Thora had researched the Earthlings' databases with Noymus and had come up with a plan for how to pick her up. Hiring a Human to bring her to us would decrease the chance of our presence being detected because, even though we had the Cardinal Prime's permission to be here, we didn't have the Human ruler's consent.

So tomorrow we'd leave this planet with our mate.

We had to remain patient for a little bit longer, to resist claiming her as my sabertooth was demanding we do. I'd told Grim to keep our distance, to make this arduous task a little easier on ourselves. He wouldn't hear of it, and that was how I'd ended up crouched low on a tree branch across from her house at such a late hour.

This planet's single moon was high in the sky, bathing every-thing in its silvery hue. Humans were a loud species. Instead of choosing a balanced life in harmony with nature, they relied heavily on machinery for their daily needs. Technology had its advantages and uses, but not at the cost of its creators' lives. The metal contraptions they used for transport polluted the very same air the Earthlings breathed. The concrete dwellings they stayed in were small and restricting, and not everyone was given one. The Healers' Centers—hospitals Noymus informed us they were called—turned away some of their sick and injured. It seemed the leaders of this world were doing a poor job managing the bountiful resources freely available to them.

My female stepping out of her dwelling pulled me out of my musings. Where was she heading?

We can grab her now. No one will see us, Grim said, his focus solely on her.

No. We'll follow her, to make sure she's safe, I contradicted.

I like your plan. We'll see who she's meeting, and if it's another male, we'll kill him.

My body suddenly felt too tight. *Fuck!* His possessiveness was bound to complicate things. This Earthling wasn't our Sacred Mate. A mind-link wouldn't exist between us. Grim wouldn't be able to communicate with our female. How would I ever explain my sabertooth to her?

Our Queen was Changed. We will Change her, he declared.

Bile burned the back of my throat, and an uncontrollable shudder swept through my entire body. *Attempting such a thing without a Sacred Bond....No. She might die...we might end up killing her.* He knew I spoke the truth, yet he didn't want to listen. He answered with a snarl and pushed to take over our body. Breathing deeply through my nose, I focused on keeping him back. He didn't like it, and I'd pay for it the next time we shifted, but he needed to accept the limits I set too.

The door of her house opening interrupted our battle of wills. My jaw hit the floor. She was a vision. The black garment she wore barely covered her generous breasts and the treasure between her legs; her face was transformed.

Do Earthlings have the ability to camouflage their skin too? I hadn't thought to ask Kali.

My female's lips had turned from pink to a vibrant red color, her golden cheeks were now a rosy color, and there was a black line on her top eyelids.

My cock instantly stood at full mast, and a groan full of desire escaped my lips. The sound traveled, and she looked up —brows furrowed. She took something out of her small satchel and held it firmly.

I wasn't worried she'd see me—even a Saberian would have a hard time spotting me, and Humans' eyesight was far inferior—but I didn't care for the fear that made her take a step back toward her dwelling.

One of their traveling contraptions stopped near her, and she got in.

My speed, even in my biped form, far surpassed the one generated by their primitive technology, so it was easy to tail them. Stealth was of the utmost importance, and I made sure to keep my distance.

When the vehicle stopped, I scanned the area for a location that would conceal my presence but allow me to observe. Across the street from where my female was standing, another structure sat. It seemed to be unoccupied for the moment and would provide adequate cover while I waited.

Hiding from one's mate is unheard of. You're a coward—

Grim had more to say, but I interrupted him. *I'm not, and you know it. Now stop being such a grouch and help me watch our mate.*

Thankfully, he was on board with the task.

I settled on a spot and let our senses expand.

The acrid scents of urine and rotten remains of things that once were edible burned our nose. Loud music blasted through the night, overpowering the pitter patter of little feet scurrying behind me every time the door opened. Noymus had uploaded both the spoken and the written languages of this planet onto my translator, allowing me to read the lit sign with the name of this place—Dark Angel.

A long line of both female and male Earthlings waited to get inside. River walked parallel to them and straight toward the door. *Important female.*

It seemed Humans respected their Healers as much as we did. A satisfied rumble vibrated in my chest, but it soon turned to a snarl of annoyance as I picked up the scents of the males she passed in the night breeze. The only thing that saved them from our fury was the fact that she didn't pay any attention to them.

Until she reached the male by the door. He was almost as tall as me, his body thick with muscles, and he smelled dominant too. If I didn't know better, I would assume he was a Saberian too. His skin was full of markings like ours, and his build was similar as well. That's where the similarities ended, though.

A worthy opponent. Let's kill him! my sabertooth demanded.

We can't kill a rival without provocation, Grim. You know the rules.

The male's eyes diverted my way multiple times. Of course he couldn't see anything, but he seemed to be more perceptive than the rest of the Earthlings, who didn't realize the predator nearby.

Suddenly, my female took a step closer to him, and I reacted, letting out a loud growl. Her scent, tinged with fear, reached me almost instantly. I retreated farther into the shadows and away from her. The extra distance seemed to help her settle, and her face transformed into a breathtaking vision. But her animated smile was for the Human who was quickly approaching her, not me. Soon they entered this establishment that was obviously used for entertainment and were out of my sight.

Even though I had stalked many a prey before, I'd never been so impatient in my life. The spires passed slowly, turning the wait into plain torture. Grim didn't like not having our eyes on her, not knowing whether she was safe.

How could the bond be so strong already? I wondered if she felt it too when my mate's scared voice asking to be released reached my ears. I raced toward her, revealing myself. The matgen on the ship had generated the outfit I was wearing—which many other males donned too—and my skin was camouflaged; the only difference these Earthlings would discern had to do with our height difference, but I didn't care.

I didn't hear footsteps of the being trailing behind me, but the night air gave away his identity—Daemon, my female had called him. I was not sure whether he'd heard the women or was just following my lead, but he was not the enemy. I got the impression he wanted to help.

Fury almost had my sabertooth ripping out from me the moment I turned at the corner of the alley.

Earthling males don't pose a danger to us—I admonished,

trying to avoid a disaster, then added—*and you will scare our mate.*

These vermin dare threaten our female...if you don't dispense them in the next few ticks, I will do it for us, Grim warned, his matter-of-fact voice carrying menace.

The Humans had not seen or heard me yet. Neither had they seen the eerily quiet male behind me. He was probably one of their warriors who had some training.

One of the fools took a weapon out, aimed it at River's friend, and said, "You will give us what you promised, bitches, or we will take it from you."

The second pushed my mate against the wall and held something shiny to her neck—a blade.

She froze.

My hearts stuttered in my chest. One reckless move was all it would take to end her fragile life. I wouldn't lose her before I even got to live a life with her.

Wanting their attention on me, I made noise as my big strides covered the distance in a few ticks.

The two men startled. The one holding the weapon pointed it my way, and yelled, "Hey dude, if you cherish your life, leave!"

I didn't hesitate. Their archaic weapons would never be able to pierce my armor, much less my skin. Ripping the sharp implement away from her delicate neck, I grabbed the male by the arm and threw him at the other attacker. As he stumbled backward, his body turned toward River, and I saw him squeeze his fingers. The instinct to protect our mate on overdrive, I used my speed—uncaring of revealing my true self—to get in front of River before he pressed the trigger. I felt the projectile hit my back. The impact made a hollow thud, and the shell fell to the floor, destroyed.

Daemon was on them next. He disarmed the fallen males and then spoke into a device. His eyes took everything in; he cocked his head sideways as he looked at me, screwing his brows in puzzlement.

"Daemon," Seri murmured, her voice trembling.

He immediately pulled her under his arm and held tight as she burrowed deeper into his embrace. He spared a last stare full of murderous intent at the two unconscious males on the ground. This female was important to him—he'd take care of her.

Keeping my movements nonthreatening, I turned toward River, praying to the Creator she did not look at me with fear in her eyes. Earlier I may have used more force than necessary, but still less than what Grim demanded. I'd sooner kill myself than hurt a hair on her head, but she didn't know that, and now wasn't the time for me to tell her. I reluctantly lowered my gaze and met her eyes. She still took my breath away.

Although the acrid scent of fear permeated the air, I did not see it reflected in her eyes. What I saw was curiosity and something else I could not identify.

"Are you okay?" I rasped out.

Grim—as enamored by her as I was—hovered too close to the surface, and it was difficult to speak without frightening her further. He wanted to come out, smell her, lick her, rub his fur all over her body, and then sting her. He didn't want to wait to make this female ours.

Upon hearing my voice, she startled, and her eyes dilated.

A sweet, alluring scent emanated from her, and I sniffed the air to draw more of it in my lungs.

Was it her arousal? The need to taste her right there rose sharply and tested my restraint.

My mouth salivated and my cock got hard, pulsing for her.

"Yes," she whispered, then said, "who are you?" as her gaze dropped to my body. But just as quickly, her shocked eyes snapped back up to mine. "Are you hurt?" she asked, and put her palms on my chest, looking for injuries that weren't there. Her touch jolted through me, electrifying all my nerve endings. She was unknowingly wreaking havoc on my body.

Unfortunately, my Human garments hadn't fared as well as I, and her thumb caught in the hole the bullet had created.

Her heartbeat kicked up while her hands remained steady. *'How can he still be alive? He isn't even bleeding. I saw the bullet...'*

Startled, I jerked back, breaking the contact. The husky voice I'd just heard was feminine and unfamiliar.

The bond between Chosen Mates was weaker than the Sacred one. What had just happened should have been impossible, but I hadn't imagined it. I raised my mental walls because establishing a connection now that we'd still have to remain apart would only bring pain.

I can mark her now, initiate her Change, Grim said.

A loud, high noise assaulted my ears, and I hunched my shoulders.

"Are you all right? I'm a doctor," my female said, and placed her arm around my waist as if wanting to share my weight. "The police are coming, and I'll call for an ambulance. You're hurt."

The police were this world's authority figures, and I

couldn't let them see me. In the time I spent torn between my desire and my duty, she found the chance to pull a device from her purse and was about to tap on the screen when I wrapped my hand over hers. She froze and lifted her questioning eyes to mine.

"I'm not hurt," I replied because I couldn't have her worrying about me for no reason.

Daemon was here, keeping the two vermin on the ground, and he seemed to be a decent male.

The sirens were getting louder.

I wanted—no, I needed to stay with her, explain everything, and convince her to choose me in return. But I couldn't ruin the plan. My Queen and her cubs' lives depended on it. So I let go of her hand and disentangled her fingers from the top I was wearing before I turned around and left.

Walking away from my mate and deeper into the shadows was the hardest thing I'd ever done.

My sabertooth snarled and clawed my insides, trying to make me turn around. *Go back to her! She needs us.*

I sighed. I missed the days when Grim and I were in harmony with each other.

You used to be a patient hunter. What happened? We both have orders, I reminded him—my tone unyielding. *We're not going to compromise our mission because you can't wait.*

Fine, he grumbled, *we'll watch her from here.*

Darkness didn't hinder my eyesight, and I noticed the troubled frown marring her face while she examined the shell of the bullet. I held my breath, wondering what she'd do. I hadn't thought of retrieving it, and not leaving evidence behind was important.

She turned her head and looked the way I'd gone, then pocketed it.

I smiled because she wouldn't try to protect me unless she felt something for me too.

The alley soon overflowed with Human contraptions and people in uniforms. This was how the species policed their own. I didn't take my eyes off her. A female approached River and asked questions. I heard my female describing me, reporting that a stranger along with Daemon had saved them. When she talked about me, the huskiness was back in her voice, and the sweet scent of her arousal filled the air.

This time it was Grim who put on the brakes when I'd unconsciously taken a step toward her. *Remember our mission,* he laughed mockingly at me.

Fuck! Being patient sucked.

WHAT IS SHE TO YOU?

THORA

I sensed Urien outside the ship. Why had he returned earlier than planned? Had the incompetent Saberian failed the one mission he'd been assigned? He was supposed to pick her up at the airport, where the transportation we'd hired would drop her off. Then he'd knock her unconscious and bring her back to the ship.

Stopping the maintenance job midway, I stormed toward the entrance and blocked his way the moment the door closed behind him. "What the fuck happened?" I demanded, waves of fury rolling off me in tandem with my breathing—I could even feel the walls of the ship pulse with it.

He didn't lower his eyes respectfully, nor did he back down.

Stupid warrior wanted a fight...I'd give him one.

"She saw me. You have to pick her up tomorrow," he growled, pushing me out of the way.

I grabbed his arm, stopping his momentum. He spun around, his teeth sharper and longer than a moment ago.

"Let. Go. Of. My. Arm."

Did he think he'd frighten me? I had fought his kind before. I wasn't afraid.

Without loosening my grip, I repeated my question. "What the fuck happened?" His muscles contracted under my fingers, and something seemed to crawl under his skin. Was he about to shift? My other hand instinctively gripped the blaster on my hip.

He closed his eyes and inhaled deeply a few times, then spoke through clenched teeth.

"The Healer was attacked tonight. I saved her, and she saw me get hit by one of their primitive weapons' projectiles."

I dropped his arm and scanned his garments for evidence. There was a hole close to his hearts. "Were there witnesses?"

He lifted his eyelids, and the orange of his sabertooth shone bright. "Yes."

Damn it. We had orders to stay hidden. "Did you eliminate them?"

"I couldn't," he murmured, and his whole body shook.

Something was wrong with him. "You couldn't?" My voice had gone dangerously low. "You are a fucking warrior and you couldn't take care of a few weak Earthlings?" I started seeing red.

"You weren't there. She had a bond with these people. I could see it. It would destroy her."

He was making excuses, and I didn't tolerate soldiers who disobeyed. I pulled my arm back and punched him in the face. I must have taken him by surprise because my fist

connected with his jaw and he stumbled backward. A ferocious snarl echoed in the ship, rattling the walls. I let the
sound wave pass through me. For a tick the pain of the
vibration immobilized me, but then I turned my pain recep-
tors off—a very useful skill, that every Wravukian learned
when they were young—and I regained control over my
body.

"Touch me again, and neither I nor Grim will hold back
from mauling you," he said as he turned, giving me his back,
blatantly disregarding me as a threat.

I had half a mind to go after him, but I clenched my fists
and took a step back. It bothered me that he had referred to
his sabertooth as separate. Very few things were known about
his kind, for they were a secretive species. Rumors had it that
their sabertooths took over when they were far gone into
madness. But Urien didn't seem to be out of control. He
hadn't shifted; he hadn't even fought back.

"Fuck," I yelled, hoping to expel my frustration and failing.

Now I had no choice but to go fetch her. Dragging my feet
to the personal quarters where the matgen was located, I
punched in my selection, uncaring of the red warning light
flashing. If the machine broke, the Saberians would fix it. I
then waited for the purple light to scan my body and take my
measurements. In a few ticks, the clothes appeared near my
feet out of thin air. I glared at them, my anger rising once
again, for if Urien had done his job, I wouldn't have been
saddled with the tedious task of picking up the Earthling
from the arranged location.

*What would you have done? Let her get injured or die? Humans
are so fragile.* The thought crept in, dousing the fire within me

because, yes, I'd have done the exact same thing as the warrior.

I'd never abandon a female in need.

Creator this planet was messing with my head. The more I learned about its history, the less sense it made, and the less I liked this destructive species. Such arrogance was rare. Such supposed superiority was laughable. Humans destroyed any and every thing they feared. They didn't take care of their planet or the more vulnerable species on it, but most importantly, they did not treat each other with equality.

I wanted this mission over, and I believed that if you wanted something done right, you had to do it yourself. Revenge was within my grasp. I just had to be patient for a little while longer because I'd never failed to do my duty before, and this time wouldn't be the first.

The roar of engines firing up assaulted my ears, and the scent of fuel fumes permeated the air. One of their cargo crafts was heading toward a runway. There were a few small airships scattered around the airfield, and dust covered most everything. A small structure that had seen better days was still standing, and a few Humans pulling their luggage were hurrying toward their destinations.

Scanning the small airport for the twentieth time, I sighed and instantly regretted inhaling the sandy particles. Despite my coughing fit, I picked up the loud rumble of an approaching land vehicle.

I moved to the front of the building's gates to greet her

and keep the Healer from going in there. The less we were seen, the better.

Soon the transport contraption stopped in front of me.

The driver got out first, never taking his eyes off me—his gaze scrutinizing while he furrowed his brows and clenched his jaw.

I'd made sure the facade they'd see would be of a common Human face; none of my characteristics were memorable besides my height. That I couldn't disguise, but Noymus had searched their databases and assured me I wouldn't stand out too much because there were a few Earthlings who were almost as tall as me. But this male in particular seemed to suspect something.

The side door opened, and my body buzzed with excitement.

She stepped out, and my breath caught in my throat.

A light breeze carried her scent to me, and it was like some unseen force punched me in the gut.

What the fuck? The discipline I'd honed during countless battles was the only thing keeping me from folding my body in half and gasping for air.

"Thank you," she told the male when he unloaded her suitcase.

Her soft voice caressed my ears, lifting the spell I was under. A calming aura surrounded me, and the weight I always carried on my shoulders was momentarily gone.

Wary of the power she seemed to have over me, I stepped backward. Was she a spell-yielder? What witchcraft was this?

No one had ever had this effect on me.

She had to be a Mystique—a creature who could wield the elements and bind with magic—a powerful one at that.

I snarled, vocalizing my discomfort, and she gasped.

The driver looked at me sharply and moved in front of her...as if to protect her from me.

Foolish Earthling, thinking he was powerful enough to stop me; thinking he could keep what was mine from me.

The pungent scent of fear permeated the air, bringing me to my senses. She was afraid of me, and I hated it.

Mine. The single thought was louder than all others in my head.

No, no, no! That couldn't be. I would never pair with another female—I had failed to protect one already, and I wasn't going to make the same mistake by choosing another one.

"Excuse me?" Her inquiring voice was soft and unsteady.

Fuck, I had spoken out loud. She made me lose my equilibrium, her effect on me...unsettling.

Clearing my throat, I tried to soften my tone. "Miss Margeaux, my name is John, and I'll be escorting you to the Queen."

The driver was still shielding her from me, but it didn't matter. I chuckled, finding his ignorance amusing. One blink of his eyes would be all it took for me to reach him and snap his neck in two as easily as I would a dry twig.

"Um, nice to meet you, John," she said as she sidestepped the driver, who reached out and blocked her with his arm.

I tensed and pictured the exact steps I'd make to dispense with the annoying male. To touch another's female without permission was a crime, and his life was of no consequence to me. I had no qualms about serving the required punishment and being done with it.

If he had a smidgen of self-preservation, he'd fall back.

Now.

She lifted her face to look at him while her fingers wrapped around his forearm. She had no business touching him either.

I glared at them. The fury blazing in my veins was unprecedented. Why was she evoking such visceral emotions from me? I tried to calm myself and use my logic. I had frowned upon Urien messing up his part when I was about to do the same.

This female was more powerful than I'd assumed, eliciting such strong reactions from seasoned warriors.

"Which Queen? Where will we be heading?" Her voice pulled my attention back to her.

I noticed the driver had dropped his arm, but still remained next to her.

"Everything you need to know is in the file on the plane. The hospital has already received the necessary data pertaining to our Queen. I'm not at liberty to say more than that."

My answer seemed to satisfy her—not the driver, though.

"Thank you, Stephen, for bringing me here," she politely dismissed him, and I smirked. He opened his mouth, about to speak up, but he must have decided against it because, with a shrug of his shoulder and a last look full of suspicion my way, he got in the car and drove away.

Thank the Creator for small blessings because his

behavior toward her drew every possessive trait I had to the surface.

"I'll carry your luggage," I said, picking up her baggage, my tone gruffer than usual, then I turned on my heels and walked toward the plane parked the farthest from the building and out of sight of the Humans in this place, expecting her to follow my lead.

After a moment of hesitation I heard her footsteps behind me.

*Submissive female...*I liked that.

She was quiet, and I didn't mind the silence—it would make everything much easier.

The moment we passed the last craft, I was on her. She gasped in surprise, but I'd already sprayed her, and she instantly fell into a deep sleep. Her muscles gave in to the drug, and she collapsed, but I caught her before she hit the ground.

Her body was soft, plush—such a contrast to mine. My cock had awoken the moment I saw her, but now that I was touching her...it hardened even more, and walking became painful. Her alluring scent, right under my nose, tested my patience to the point I couldn't resist bending and smelling her neck. A flowery aroma mixed with an underlying sweet scent wafted from her smooth skin and went straight to my head, making me feel light-headed...drunk...tethered.

Had she somehow spellbound me already? She couldn't have. Noymus had not found any files on Mystiques. They didn't exist on this planet.

I shook my head, trying to dissolve the fog clouding my mind, then activated a stealth shield around us. Securing her tightly in my arms, I picked up her luggage and started running toward my ship. On the way, my eyes kept drifting downward. I told myself it was because I had to safely deliver her to Saber. It didn't mean anything else. I wasn't making sure that she was still breathing, and I definitely wasn't admiring her beauty.

The female was still soundly asleep in my arms when we reached our S-970. I deactivated the shield and placed my palm on the reader next to the ship's hatch.

The second it opened, Urien leaped in front of me, blocking the way.

"Give her to me," he ordered. His voice had more gravel that warned me his sabertooth was close to the surface.

His demand rubbed me the wrong way, and I tightened my hold on her. "I'll take her to the ship's quarters." I couldn't keep the growl from my voice, nor did I care to do so either.

He didn't move, and his hands no longer had fingers but claws. "If you value your life, Wravukian, you'll give her to me."

The desire to keep her sharply arose in me, taking me by surprise. She was just a mission, nothing more, but I couldn't make my arms pass her to him. "What is she to you?"

"Mate."

The single edict that was more of a snarl than an actual word rocked me to my core.

Fuck. Fuck! My body revolted at what I was about to do, but I had to. No one got between mates. No matter the unfamiliar emotions this female was evoking in me, she was not mine. Nor did I want her to be. A puny, fragile, lowly Human.

Keep lying to yourself...

I ignored what my mind was saying and offered her to him. His growl turned into a purr the moment he drew her close to his chest. He turned around and disappeared, while I was left behind, feeling baffled and uncertain. I ached to follow him. *What the fuck am I doing?* Locking my feelings down, I squashed every emotion she had awakened so far to smithereens and headed to the bridge.

It was time we left this primitive planet and returned to Saber. I'd done my duty, and now I'd demand my reward. I brought up the galactic maps on the viewscreen and studied the path we'd taken before. "Noymus, set a course for Saber; keep to the same route."

"Speed and mode, Admiral?" the ship's AI asked.

"Activate stealth mode, engines full force the whole way," I ordered, certain that our journey back would again be uneventful.

"Yes, Admiral."

Flying was freedom—a joy unlike any in the worlds. The exhilaration was indescribable, yet I couldn't focus on the task at hand. I ground my teeth, my desires at war with my logic. "Report status of the female," I said—trying to keep from checking on her and failing.

The AI complied at once. "Vitals are normal. She is in deep sleep in the Healers' Bay." After a while he added, "We are ready for liftoff."

I strapped into my seat and took my time to check all the S-970's systems, using both the control panels and my senses. When I was satisfied everything was in working order, there was only one thing left to do. "Inform Urien to prepare for liftoff in ten ticks and start countdown."

"Ten, nine, eight,…,three, two, one."

I blasted off the surface of this planet, with our precious cargo along with all the information about this species Noymus copied from their own digital networks without anyone having the slightest idea we were ever there.

WHAT ARE YOU?
RIVER

Ouch! Something had just jolted me awake.

My temples were throbbing, and I raised my hand to massage the sore spots—only, it didn't move.

I was trapped.

A shiver of fear raced down my spine, and I started trembling.

My brain felt foggy, and I couldn't remember what had happened.

I tried to breathe air into my lungs, but some kind of film was blocking my airways. I was suffocating and couldn't do anything about it.

Suddenly, two big, steady palms applied pressure to my sternum.

"Breathe." The rich, gravelly voice was low—barely above a whisper—but my body obeyed, and I hungrily gulped sweet oxygen.

"Open your eyes," he ordered, and I squeezed them tighter.

A peculiar feeling insisted that something was very, very wrong. And, like the coward I was, I tried to avoid confrontation for a little bit longer.

A feline's purr, as loud as an engine's, sounded near me, then was cut off abruptly.

Oh my God, there was a big cat with us. Was it planning to eat me? I started panicking and hyperventilating again as thoughts of me becoming an animal's main dish invaded my mind.

"I'm not going to hurt you. You're safe," the man, whose hands still remained on my body, vowed in a solemn tone.

I was certain he was trying to reassure me, alas it was not him I was afraid at the moment, but the feline that seemed to be in the same room with us. Although, on second thought, I couldn't fathom why I didn't fear this stranger. We clearly weren't acquainted.

"What about the lion, or is it a tiger? Is it your pet?" I hated the tremble in my voice.

Butterflies took flight in my stomach upon hearing his husky laugh. Sweet Jesus, this man sounded gorgeous.

"Grim is a sabertooth, and he won't hurt you either." What was he talking about? Sabertooths were extinct. "Open your eyes, psehimou," he demanded, and I could no longer deny him.

I slowly opened my eyes, but everything was hazy. "What does that mean?" I asked and blinked a few times, trying to get my vision to clear.

What is wrong with me? I wondered as I took stock of my situation. I couldn't remember how I'd gotten here, and I didn't know where here was. My eyesight was blurry, my mouth was dry, and my throat was parched. *Shit.*

"Did you drug me?" Shock raised my voice a couple octaves. "Who are you?"

Bits and pieces of what had happened the last time I was conscious were coming back to me in flashbacks as the room and the man standing above me came into focus.

I blinked and gaped. Was I hallucinating? Because the term man didn't apply to him. He looked humanoid, with two arms, two legs, and one head. He was tall, with wide shoulders and a uniform showcasing his defined musculature. But his skin was a few shades of orange, with markings, or maybe they were tattoos, the same color as his hair—dark green. He seemed familiar, and yet I was pretty sure I wouldn't have forgotten meeting him. His facial features were just...more... more pronounced, more intense, more masculine, but the most striking feature on his face were his eyes—wholly focused on me; their intense alien-green color captivating.

This was no man; and when I took in the whole room with the foreign instruments, I realized that this was like no place I'd ever seen in my life.

My fight or flight instinct kicked in, and I hastily scrambled off the surface I lay on, moving toward the wall farthest away from him.

Weapon. I need a weapon.

But there was nothing. Everything was neatly put away.

There weren't any exits either.

My short and fast huffing breaths sounded loud even in my own ears. If I didn't calm myself, I'd soon pass out, and what good would that do? My eyes were drawn to him again as he raised his arms, palms up and facing outward in a calming gesture.

A deep sound, like a low purr, reached my ears, the cadence slipping slowly into me, communicating in a primal way that I was safe.

"My name is Urien, and I'm not going to hurt you," he repeated calmly. "Please, sit down, and I'll explain everything."

"How could I possibly trust my kidnapper? Where are you taking me?" The words tumbled out of my mouth, one on top of the other, with little to no control from me, broadcasting my agitation and fear.

He lifted his nose slightly and his nostrils flared. He grimaced, but was quick to school his features. "I was the one who thwarted your offenders, and guarded you and the other female. We didn't kidnap you. We are taking you to our Queen," he said matter-of-factly, making my head spin.

What the heck? This was the guy from Dark Angel? He wasn't orange with green spots and stripes at the time, but I guess disguising one's appearance wasn't that difficult to achieve. He'd stood in front of me and taken a bullet.

My heart be still.

I doubted anyone else would dare defend me against a freaking bullet. A slew of emotions swamped me, for he was checking all the boxes for the ideal man...but he was clearly not a man but an alien. *How can I possibly feel attraction toward him?*

Confused, and a little bit scared, I chose to focus on him instead of inwardly. "Did you just sniff me?" The shrill in my voice was nearing hysterical proportions, something that had never happened to me before. Usually I was very calm and levelheaded when dealing with crises.

He hunched his shoulders but stood his ground. "You're safe with us. Both Grim and I will protect you with our lives."

Whoever this Grim was...his name wasn't very encouraging.

"Please," he said tenderly, and motioned toward the table with his big-as-a-plate hand.

Oh my God! I bet my breasts would not spill out of his palms, I bet it'd feel good if he squeezed them.

What the heck! I chided my inner hussy. The man...alien was making an effort to try to appeal to my logic, but it had currently left the building.

Wait, were we even in a building? Were we even on Earth?

I didn't know whether he could hear my inner turmoil, or whether my face was so transparent that he saw I was driving myself insane out of fear, but his next words were not uttered softly, or gently.

"Sit." A single word. A definite order.

I hated orders. I had worked long and hard to be the best at what I did, to make sure I was the one giving them, but my body didn't seem to mind because it immediately obeyed him. My feet led me to the table while my mind was screaming at me to stop moving, to run away from and not toward him.

His deep baritone elicited more reactions from my body than any other guy before. *What is it with this male and my libido?* I felt heat pooling in my core and warmth trickling onto my panties. Embarrassment flooded me, and I was sure my cheeks were crimson by now.

He canted his head sideways, his nostrils flaring again.

I buried my face in my hands. He had definitely smelled the air. Could he scent my arousal? Mortified, I wished for the ground to open up and swallow me whole, when a growl similar to the sound of an engine on idle filled the space.

Startled, I dropped my hands and scanned the place.

It was clear that the predatory tone was coming from him. Weird, but then again, he was an alien.

Well, on the bright side, a sabertooth wasn't about to devour my body.

I hoped.

Standing in front of the table, I wondered how I'd get on—it was too tall for me to climb in the state I was in—when movement caught my eye. He was coming my way. I shivered. The lethal grace with which he moved, combined with his laser-focused gaze was mesmerizing, wreaking havoc on my body and will because I found him beautiful.

They must have done something to me. Maybe it was the drug they'd given me, because I had never had such a reaction to men.

As he inched closer, I tried to step back, but the table blocked my escape, and before I could think of anything else to do, he was standing in front of me.

I lifted my head to look up, and up, and up to reach his eyes.

His heat enveloped me, and the plain-to-see hunger in his exotic eyes caused my heart to beat double time. *So now you decide to beat for a man? For an alien? Traitor,* I chastised myself because, seriously, someone had to stay responsible in this train wreck waiting to happen.

He placed his hands on my hips, flexed his fingers—

squeezing me just right—before picking me up and lifting me onto the table.

Goosebumps erupted all my over body. I wasn't thin. I had meat on my bones, and yet the ease with which he just manhandled me threw my mind straight into the gutter.

He's an alien, for God's sake, a little voice admonished.

But then his thumbs found their way under my top and drew smooth circles on my skin—the touch electric. I felt it to my bones, and the unexpected intensity made me flinch.

Undeterred, he didn't drop his hands. After a few seconds —an eternity—his right palm covered my hand before he trailed the back of his nails slowly upward, igniting a burning desire with his seductive touch. Then, as if having teased me or himself enough, he cupped my shoulder, splaying his long fingers and grazing the top of my left breast.

A full-body tremble I couldn't control started in my core and spread all over my body.

The tips of his lips lifted before he continued his exploration by circling my throat. I stiffened, and he tightened his hold for a second before his hand slid to the nape of my neck, where he gathered my hair in his fist and pulled my head backward.

The slight bite of pain transformed to pleasure, traveling straight to my core and making me fidget against something rock solid.

Under his spell and completely focused on the path his hand was taking, I hadn't noticed him wedge himself between my now spread thighs, our clothes the only barrier separating us.

God, he's hard all over.

Eyes glued to his, I was unable to move my head. This close I could see thin orange lines like jagged streaks of lightning within his vivid green irises. The long lashes should have looked feminine, yet they didn't. Mesmerized, I was so lost in my observations that I almost missed him lowering his head toward me. Almost missed his lips coming for mine.

He pulled me flush against his body and kissed me—*no that is not what he did*—he devoured me. His hunger was insatiable. As his lips moved with mine, his tongue licked my seam and demanded entry. I couldn't resist, needing to know how he tasted. My whole body was on fire, and he was the only one who could put it out. The moment he gained entry, a rumble started somewhere in his chest. The vibration on my hardened nipples was more than I could handle.

I moaned, and his kiss turned frantic.

I was making out with an alien.

That thought was a bucket of cold water over my inflamed libido, and I froze.

Instantly, he pulled back. For a second he looked at me questioningly, but then his eyebrows lifted, and his mouth fell open in a horrified expression.

Oh my God! Was my kiss so bad? Did aliens do it differently?

"What?" I could barely push the word out—fear overtaking my senses. What would he do since it was obvious I'd messed up?

"Your lips are melting," he cried.

"Melting?" I asked, confused, my voice steadier than earlier. What was he talking about? I brought my fingers to my lips. When I pulled them away, part of my pink lipstick was smeared on them.

The relief over not being such a horrible kisser was instantaneous, and I giggled. I wanted to reassure him that I was all right, but the giggles turned into loud laughter, and I couldn't speak. My abs were hurting, but I couldn't stop. This had been such a weird day so far, and I still had so many questions, but laughing helped drain the tension I'd been carrying.

Suddenly, he grabbed me by the arms, turning his head left and right, unsure what to do. I could almost feel the horror rolling off him.

"I'm okay. It was just my lipstick."

My words seemed to fall on deaf ears, so I took my sleeve and wiped it all off, then grabbed his face, trying to get his attention and failing.

"Sweetheart, that was just my lipstick." What had gotten into me and made me call him sweetheart? I would blame it on stress and move on. "Look. My face is fine," I insisted, raising my tone.

He did look at me then. The breath rushed from his lips, and he sagged before shaking himself and straightening again.

"Why would you hide such beautiful lips?" He seemed to truly be baffled.

I pondered his words for a minute. Perhaps he didn't know what makeup was. Maybe where he was from females didn't have to enhance or change their appearance to attract a male. The notion seemed so foreign to me. *Imagine that.* I realized with a sinking heart that it was a terrible thing we women did to ourselves. We felt obligated to change ourselves in order to find a man—often via painful procedures too. And we just took it all in stride, as a given, as the only way of appropriate behavior.

It saddened me immensely, but, on the bright side, I probably wasn't on Earth anymore—I'd been abducted by smoking hot alien, who was currently raising an eyebrow at me, making me swoon.

"That is what women do on Earth," I explained.

"Why?" His question was valid, but I didn't like the answer I had for him.

"Because that's the way it is if we want to find a boyfriend. Natural beauty is rarely appreciated, unless a woman is already perfect."

His eyes traveled from the top of my head to where our bodies still touched, and the rumble returned. "You are perfect, you don't need...lipstick. What is a boyfriend?" he asked.

I gasped, and did a double take. He thought I was perfect? He must not have known many women, then. Which could very well be the case. He was an alien, after all. "A boyfriend is a man who a woman has an intimate relationship with," I explained, but every word leaving my mouth made him tense more; the throaty purr coming from him went deeper and rougher, turning into an aggravated growl by the time I closed my mouth.

"Do you have a boyfriend?" His gravelly tone gave me the impression that if that was the case, we'd turn back and he'd erase him from existence.

Suddenly, fleeing was the only thing on my mind.

A loud snarl froze me in place and made me focus on him again.

Fear warred with curiosity and lust. How often did one have the opportunity to study another species? The scientist in me took over, puzzled by this animalistic sound he was producing. How different was his anatomy from a human's, I wondered?

"River," he growled, a warning over the purring.

My name rolled off his tongue, causing butterflies to take flight in my stomach. "No," I answered, needing to pacify his anger. I never liked confrontation.

That seemed to satisfy him until another thought crossed his mind. Scowling, he clenched the fist holding my hair. Such a sexy yet intimidating sight. "Did you ever have a boyfriend?" he continued with his inquisition.

I couldn't understand how the deep timbre of his voice had such an effect on me. It was like an electrical current ran through my body and ended in my core, waking up synapses along the way that had been dormant my whole life. I was drenched. How could that be? I'd never met a man I'd had such a visceral reaction to, and, okay, technically he wasn't a man, so why did my body choose to wake up now? *Hello, Stockholm syndrome.* I needed to snap out of this trance. "No," I replied.

"No one has touched you before." A statement, not a question.

How could he tell? Did I have a sign on my forehead that said virgin?

His other hand—still on my hip—snaked down my leg, reached my knee, then slid upward once again, caressing the inside of my thigh.

What was he doing? I felt my cheeks burn. I bet my face was as red as a tomato by now.

He cupped my mons over my pants and I stilled—afraid he'd move, afraid he wouldn't.

"No one has touched your pussy before." Another statement. I shook my head in denial because he was successfully scrambling my mind.

He lightly applied pressure with the heel of his palm right on my clit, making me moan.

Kill me now...on second thought, do not kill me. Will he make me come? That had never happened before. When I masturbated, it was either a hit or a miss, and I couldn't understand the fascination people had with the act.

His hand sneaked into my panties, bringing me out of my musings. "What are you doing?" I managed to stutter, before another moan escaped my lips.

"You saved yourself for me, Mate, and it's time for your reward," he said, his husky tone revealing his determination. "Will you allow me to give it to you?" His lips tilted upward, the smile taking my breath away.

Clearly, he was stronger than me. If he'd wanted to force himself on me, he could have done so already, and I would've been incapable of stopping him, yet he'd just stopped to ask for permission to give me pleasure. He couldn't possibly be that bad.

I nodded my assent and gasped when he slowly started exploring my most private area before he found the entrance —the whole time his focus remained on my face.

He slowly inserted a single digit in me, and I was ready to come apart. The thickness caused a variety of reactions; pain and pleasure vying for first place.

His fingers were way thicker than mine, but then again he

was way bigger than me. Unbidden, a dirtier thought crossed my mind, was he big all over? Was his cock bigger as well?

I thought I didn't have a G-spot, having never found it, yet he located it so easily, making me whimper as he used a come-hither motion to stimulate it. How did he even know it was there?

Sweat coated my skin. My heart raced, and my panting sounded too loud in my ears. A pressure was building low in my belly, and it was unlike any I'd felt before. I closed my eyes and he stopped stimulating my magic button. I snapped them open, mad at him for stopping.

He chuckled, and inserted his finger deeper. The sharp sting made me jump on the spot, and he instantly stopped.

"This pussy is mine," he growled, his earlier mirth gone. "No one touches what is mine, unless they want to die," he threatened, and I shuddered as he slowly pulled his finger outward and resumed playing with my G-spot. "Do you understand, little one?"

It was so hard to focus on his words. The come-hither motion he was using had brought me close to the brink again, but would he let me tip over this time? I was panting and moaning, begging without words to be allowed release, when he stopped abruptly. I whimpered, but managed to give him my full attention.

The hunger in his eyes was scary as he said, "When I ask a question, I expect an answer…unless you wish to be punished. Then I'll happily oblige you."

I gasped at how nonchalantly he had stated that. What punishment? Would he beat me? This time the shudder going through me was not from arousal but from fear, turning my blood cold, and I unconsciously recoiled.

He instantly picked up the change in my demeanor. And tightened his hold, blocking any movement I might have made.

"I will never hurt you, psehimou," he vowed, and I wanted to believe him. "When you earn your punishments, I'll make sure you enjoy every bit of them." Inwardly, I rolled my eyes at him. Somehow his certainty that he'd be the one punishing me helped me relax. "I'll never give you more then you can handle." His voice softened at the end, and he resumed his come-hither motion.

"You are mine. Anyone who puts his hands on you forfeits his life. Do you understand?"

This male was intense, but I didn't mind playing his game for now. "Yes," I whispered, giving him the answer he wanted to hear, so he continued what he'd been doing. "Please…" My begging did the trick, and he intensified the pumping of his finger at the same time his thumb started rubbing delicious circles on my clit.

I came apart. I might have screamed, but he covered my lips with his and swallowed the sound.

He held me upright on the table, when I would have crumbled to the floor in a puddle at his feet.

Then, when the last waves rocking my body faded, he slowly withdrew his finger and brought it to his mouth, tasting me.

My face burned similarly to that time I'd accidentally stepped too close to my fireplace, and I was certain my skin had turned beetroot-red.

Licking it clean, he groaned a sexy sound. Just the sight of him had my pussy clenching again.

He chuckled and locked his lips with mine in an exploratory kiss that quickly turned into more when I tasted myself on his tongue. Inching my hands along the roped muscles of his forearms, I wrapped them around his neck and pulled him closer. The feel of the texture of his tongue, unexpectedly rough and sandpapery, made me gasp. Taking advantage of the opportunity, he explored my mouth. His tongue duelled with mine, before he retreated, sucking my lips, gently nipping my flesh, adding fuel to the fire he'd ignited in me.

He started the kiss, and he was the one to end it while I stared at him with starstruck eyes.

But then something stung the side of my neck, and on instinct, I swatted the bug, only to hit a furry tail.

It was just the two of us here, when had the animal come in? I looked down to search for it.

"What are you?" I gasped. The alien stood on two paws instead of the feet I'd seen earlier, and a tail that curled at the top like a question mark sat still on the floor behind him. I blinked multiple times. There was no other explanation; my eyes were deceiving me.

Suddenly, a sharp ache made my heart throb. I pressed my palm to my chest, but it didn't lessen. The doctor in me insisted I was too young and healthy to be having a heart attack. My breathing became quick and shallow, and the room spun around me.

The alien picked up my sweaty hand and placed it on his

chest, spreading his other palm on top of it. *'Feel my hearts, little one, let yours follow mine. It will be over soon.'*

Something had gone horribly wrong—probably, my sanity. I'd just heard his voice, but his mouth had not moved. I was certain of that fact because my eyes were glued to the lips that had wreaked havoc on my senses.

My brain must have had too much excitement for one day, though, because suddenly the lights were out and I lost consciousness.

I WAS IN SERIOUS TROUBLE
RIVER

Aw shiznit! Not again.

Something jostled me awake, but my eyelids weren't cooperating when I tried to lift them.

That meant I had checked out, only this time, my brain was not fuzzy, and all the details came rushing back. I wasn't on my bed, but somewhere with an alien who was half animal, half humanoid. We were definitely not in a building because it was shaking too much and breathing was difficult.

Come to think of it, I had trouble drawing in air because something heavy was sitting on my chest. Taking stock of the situation, I sneaked a peek.

No sooner had I opened my eyes than I closed them again. My voice thick in my throat, I was too terrified to even scream.

There was a huge animal on top of me, the constant growl bubbling in its chest low and menacing. The sound turned into sensation as the vibrations spread from its neck to its chest, and then to my breasts that were grazing its broad underside, my clothes the only barrier between us. I was engulfed under its gigantic body, caged between its paws. When I tipped my head backward, the only thing visible was its two knifelike canines.

Oh my God, it would eat me alive. Not only was I frozen in place, but I was unable to move a muscle because it kept me pinned to the floor. Resigned to my inevitable fate, I took however long I had left to explore the creature. Its dark-green fur was interspersed with orange spots and lines —a mix of a leopard's rosettes and a tiger's stripes. Never having been near any of the Earth's lethal felines, I wondered how it'd feel if I plunged my fingers in the thick pelt. Making a snap decision, I sank my splayed hands in its coat.

"So soft," I mumbled, surprised. I had expected it to be coarse.

The menacing growl stopped abruptly and was replaced by a softer sound emanating from its chest. The low and rich notes filled me with warmth, and I felt my muscles relax a bit. When it lifted slightly off me, I looked upward, curious to see what it was doing, and was met with two bright orange orbs, full of intelligence, staring back at me.

Was the false sense of security one of the tactics it used prior to attacking? *Darn it, this is it,* I thought while waiting for the lethal bite...but it never came. Instead, a moist, rough tongue licked my cheek, my mouth, and then the side of my neck at the spot that was still sore from the sting.

Oh my God, it's tasting me.

As soon as the thought crossed my mind, it opened its

muzzle slightly, lolled its tongue to the side, and let out a chuffing sound that echoed in the room.

Great. The animal was laughing at me.

'Not animal. Protector.' The deep, raspy voice—belonging to a male and not me—rang clear in my head. *'I'm Grim, Mate.'*

It could talk...telepathically. My lips trembled and my teeth chattered, then the quiver spread to my limbs. So far I'd considered myself steady when faced with adversity, but this was asking too much of myself. I curled into the fetal position and clenched my eyes shut, praying to wake up from this nightmare.

The shaking intensified, and the predator lowered his body, securing me in place without suffocating me.

I hadn't wanted to acknowledge the fact, but all the shaking, the turbulence, and the steep angle of the floor, meant we were on an aircraft that was falling. *Please, God, I don't want to die...I don't want to die...* I kept repeating the mantra in my head when I thought I heard someone yelling, but it was hard to tell. The soul-cringing noise of metal being distorted and abused drowned all other sounds.

The aircraft jerked this way and that, nearly dislodging the being on top of me. I snapped my eyes open when I felt its muscles bunch. Then, from paws that were as big as my head, it extended its huge claws, and tore the metal floor.

I think it was trying to get a better grip, but that didn't stop the entreaty from tumbling out of my mouth. "Please don't hurt me," I begged.

'Never,' Grim vowed and placed his big head protectively over mine, tucking me in, careful not to hurt me with his knifelike canines.

It was such a profound moment. The noise quieted. The room disappeared. It was just the sabertooth and me. A blanket of peace enveloping me—I felt safe...until the shaking and the noise intensified tenfold in a matter of seconds. I wanted to cover my ears; I wanted to scream my lungs out. I tried to say a prayer because I knew these were my last moments, but I kept messing up the words. My body was rattled violently even though I was encased in a fluffy embrace. Pain exploded from within and all around me, and then blessed darkness. I existed no more.

This has to stop..., I groaned inwardly as consciousness slowly seeped into me.

Touch came first. Something wet and warm kept nudging my face and tickling my neck. I wanted to push it away, but I couldn't move my arms.

Sound came next. Whining...was an animal close by hurt? The sound it was emitting was one of pain.

I needed to open my eyes. I wasn't a vet but I could still help.

Trying to move my limbs was a big mistake. Everything hurt. The pain was sharp and intense, and it jogged my memory. I had been in an accident. The ground wasn't shaking anymore, so the aircraft we were in must have crashed or something.

It took effort to open my eyes, and when I managed it, I was momentarily blinded by all the intense colors around me. Trees shouldn't have pink trunks and white leaves.

Where am I? Were we flung out of the aircraft?

A ferocious sabertooth's muzzle nudged my cheek and licked me from chin to forehead. And if the loud whining noise wasn't coming from it, I would have been screaming my lungs out while running for the hills…although I wasn't sure if this place had any.

"Are you hurt?" I had no idea why I was talking to the animal. The whole ordeal was messing with my mind.

It shook its head negatively.

Did it just reply? I must have hit my head pretty hard, or I'm just plain losing it.

The sabertooth arose from on top of me and I gasped. It was bigger than a horse. It did a thorough sniff test all over my body, and just as I was about to freak out, I noticed another man.

No, no man, unless humans suddenly had blue skin with shimmering navy-blue markings, and were at least seven feet tall, with broad shoulders and sculpted bodies.

Another alien was approaching us…a gorgeous masculine specimen really.

"Urien, move away from her. We have orders. She is to reach the Queen unharmed." This imposing figure with the commanding tone meant business.

He hadn't spoken English, but for some reason I'd understood the unfamiliar language. That was weird.

Weirder, though, was the fact that I found his gritty voice panty-melting. What was going on with my libido? This was such an inopportune time for her to rear her unwanted head. I'd never had such an instant reaction to a man, and I had it twice now for these aliens, nonetheless.

The sabertooth sniffed the air, then turned his head, zeroed in on the other alien, and curled his upper lip in a snarl.

Holy moly. The predator's teeth on full display were a frightening sight.

I was relieved to not be the target of his ire, but as Grim took a couple menacing steps toward the other male, I felt scared for him. That guy, though, didn't share my sentiment, because he stood still, seemingly unfazed by the intimidating display.

The sabertooth roared an earsplitting sound while the other alien uttered a battle cry, conjuring two swords out of thin air. Before I could try to stop them, the fight erupted, and it was violent, terrifying, and quite overwhelming. They moved so fast my eyes couldn't track their movements, but I noticed the blood spatters staining the purple grass.

What if they killed each other, and I was left stranded here, wherever this here was? That thought gave me the incentive I needed to speak up.

"Stop." My voice came out soft and unsteady. There was no chance they would have heard me over the ruckus they were causing. I cleared my throat, stepped a little closer to them and tried again. "Stop!" I yelled. This time my voice didn't tremble. It was loud enough to be heard above their growls and snarls.

I had expected them to ignore me and keep fighting, but they both froze, as if I had cast a spell trapping them on the spot...and oh leapin' lizards, I had cast something all right because a green line formed, connecting us all in a circle.

Looking down, I tried to run my hand through it and failed, as if it were tangible...like it was real, but it couldn't be. First of all, I wasn't a witch and I didn't know any spells. But even if I did, I had only told them to stop. Yet, there was a line coming out of my body where my heart was. Turning sideways and looking at my back, I saw that it was also coming out of my back as well.

I looked at the aliens shell-shocked. The same thing was happening to them, only now in the place of the sabertooth, the alien who had claimed I was his and had earlier given me an earth-shattering orgasm was standing. I took a step back and the line contracted and expanded but did not break.

Confused, scared—terrified to be exact, and quite lost, I expected my voice to waver when I asked, "What the drat is going on?" Yet, it didn't.

"A Sacred Union. We are Sacred Mates," the orange-skinned one murmured, awe suffusing his deep throaty timbre.

"No," the other one said—the word full of vehemence—and abruptly pulled away, breaking the line and making it disappear.

I squeezed my eyes shut to keep from seeing his retreating form. His rejection hurt more than I'd like to admit. What was so wrong with me that I didn't just repel men, but alien males as well? My heart actually ached, and I rubbed the pained area with the heel of my hand.

A heavy sigh sounded near me, right before two strong arms enveloped me in a tight hug, and my head was peppered with light kisses.

The tears I'd been holding back threatened to escape. I

didn't want or need anyone's pity. So I struggled against the hold, but didn't manage to break it, and then the floodgates opened, and all my bottled up feelings spilled in a torrent I couldn't stop.

"Shhh, he'll come around," the male, whose whole attention was on me, said. "I'll make the cur feel the pain he's caused you," he murmured under his breath, more to himself than me, and it was what brought me out of the trance I was in.

Slowly, I stopped gulping like a fish out of water, and breathing became easier. "What just happened?" I asked, then on a second thought added, "What are you?"

"I'm Saberian, and you are our mate." Beneath his seductive voice I could hear an underlying snarl, and somehow, I knew it was not directed at me, but toward the other alien.

How could I possibly know that?

"Because that happens between mates." He managed to shock me by answering the question I hadn't asked aloud.

"How—" Yup, there was no way I could finish that sentence. It sounded crazy in my head, let alone if I uttered it out loud. Telepathy had been studied in the past, and there was evidence that people had that gift, but I wasn't one of them.

"Everything will be all right. You're safe, and both I and Grim will protect you with our life," he vowed.

This wasn't what I had signed up for. "Will you take me back to Earth?" I asked, hoping against all odds, but maybe deep down I already knew the answer.

He drew me closer, the warmth from his bodysuit seeping into mine. "Ask me anything but that. You're our mate. We've been waiting for you for too long," he said in a low voice, giving me the impression that he hated disappointing me.

"I don't know what that means. Who's we?" If I could hear the tremble in my voice, so could he, and my cheeks heated. Showing weakness was something I avoided at all costs, but the past few hours had been a bit much.

"My sabertooth—Grim—and I. You saw him earlier on the ship—"

It seemed I'd left my manners back on Earth. "Wait," I interrupted. "You mean you are a were…sabertooth or something?" Like in the books I indulged in from time to time?

"I don't know what a were-sabertooth is. Grim and I share a body. We are Saberian, and like everyone else in my species, we have two forms," he tried to explain, and I felt like I was living one of my shifter novels.

Hot MC? Check.

Inner animal? Check.

Alpha dominant male? Check.

Spankings? We'd see.

Great, River. Keep your freaking mind out of the gutter. I chastised myself, and Urien cocked his head sideways and looked at me funny—like I was an alien.

I giggled. For him, I was.

Something from earlier kept nagging at the edges of my mind. What had he said? I was still in his arms, and that didn't help clear my thoughts. Wherever his body came into contact with mine, it burned in a good way, and that fire was heating my core.

The sensations were unfamiliar and confusing. There we were, still in danger, having crashed on this place, and my body had other ideas. I started squirming, trying politely to get out of his embrace. He tightened his hold for a second, but then released me before he stepped backward.

As soon as he put space between us, I started shivering. I looked around us, wishing for a jacket, when the colorfulness of this place distracted me. Full of neon colors, it made for a pretty sight...a girly girl's dream, but the air was freezing and breathing was difficult.

On top of that, a killer headache was slowly making its presence known. On the bright side, though, it could have been a lot worse. We could have died when we crash-landed. Then my gaze was drawn to the fine male specimen in front of me.

How was Urien not cold? His breathing wasn't labored. The scientific side of my brain lit up, analyzing the possibilities and hypothesizing about what his biology was like.

"Why are you looking at me like that?" he asked, a deep frown marring his handsome face.

"Um...sorry." I knew what he was talking about. Serina had pointed out this annoying little habit of mine multiple times.

Serina. A sob escaped at the thought of my best friend's name. Would I ever see her again?

Urien took a step toward me, and, in an instinctive reaction, I raised my hand—palm out—in what I hoped to be a universal sign for stop.

I couldn't let him touch me now. I needed to think, to find a way to escape from here. I looked around.

The spaceship we traveled in was sitting at a weird angle. It was not that big, but it was definitely damaged. I wondered if they could make it fly again. Besides the clearing the ship had created when it crashed, we were surrounded by trees as tall as mountains and dense vegetation.

"Where are we?"

"Thora will be able to verify it, but if my calculations are correct, we are on XT-145," he answered swiftly, not missing a beat and uncaring of our surroundings—never taking his eyes off me.

His direct gaze was unnerving. Hunger as clear as day clouding his eyes. Would he turn sabertooth and eat me? Fear gripped me and made my heart constrict painfully.

Urien furrowed his brows, and his gaze darkened dangerously, scaring me even more.

Fudge nuggets! I was out of my depth here. *Think, River, what is the best way to handle this?* Maybe a diversion would work.

I blurted the first thing that came to mind, "Thora is the other guy, right?"

He bared his teeth—so much like his animal counterpart—and a loud growl erupted from his mouth at my poor attempt at distraction.

"He is your other mate." From his tone it was evident he didn't like the idea either.

This felt very important but I had no clue as to what it meant. I needed to understand.

"You mentioned 'mate' earlier when...that line appeared out of thin air, I didn't imagine it, right?" He shook his head, and I gulped a big mouthful of air, only to choke when not enough air entered my lungs. The atmosphere here was more dense, as if we were high on a mountain when in reality we were in a valley. "What does that mean?" I croaked, my voice even smaller than before, mainly because I was afraid of the answer.

"It means we are meant to be together. The three of us—"

"Whoa mister," I interrupted. Already not liking the direction of his answer. "You, your sabertooth, and I, three of us?"

"Grim and I are one and the same. We aren't separate," he said, and suddenly my clothes felt too hot, too restrictive.

"You aren't separate," I mumbled, repeating his words to myself, and I had to swallow quite a few times before I found the courage to ask, "Then who three?"

"You, Thora, and I," he replied calmly, nonchalantly, as if we were talking about the weather and not our future.

And had he just talked about a threesome? "No, no, no. That can't be." I was monogamous. Or I would have been, if I'd been in a relationship before.

Son of a gun. Had I started hyperventilating again? This was not the right time to pass out.

"The green line that connected us when you spoke? It is proof that we formed a Saberian Sacred Union. It's very rare, and there hadn't been any for more than two hundred rotations, not until recently. We are mates." He stopped and scrunched his nose—such an adorable gesture—before he continued, "It's permanent."

There was finality in his voice, and I didn't like it. "What you are proposing is preposterous. An abomination. One woman marries one man. One wife, one husband." This was not happening, no freaking way.

"I'm not proposing, female." Shoot, I'd angered him. "Your line," he emphasized "united us, and there is nothing to be done about it. Human notions are of no consequence here. It is an honor to belong to a Sacred Union. Not an abomination, as you so eloquently put it." The grittiness in his low voice along with the snarling undertone were a clear sign that I had just offended him.

Maybe it wasn't the brightest idea to enrage the alien I depended on for survival. Especially when he could do anything he wanted to me and none would be the wiser.

God, would he hurt me? I hoped not.

He abruptly turned the other way, and I had to cover my ears, lest I wanted my eardrums busted while he let out a ground-shaking roar. Shivers seemed to rack his big frame too.

I was not above begging, not when I was stranded on an alien planet with beings bigger and stronger than me. "Please don't hurt me," I pleaded.

If I hadn't been so focused on him, I'd have missed him move. He was so fast, he almost blurred—standing a few feet across from me one second, and the next towering over me. He grabbed my arms, pulling me roughly to his chest, and pinning my head there with his huge palm.

His heartbeats—because I could clearly hear two and not one—were loud and pitter-pattering like the winds of a hummingbird.

"I'm incapable of hurting you. We are a perfect match, the Creator made sure of that." His chest rose high with his deep inhale, and he pressed my head tighter to his chest, as if he were afraid I'd disappear. "I'd die to protect you. I will do whatever is needed to provide a full, happy life for you. Don't fear me," he murmured his vows to me. But the last one was an order, and again my body chose to melt at his command.

I was turning into a hussy in his presence. I heard him sniff the air and chuckle. The deep vibration doing all sorts of things to my insides and short-circuiting my brain.

I was in serious trouble.

"Don't worry, little one, you are safe with me, and Thora will come around. He doesn't have a choice. I can feel your worry beating at me, but I promise you this. We will not take you"—he bent his head, and his lips tickled the shell of my ear —"not until you beg us. And you will. That is my vow to you." His deep, throaty timbre caused liquid fire to pool in my core, and I began to worry that he might actually be right.

WHAT THE FUCK DID YOU DO?
THORA

I tried to run away, to escape her and failed. My feet took me as far as the rear end of the ship but would move no farther. A roiling sea of emotions battered at me, shredding my insides. My hearts beating painfully. My soul screaming for her.

My mate.

But she wouldn't be just mine.

I'd heard stories when I was just a youngling of the Saberian warrior tribes forming powerful unions. The offspring from those were superior to all others, both physically and mentally. But I'd never heard of an interspecies one, though.

How could it be, when I was a Wravukian, and she was an Earthling—powerless, primitive, ignorant?

Mine! My conscience insisted.

No, I'd never be the Pair-bond of my sworn enemy. I'd gone so far without a mate that keeping myself from forming an attachment to her wouldn't be a big deal.

My chest caved in, and my legs could no longer hold me. I dropped to my knees. Panting, trying to gain the control of my body back.

This fragile female won't be able to handle me or my appetite, I reminded myself. By staying away, I'd do her a service, and she wouldn't end up ruined by her own mate.

Focusing all my efforts on regaining control of my body, I consciously unlocked every single muscle slowly, painfully, and I managed to stand up again.

I wouldn't have been the Vice Admiral of the Wravukian fleet if I did not have discipline and a certain tolerance to pain. Gritting my teeth, I straightened my spine.

I did it. The first step toward victory.

But then the stifling air of this planet carried Urien's gravelly voice my way. "I'm not proposing, female. Your line united us, and there is nothing to be done about it. Human notions are of no consequence here. It is an honor to belong to a Sacred Union. Not an abomination as you so eloquently put it," he said, his timbre deeper than usual. Was he losing control to his sabertooth?

"Please don't hurt me," the female begged, breaking the wall I had painstakingly erected around my hearts. Her terror elicited a visceral reaction from my body; It forced my feet to move toward her without permission.

"I am incapable of hurting you. We are a perfect match, the Creator made sure of that. I'd die to protect you. I will do whatever is needed to provide a full, happy life for you. Don't fear me." I felt a pang of jealousy upon hearing Urien's solemn words, but he hadn't finished. "Don't worry little one, you are safe with me, and Thora will come around. He doesn't have a choice." The Saberian should learn to talk about himself and no one else. "I can feel your worry beating at me, but I promise you this. We will not take you...not until you beg us. And you will. That is my vow to you."

The image he drew was pure temptation...but I had to stand strong, I had to resist. Seeing him embrace her, though, messed with my brain, and I wished my arms were around her instead of his. Schemes to steal her away and leave the warrior behind filled my thoughts.

Realizing I was going down a dark path fast, I shook my head in an effort to dislodge the unwanted emotions coursing through me, when I sensed the power of other ships. It started as a small electrical current zapping my fingertips and steadily intensified in volume as it spread to the rest of my body.

"Hide," I yelled, running toward them, one thought foremost in my mind—to keep my female safe, but Urien picked her up before I reached them, turned, and headed into the forest.

My gut was screaming at me that this planet wasn't a safe place for us. Right before the Sacred Line had distracted us, I'd noticed it was too quiet.

Something was amiss.

Where were all the animals?

I didn't hear the chirping of feathered creatures, nor the growls of predators.

Just absolute silence. Eerie stillness.

This planet had been charted, and all data on the flora and fauna had been uploaded on the Intergalactic Enosis' database, which was available to all. I had read the reports, but when I tried to recall the details, nothing came to mind but unease. Fear, not for myself, but for our precious cargo—she was too fragile, too breakable, and she didn't have any armor on. *Why hadn't I insisted on Urien putting her in some?*

Such a fledgling mistake that could cost us her life. *Fuck!*

Urien, who'd been running ahead of me, stopped abruptly, and I crashed into his back, not having anticipated his move. He must have been expecting it, though, because he barely moved a muscle.

"What the fuck—" I started to curse him, we were being hunted, we didn't have time to lose, but then I noticed what had made him freeze.

We were surrounded by carnivorous plants. Flowers bigger than me, with toothlike petals—a parody of blooms—ready to ravish ignorant prey.

And like obtuse fledglings, we raced into their trap. Well, that explains the absence of animal life.

Roots above ground were already slithering their way toward our feet.

We had to move, and move fast.

"I need to shift," Urien said. "Don't have any weapons on me."

Knowing what the request must have cost him, I still didn't want to do it. He wanted me to hold River, so he could cover our backs. I didn't want to touch her—to feel the weight of her body in my arms...to have her scent clinging to mine.

The contact would only intensify the bond, but what choice did I have? I had to protect her.

My inner turmoil lasted for a millisecond before I grabbed her from Urien's arms and threw her over my shoulder.

Less intimate this way, a mistake nonetheless.

She screamed, and I instinctively slapped her ass. Her yell was abruptly cut off.

The moment my palm connected to her delectable back side, my cock went semi hard. Her instant obedience made my blood boil and planted all sorts of imagery of her sprawled naked on my bed in my head...until I realized she'd stopped because I scared her. And even though her fear was a knife to my insides, it was for the best. She'd understand in the end.

The sabertooth's roar and the sounds of battle pulled me back to the present. Holding the back of her legs securely, I palmed one of my two trusted weapons, Ksi—a sword black-smithed by my grandfather, an extension of my arm.

The roots of the trees around us, which had been slith-ering slowly, inconspicuously, started ripping from the ground, trying to wrap around our legs, to trap us in their grasps.

Swinging Ksi with every exhale and jumping around the deadly arms, I believed we'd make it out unscathed, when a branch from above hit me sideways. I almost lost my grip on the female.

Before the tree had the chance to attack again, Urien jumped and caught it in the air. With a powerful chomp of his jaws, the flexible bark broke in two.

Securing her more firmly, we slowly but steadily cleared a path out of the deadly forest, only to find ourselves between a rock and a hard place. The moment we stepped into the clear-ing, I lowered my fragile cargo to the ground.

"Don't go close to the trees and stay out of the fight." I

infused command into my words. Seasoned warriors didn't dare disobey me when I used that tone. Surely she—a mere Human female—wouldn't either. So without waiting for a reply, I turned and joined Urien in the upcoming fight.

When we'd exited the wormhole—the most vulnerable moment of a space leap—we'd been caught in the crossfire. A stray blast had hit the main connection to our energy core, rendering the S-970 unmanageable. We'd spiraled out of control, and the gravitational force of this planet had pulled us down.

I'd done my best to land the ship in one piece, but I couldn't do anything about the filthy pirates, who had already followed us, not missing a chance to pillage new material. *Scums without honor, trying to steal what didn't belong to them.* There were seven of them and two of us. The odds weren't in their favor, and the battle would be short-lived...but currently luck wasn't on our side. The blast we received had been intended for another ship, which was now hovering not far above the ground, in the middle of the field, between us and the S-970.

Urien's sabertooth was descending on the pirates when he stopped and stood still. The continuous chuffs that sounded in tandem with his exhales went deeper and rougher, changing into a fierce growl as the second spacecraft opened the hatches of its underbelly and four round, black hostiles fell to the ground, raising a purple cloud of dust around them.

"Move back, it could be toxic," I said, not knowing whether Grim was immune, and whether Urien remained safe in this form.

As a rule of thumb, the more colorful a creature or a plant, the more deadly it was, and it was always better to be safe than sorry. I pressed my thumb to the collar of my uniform to activate my mask. The flexible membrane covered my entire head; it would filter the air and seal my uniform from external pathogens.

I glanced backward to check on the female. She hadn't moved; she also didn't have a mask on, but I hoped the distance from the purple cloud would keep her safe. But we'd make sure to end this fight sooner rather than later, and take her straight into a med pod in case she had gotten exposed to any harmful organisms while we dealt with our current predicament.

Speaking of which, the creatures unfurled and stood on four limbs. I'd never seen this species before. They had multiple sets of arms, some three pairs others more, but on all of them, the top two ended in serrated spears.

In the blink of an eye, the sabertooth in front of me had disappeared and Urien stood in his place. "You need to decapitate them to kill them," he warned. "The spears are the only weapons they use."

That was pretty obvious since these aliens weren't armed. I wasn't sure they were wearing any type of armor either—only dark-brown shell-like pieces covered their bodies. "You've fought them before."

He opened his mouth to reply, when the creatures stridulated wings that had been tucked tight behind their backs. The sound ominous as their gazes focused on the Saberian.

Urien cursed and shifted to his sabertooth form. He was preparing for battle, and I followed suit by unsheathing my second sword, bending my knees, and centering my weight. We wouldn't escape without a fight.

Suddenly the ground shook and another puff of purple particles exploded upward, forming another cloud. Through it, another species I'd never encountered before stepped forward, emerging from the smoke, revealing a hideous sight.

At least three heads taller than me, his round head was disproportionately smaller than his body. The only discernible features on it were a wide mouth that lacked lips over pointy teeth, and two long, oval, pearly-white eyes. Three sets of arms were stacked one on top of the other— three armed limbs on each side—across its long torso.

He extended a long forked tongue, tasting the air, right before he turned and focused on the Human in our midst. "Capture the Saberian, and kill the rest of the males, but leave the female to me," he ordered, and the others obeyed instantly.

One of the soldiers turned and headed toward the pirates. I didn't mind it one bit that he'd do our job for us, but the other three descended upon me and Urien, making any traces of gracefulness I felt flee like a creature startled into flight.

"Protect the Human," I ordered Urien, knowing he was somewhere in that body.

The sabertooth had been focused on the newest threat, but he spared a murderous glance that promised retribution my way. He could fucking wait in line because the four-legged beings advanced on me all at the same time.

I cursed myself for not grabbing a blaster, but the only thing on my mind had been whether the female had survived the rough landing unharmed. The worry about her health overriding years of training and rigid routines.

More proof that she was a distraction I didn't need.

At least I had my blades. The Saberian had said the way to kill them was to remove their heads, and even though I didn't like him, his kind were one of the best allies to have in a battle. Fuck, that meant I needed to get up close, and personal with them.

They were bulkier than me, and they kept a small distance between them to give each other room to fight as they advanced my way. I'd use this fact to my advantage, as they wouldn't be as agile as me. A high pitched sound made me want to cover my ears, no way, though, was I dropping my only weapons to do so.

With a hasty plan in mind, I didn't give them time to communicate further. I ran straight at the one on the right, and just as I put myself within striking distance, I tucked my arms to my sides and dropped to the ground—my momentum helping me slide underneath his four legs. The moment I was clear, I jumped upward and onto the creature's back.

I'd taken a calculated risk, assuming that these beings couldn't swing their speared arms backward, and I was right. Swiftly crossing my arms behind his neck, I pulled them outward, my blades cutting cleanly through tissue, muscles and bones, severing the enemy's head. I jumped off him before the body hit the ground.

For one tick they stood frozen, their eyes locked on the dead soldier. They emitted a screech that made me hunch, and then they attacked. My swords clashed and bounced off their serrated spears...for the most part. They had managed to inflict shallow cuts when my reflexes had been too slow. But no matter how many successful hits I'd delivered, they weren't slowing down.

Damn it, I'd have to get closer to finish them off, and that meant opening myself to injury. Putting on another burst of speed, I collided with the torso of the one in front of me—my weight momentarily throwing him off balance. Before he had the chance to embrace me with the deadly arms, I brought my right forearm upward—blade tucked against it—and pressed it against the being's neck—the one soft spot on his body. The skin separated, and his blood sputtered and hit my mask, but I didn't stop. Putting all my weight behind the move, I managed to push the blade through and out to the other side, detaching his head from the rest of him.

This time, though, the last hostile didn't freeze, but took advantage of the fact that I was preoccupied, and positioned himself behind me. Trapped between the dead heap in front of me and the body behind me, I had nowhere to go, no way to defend myself against the attack as he thrust one of his serrated limbs into my back with such force that the pointy end stuck out of my left shoulder at the front.

One of my swords fell to the ground with a hollow thud—my fingers no longer able to hold its hefty load.

A pained hiss left my lips in a rush. The nanites in my blood scurrying to the injured site to control the damage.

Through the foreign limb, I felt the being's muscles contract. I only had a few ticks before he delivered a lethal hit. Grinding my teeth and bracing myself, I threw all my weight forward, tearing my body off my enemy's weapon. "Fuck," I yelled, black spots filling my vision, but I couldn't let go, my job wasn't done yet.

I spun around at the same time I brought the sword I was still holding up and into his neck. A gurgled sound escaped its labrum, and the mandibles that formed his bottom jaw opened wide.

Switching the hold I had on the hilt, I placed the pommel in the center of my palm, and pushed until the sword started moving sideways. One handed, it was a difficult maneuver to execute, and the creature flayed its limbs, inflicting damage across my dorsal sides before its body crumbled and the head was finally severed.

It seemed my nanites weren't enough to fix my many injuries because I was panting from the effort, and swaying on the spot from the loss of blood, when a feminine scream of terror caused a flood of adrenaline to rush my system.

The Human was in danger.

Sheathing the weapon I was holding and picking up the one from the ground, my vision tunneled to the point the world included only her.

Three pirates had surrounded her, and she'd retreated into the deadly forest. A bad choice since she'd now found herself being pulled even deeper by the bloodthirsty vegetation. Tree roots had criss-crossed around her body, immobilizing her, while vines wrapped around her neck, cutting off her air supply.

"Grim," she screamed, and red hot anger seared my veins, for she was not calling out my name in her time of need but the predator's.

Fuck, why would I want her to call out my name?

Mine, an inner voice whispered, but it was wrong. She wasn't mine, and I didn't want to be saddled with a mate. Having a female meant debilitating pain, meant becoming vulnerable and having a weakness.

Nonetheless, I raced to her aid. Disposing of the pirates first was easy because the moment the jungle turned against them, they gave up on their effort to capture her, and focused on saving themselves from the vicious meat-eating plants. Next, I cut the vines that were slowly suffocating her. The moment she was free, she threw her body on me and hugged me tight.

I hadn't realized I was freezing until the moment her body lent its warmth to mine. The innocent gesture threatened my composure, and made the walls around my hearts quake. Out of reflex I pushed her away from me—more abruptly than I'd intended—and she stumbled and fell on her delectable ass.

"You're hurt," she gasped, and I ignored her.

This wasn't the first time, nor would it be the last. I'd heal like before. "Get up," I growled, mad at her for making me feel emotions I had no business feeling.

Big, round, watery eyes found mine. "I'm sorry, I didn't—"

She didn't get to finish the sentence because a powerful roar overpowered all other sounds, right before what felt like a fucking spacecraft hit me sideways.

I'd been so focused on her that I'd forgotten we weren't alone. It was my first mistake in however long I could remember. I'd never turned my back on a sabertooth before, and now that I had, I'd pay the price, maybe even with my life.

The impact with the ground stole my breath away, and the

wound on my shoulder gushed out a significant amount of my blood instantly making me feel lightheaded.

Grim with his bulk was sitting on top of me, trapping my good arm and my legs. His muzzle was in my face—the tips of his long teeth grazing my collarbone.

"If you kill me, how will you fly out of here? Is this where you will bond with your mate?" I rasped, his weight making breathing nearly impossible.

I felt the vibration that started in his chest then moved to his throat, a moment before the roar nearly burst my eardrums.

"No," River yelled while getting up and running toward us.

Silly female, trying to get between a sabertooth and his prey—for in my weakened state that was all I was.

"Get off him, I need to stop the bleeding," she ordered while placing her hands on Grim and pushing to shove him off me.

Brave female, showing no fear to the predator on top of me.

Miraculously, he obeyed her and lifted off me, but not before he delivered one final blow. As he turned to leave he stung me with his tail. It felt as if I had been injected with liquid fire. His venom spread through my bloodstream, paralyzing my body, condemning me to sheer agony until my hearts would beat for the last time.

The deadly predator sat on his laurels, and brought his big head in my face. *'I should kill you for the pain you're inflicting on River'*—the sabertooth's gravelly voice sounded in my head to torture me some more with what was to come—*'but you're my*

Pair-bond, and I don't want to cause more damage than you already have to our female.'

"Heal him," she said, and my gaze jumped to her exotic eyes upon hearing her demanding tone.

Her voice sounded strong, yet tears streaked her cheeks. I hated them. We were the reason she was crying.

'We both know you want her all to yourself, so get it over with,' I ordered, knowing no one had ever survived a sabertooth's venom.

The eerie silence of this place had returned, my wheezing the only noise interrupting the unnatural balance, until my lungs gave up, and that too quieted.

This was it.

Looking at her beautiful alien face, I wished I could touch her soft skin one last time, but my body had failed me.

My gaze dropped to her plump lips, and I wished I could taste them just once, but my actions had pushed her away.

So few males were blessed with Sacred Unions…I wished I had given us a chance, but it was too late now.

My oxygen deprived brain started shutting down, the sides of my vision blurred, and my eyelids closed of their own accord. *No, no, no, I want more time with her!*

'And you will have more.' Grim's whispered promise echoed in my head right before I felt his wet tongue lapping my neck.

After a few ticks I was able to draw big gulps of air into my lungs, and just as fast as I'd been incapacitated, I recovered fully…well, almost fully. The hole in my shoulder still needed to be treated. I should have died; something wasn't adding up.

"What the fuck have you done?"

The Saberian shifted to his biped form. "If I wanted to kill you, you'd be dead," he said in response to my thoughts instead of my question.

"Thora, please let me take a look at the wound on your shoulder. You're still bleeding." Her gentle tone conveyed caring, and it angered me more.

Raising my voice, I growled at the warrior, "What the fuck have you done?" Not liking what my gut was telling me.

He sighed.

I steeled myself. This was going to be bad.

"I initiated the Saberian Mating Ritual," he said, turning to the female instead of looking at me. "I'm Changing you."

The ground fell from underneath my feet as two realizations hit me at once.

One, I was no longer just Wravukian, but a fucking hybrid, and two, he had already done this to her.

BETWEEN A ROCK AND A HARD PLACE
RIVER

The big blue alien hated me for some reason and it hurt, but I couldn't stand by while he died. "Heal him," I ordered Grim. He had done so with me; he could do it again, yet the sabertooth ignored me, and I watched helplessly as Thora's body started shutting down. He wasn't indestructible even though that was the impression the proud soldier gave.

The wind rustling through leaves had been loud a second ago, but now all I could hear was the gurgling sound Thora made when he inhaled.

I knew that sound—the death rattle. I hated hearing it, hated what it entailed.

The alien's yellow-amber eyes closed, and the world's brightness diminished. My heart stuttered; pain lanced through my chest as his body succumbed to the sabertooth's venom.

Grim, who hadn't taken his eyes off him, lowered his

muzzle and started licking Thora's neck. He didn't stop, not until the soldier's breathing returned to normal.

"What the fuck have you done?" the blue alien croaked, and it took tremendous effort on my part to keep myself from sinking to my knees and tending to his injuries.

I noticed the way he'd looked at me, he didn't want my help, but I had to try.

"If I wanted to kill you, you'd be dead," Urien said with an air of disdain, like someone had implied otherwise, affronting him in the process.

I jumped on the spot, and pressed my hand to my chest. God, I'd been so focused on the wounded alien that his voice startled me—I hadn't known he'd shifted forms.

"Thora, please let me take a look at the wound on your shoulder. You're still bleeding."

He ignored my request. My words, or maybe Urien's seemed to enrage him more, if the rise of his voice was any indication when he snarled, "What the fuck have you done?"

I flinched. I tried to not take his behavior toward me personally…but it still hurt.

Instead of answering him, Urien turned to me, lifted a finger, and placed a lock of my hair behind my ear before he dropped his hand and spoke. "I initiated the Saberian Mating Ritual." His voice was steady, his demeanor unyielding, and his eyes focused on mine. He was trying to judge my reaction, but I had no idea what that was—he'd explained about Sacred Unions, but nothing about rituals. "I'm Changing you," he continued, and I didn't like what the word 'changing' implied.

Although the sentiment scared the bejesus out of me, the scientific side of my brain couldn't resist but be intrigued, and the worlds tumbled out of my mouth without permission. "How are you Changing us?"

"Grim's venom carries our DNA, which has the ability to alter most species' DNA. It is deadly, but when combined with the healing agent in his saliva, instead of destroying the host, the lethal agents are neutralized, and its metamorphic abilities are amplified," he explained, but I sensed there was more he wasn't saying.

"Like a retrovirus? Wouldn't the process take a while to complete? Are there any other components that contribute to this metamorphosis?" I asked, too curious to drop it and too numb to process my feelings right at this moment. But the moment I was alone...then, and only then would I allow myself to examine them and very possibly freak out as well.

"My seed and my bite will complete your transformation and release your sabertooth," he replied, his eyes tracking every single reaction shown on my face.

He'd just lost me with the talk about me having a sabertooth. I was human. "Come again?" I squeaked.

Urien stepped into my personal space and wrapped his arms around me, but before he had a chance to reply, Thora growled, "If your fucking cock comes near me, I will chop it off." He wasn't the least bit surprised by the fact he'd get a sabertooth in the process, only about how he'd get it.

If I wasn't so shocked, I would have burst out in laughter, like Urien at the moment.

"I have no sexual interest in you, Wravukian. River will be the one to release your sabertooth," he said, mirth lightening his tone and crinkling the skin at the sides of his eyes.

Thora, who was now standing, was pissed...no, he was

furious. I could feel the heat of his emotion burning my insides.

I shifted my weight from one foot to the other. *How can I possibly feel his anger?* The sudden desire to flee rose sharply as my mind became a tangled mess of questions, and if the alien whose skin looked as if he were on fire hadn't been caging me in, I would have retreated away from them, carnivorous plants be damned.

Urien's hand drew soothing circles on my back. "You are safe," he said, then dropped his arms. *'I will never hurt you. I am incapable of doing so,'* he added, but not out loud. This time his deep voice caressed the walls of my mind.

I squeezed my eyes shut, trying to come to terms with my new reality. Aliens existed, and now one claimed that I belonged to two of them. Two that apparently couldn't get along, since the sickening sound of flesh hitting flesh reached my ears. I hated violence, it went against everything I stood for. I opened my eyes and my mouth to tell them they needed to stop when Urien spoke.

"One punch is all you get, Wravukian." What came out of his clenched mouth sounded more like a growl than actual words, but it still stopped Thora, who lowered his raised fist.

"This changes nothing. I never asked for a mate, and by the Creator I'm never pairing with a Saberian and a Human." I flinched upon hearing our species being used as curses. "I reject this Union," he spat, then spun and started walking away.

Broken heart. I'd heard the expression, but never thought it would apply literally. Yet, this was exactly what I was feeling. His parting words sliced a piece of my heart and I wasn't sure it'd ever heal.

I choked back a sob. He'd rejected me.

After Urien's explanation about the permanency of Sacred Mates, I'd been slowly warming myself to the idea of belonging to two males—instead of one, as it should be. Yet Thora—with a single sentence—had managed to destroy that picture and dig up all sorts of insecurities.

Unworthy. Unwanted. Fat. Voices of men I'd shown interest in the past echoed in my head, reminding me of what I was.

How could I have even for one moment believed that I, plain old River, could hold the interest of two gorgeous men? Inexperienced me—with more meat on my body than socially acceptable, and a career that demanded most of my focus—was not what men wanted.

I'd never be enough.

Another sob racked my body, but it was nothing compared to the pain I was feeling. And only I was to blame, for none of this would have happened if I hadn't forsaken my beliefs. If I'd been vigilant and guarded my heart, those pesky feelings about the two aliens wouldn't have sneaked in.

Urien gently took my face in his palms, quieting my inner turmoil with a simple action. His thumbs swiped under my eyes, brushing away the tears I didn't realize I'd been shedding. "The fool doesn't know what he's talking about. You can't reject a Sacred Union, only death can break it apart temporarily," he said, but his words fell on deaf ears because I didn't know if it was the truth, or pretty words in an effort to appease me.

Since the latest date fiasco, I'd vowed to never let another man hurt me. Human or alien—made no difference. I wasn't a vengeful person, but the hurt of being rejected yet again made me lash out at the soldier's retreating back. "Well, I choose Urien, so you have nothing to worry about."

Thora stopped in his tracks, but didn't turn to face me. He hunched his shoulders, and balled his fists, but then he straightened his posture and strode away.

I had expected to feel some kind of satisfaction. Instead, the door that held my insecurities tucked away creaked open, letting them loose to wreak havoc on my self-esteem.

Urien's vibrant green eyes pierced me with their intensity before I heard the order in my mind. *'Stop it.'* He hadn't raised his voice, he needn't; it was laced with command.

The next instant, I found myself against his chest with his arms wrapped around me. The steady ba-bump ba-bump of his hearts was masked by a purr-like sound emanating from deep within him. It lulled me, and calmed my tumultuous emotions. I sighed, feeling some of the tension leave my body, and my mind became blissfully empty. How could a stranger's embrace bring such peace?

"Not a stranger," he whispered, his breath tickling my ear. "Mate."

Mate...did he mean it like Aussies did? Like we were friends? "I don't know what that means," I admitted, my eyes darting to where Thora had disappeared, not finding him there anymore. I told myself that I was just worrying about his injury, his absence didn't hurt for unfathomable reasons. There wasn't something between us, something I didn't understand.

Urien once again responded to my thoughts rather than

my words. "He went to fix the ship, and he doesn't want my help." He chuckled, and I felt the rich sound deep within me. "Probably for the best, lending a hand could lead to more damage in this case."

He wasn't afraid to admit his shortcomings, and that endeared him more to me.

"Let's go inside," he said, picking me up like I weighed nothing. "Don't look," he ordered as he followed the path Thora had taken.

"Why—" My voice got stuck in my throat when the mangled bodies of those who had attacked us appeared in my periphery.

Some were mauled. Some were cut in half.

I had seen my fair share of mangled bodies during my ER shifts but nothing raw like that. My body trembled uncontrollably and I dry-heaved. I was glad it had been a while since my last meal, otherwise I'd have decorated Urien's chest with the contents of my stomach. I doubted he'd find me appealing after that.

The alien seemed to be a man on a mission. Leading me straight to the spaceship and into the room I remembered from earlier. He placed me on the table and retrieved some kind of wand from an alcove in a wall that magically appeared the moment he stood in front of it.

Hovering the tool all over me, he looked intently at a small screen full of symbols I couldn't read. "You're okay," he exhaled.

Ha! It probably was some kind of portable scanner—small and cordless. What a difference such an instrument would make on Earth. Maybe I'd convince him to share.

His need to fuss over me radiated off him, so I didn't put up a struggle when he tended to every little cut and bruise I had, no matter how insignificant it was.

I took that time to go over everything I was told, because there was one burning question that needed an answer. "Can you explain mates?"

"Please?" I added, as an afterthought. Good manners always went a long way compared to demands in my book.

He took the wand back to its place, then returned and nudged himself between my thighs, bent slightly forward, and caged me in his arms.

I thought he would kiss me again when he lowered his head and closed his eyes, but he only laid his forehead on mine, letting our breaths mix for a few heartbeats.

When the green orbs with the orange streaks found mine again, I could see the array of emotions running through him. He didn't hide any from me.

Somehow this moment was more intimate than any I'd had with a man before, and if he had kept a wall up and me at arm's length, it would have hurt deeply.

He straightened, and I had to lean back to see his face. Next to him I was a petite woman. I inwardly laughed at that thought. Being close to six feet tall, I was anything but that. Both he and Thora were close to seven feet, if not taller.

Now, why had that jerk's name come to mind?

The tips of Urien's lips lifted in a smirk.

My heart be still. He was breathtaking.

"You make this hard," he rasped.

"What?"

He caressed my cheek with the back of his hand, his eyes

following the motion, before he spoke again, "You want answers, yet there you go, having these thoughts about me..."

He was yumminess on a stick, but I needed answers, so I insisted, "Please, tell me."

A brief cheeky smile lit up his face—*ooh*, he liked me begging—before he started speaking. "For Saberians there were two kinds of family units, Mated Pairs and Sacred Unions. The first was formed when a female chose a male to bond with. The connection between the pair was weaker, but no less respected." My stomach started roiling—I hadn't missed the use of past tense. "The second couldn't be formed, it could only manifest. The appearance of a Sacred Line uniting the members of the Union was always the first indication. The connection between Mates was powerful," he explained, and by the solemn tone of his voice, I started realizing how serious our situation was.

"You said 'were'. Are there other types of family units now?" I asked, afraid to know more, but too curious to let it go.

He shut his eyes, making me think our conversation was over, but then he said, "Yenoctonia claimed all our females, condemning us to death." Between my thighs his body had gone stiff. I wanted to hug him, to alleviate the obviously deep-rooted pain, yet his posture screamed: stay away. "You see, Saberians have only one mate in a lifespan, and we didn't mix well with other species"—his green-orange gaze fell on me, and a shiver raced down my spine—"until we discovered humans."

Humans? As in plural? Cases of people going missing

popped in my head one after the other in a reel. *Don't freak out, River.*

"Silly mate," he said as he lifted his hand and smoothed the lines on my forehead with his thumb. "There is only one other human female, our Queen. You will meet her soon."

I needed to stop overreacting, but God the whole situation was overwhelming. "You know, you should have added 'Queen of Saberians' in the ad. It would have made this a whole lot easier," I joked, making him smile too. Then on a more serious note I added, "Humans choose partners to marry, or sometimes they just live together and form a family without making it official legally. Neither guarantees that two people will stay together forever, though." I felt it was important that he knew where I was coming from.

"Our union is forever, like those of my ancestors—"

"You don't know that. Relationships break; people separate," I interrupted him.

Nothing was forever.

He shook his head, rejecting my words. "Sacred Mates cannot separate. Such a thing would lead to death...." His words turned to a growl as his voice trailed off. "Mates are parts of one soul that yearns to be complete. When they meet, they feel attraction, possessiveness, lust, devotion...and once the female speaks in the presence of all her males, the Line forms and begins threading the divided parts of their soul together into one again." Soul mates. I knew they existed, my parents had been proof. "Once the Union is complete, the mates become stronger, sometimes they are even blessed with new powers," he finished.

Like the ripple effect caused by a pebble thrown in a pond,

a quiver started in my stomach and spread, growing in intensity, making my whole body tremble.

"I'm monogamous, Urien. One man. One," I insisted on denying the truth, but the breathless quality of my voice broadcast loud and clear that my hesitation had started melting away.

"We are not men, and you are not on Earth anymore, sweet mate," he said and bent closer, caging me between his arms—his lips dangerously close to mine. "I can feel your struggle. Let go of your prejudices. You won't be judged, you will be revered. Females are sacred on Saber." His tone was gruffer than before, stricter, nonetheless my body reacted in an entirely inappropriate way to his close proximity.

It was turned on...I was turned on, and the woodsy, rich scent that wafted from his skin didn't help either, making me want to lick it, to taste it, to see if it was as delicious as it smelled.

"Careful, female. You're testing my patience, but I can only maintain my control for so long." A reprimand this time.

Oopsie. I had to get my mind out of the gutter. Now was the time to ask questions, not daydream about the sexy alien.

"You said once the Union is complete. How...how will it be completed?" I asked, but then noticed he broke eye contact and looked sideways at the exit.

His fidgeting surprised me because he'd been giving off this dominant alpha-male vibe the whole time. He'd been acting so sure-footed, and this sudden change in his behavior meant it was bad. The question was, though, how bad?

"Urien?" My voice came out steady and demanding, which were two emotions I wasn't feeling.

He cleared his throat and spoke through clenched teeth. "With Saberian females it used to be different, but to complete the bond with a human female there are three parts—"

A flash of anger burned through me, and jealousy clouded my good judgment. Why would he know that the process was different? Did he have another female? "How do you know that with humans it's different?" I snarled, forgetting all about him being almost double my size; forgetting all about him having an animal inside him that could rip me in two; forgetting all about the fight I had witnessed between him and Thora, who was some kind of a super soldier, if his skills were anything to go by.

He hesitated, and I was about to shove him away from me when he said, "You are my one and only mate now. There aren't any other women on Saber besides our Queen, who was human before she became Saberian."

Now? Not the answer I was expecting. I pressed down on my breastbone, trying to ease the sudden tightness there. Was I being lied to again? I was at a disadvantage here, I needed to gather information, and then I'd discover a way to reverse whatever was happening.

His eyes widened in surprise and then instantly darkened, portraying his fury as he took two steps backward, leaving me bereft.

Cold seeped into me, when a mere second ago I'd been bathing in his warmth, and goosebumps erupted all over my skin.

"Reverse what is happening?" he asked, his voice tight and guttural.

I'd heard him use this tone earlier when he'd been angry with Thora, but he'd been mostly gentle with me.

"Stop reading my mind," I demanded, feeling equally pissed. Those were my personal thoughts, and he had no right to invade my privacy like that.

"You have the same access to me, female. The only thing you have to do is reach out." His timbre turned grittier, lower than before.

He was really mad at me.

Well...the feeling was mutual.

"If you were to harm yourself in any way, Mate, it would drive me to insanity. I would lose the logical part of myself and only a crazed Grim would remain. He'd wreak havoc and kill many of his warrior brothers before they managed to put him down."

Urien's admission drew me up short. Just the idea of such a fate made me nauseous. I couldn't hurt him like that. I'd never survive the guilt. Breathing deeply, I tried to calm myself. What he was telling me was of the utmost importance. He'd already altered a part of my DNA without my consent. Furthermore, I'd have to change completely to be with him. I wouldn't be a human anymore but something else. Yet if I tried to reverse what had already started, I'd be condemning him to death.

Between a rock and a hard place.

That's where I was. I had to choose who I'd save—myself or him.

It wasn't fair I'd have to carry this burden, but that was life.

"I won't try to reverse this." That was my olive branch to him, and he didn't hesitate to take it.

He stepped closer, placing himself between my thighs and enveloping me with his warmth. He didn't seem to hold grudges.

Another quality I'd wished for in a man. He ticked all the boxes, and darn it, I wanted what was being dangled in front of me.

ONE STEP CLOSER
URIEN

Thora, the fool, didn't know Sacred Unions didn't work like that. They couldn't be rejected—only death could temporarily break them, and his ignorance had added salt to our mate's wound. She wouldn't have even thought about reversing the Changing, if he'd behaved as a mate should.

We punish him. No one is allowed to hurt our female, Grim added, his mind on the same train of thought as mine.

Yes, we will. But first we'll take care of River, I told him and watched under hooded eyes as her cheeks turned rosy.

Inhaling deeply, I took in a big whiff of the sweetest aroma in the universe—the one of her arousal, and it had an immediate effect on my cock, turning it rock hard.

My fingers itched to touch her, and completing the second step of her transformation would make it even harder for her to reverse the process. I trusted that she'd told me the truth, but it wouldn't hurt to make sure that a reversal wasn't an option.

141

Closing the distance between us, I placed my hands on her knees, pushed them farther apart, and wedged myself between her long legs. I trailed my palms upward but stopped when I reached her hips. My fingers grazed the top of her ass and I loved that she had meat on her bones. She would be able to withstand a rough pounding. A growl slipped from my lips and she tensed.

That wouldn't do. "You never have to fear me. I'll pleasure you, provide for you, and keep you safe," I vowed, meaning every word. I was prepared to die and kill for her. Loving her would be the easy part.

Flexing my fingers, I applied more pressure than usual just to test her reaction. When she remained pliant, I pulled her flush against me. Electricity zinged through me, waking up every nerve on my body when my action smooshed her big breasts against my chest. My body seemed to have a mind of its own as my hips ground on her center, eliciting a loud moan from her plump lips.

I bent my head, and traced the shell of her ear with my nose, making her shiver, before I added, "Will you let me?"

"Let you?"

"Worship your body, psehimou. I need to taste you...I need to assuage the hunger you feel."

Taking her without consent wasn't an option, but I wouldn't make it easy on her to deny me either. I fused my lips to hers. This time I didn't hold back, I took her breath away and gave her mine. I licked the delicious seam of her lips, then applied steady pressure until she opened and her tongue tentatively touched mine, but I was too ravenous to remain gentle; I led hers to a duel, an aggressive dance, showing her all the ways I wanted to take her. This, though, wasn't enough. Her body was singing for me, calling to mine, driving me crazy with lust.

I pulled back from her, gently biting her bottom lip while doing so. She trembled but couldn't really move because my left hand was wrapped around her neck, holding her in place while the other massaged her plush breast. I feathered kisses from her chin to the nook between her neck and shoulder, where my mating bite would leave a permanent mark, and bit gently.

She gasped, and that breathless sound drove me to bite harder, but I didn't break the skin—she wasn't ready for that.

The moan that left her lips nearly broke the fragile control I had over my primal urges. "Psehimou, I need your answer."

"Mmm...yes," she moaned, surrendering her body to my care; and not only would I take care of it, I'd make sure she never forgot our first time together.

The clothes on her body that hid the sweet treasure underneath had to go. Eyes locked on hers, I fisted the middle of her top and pulled sideways, tearing it in two, revealing the smoothest skin I'd ever seen. She was wearing another strip that covered her breasts. *Did she think that would protect her?* I smiled at the thought, allowing my fangs to elongate as I bent between the two mounds, bit the fabric, and tore it in two.

She gasped and lifted her arms to cover my prize.

It was too late for that.

"No," I growled, failing to keep my tone soft.

She dropped her arms immediately.

Naturally submissive...interesting.

Saberian females had been dominant. They were life-bearers, they could nurture and be gentle for their offspring, but their bodies were lithe and hard, built for war, and they had the attitude to match. I'd never have thought I'd be attracted to someone the exact opposite, someone like River, that I'd rejoice in the fact she was soft where I was hard—her luscious curves being one of the first things that caught my attention.

"Urien, what about protection?"

"Protection?" I repeated, not understanding her question. She was safe with me.

Her cheeks turned a rosy color, and it spread to her neck and chest. "Um, you know, do you have a condom? I'm not on birth control."

I furrowed my brows. She explained, but I still had no idea what she was talking about. "What do you mean, Mate?" Then the other part of what she'd said registered, 'birth control'. My stomach roiled, and I ground my teeth. Didn't she want to become a mother, and carry my offspring? Or was it me she was objecting to?

"What do you use when you have sex with other wom— females, so they don't get pregnant?" she asked, and I noticed her nostrils flaring. "Now is not the right time to get pregnant with an alien baby."

The sudden tightness in my throat made swallowing hard. Her words hurt more than I cared to admit. But she had no reason to be jealous, and I needed to put her mind at ease, so I chose to ignore the alien baby part. "I haven't mated with anyone. I've been waiting for you."

Her mouth fell open, and I chuckled, but she quickly composed herself. "That solves one of the issues. What about the other?" she insisted.

I took in her form—thick dark-gold mane, eyes shining with intelligence, and straight shoulders. She was a sight to behold, then my gaze dropped to her tummy. The soft pouch there put all kinds of images in my head of River with my offspring, and I was looking forward to seeing it grow once we completed the Mating Ritual. "Beautiful," I mumbled under my breath, and realized a purring sound was coming from deep within my chest—Grim was happy with the way our mate was built. She'd be perfectly capable of nurturing our cubs. "You can't get pregnant."

"What?" she replied instantly. "Aren't we compatible?" The cooler tone of her voice was void of its earlier huskiness. Like the flip of a switch, gone was my mate, and the Healer stood in her place.

"We are. But in the case of a Sacred Union, unless both males take their mate at once, the female cannot get with offspring," I explained, and she recoiled.

Her reaction confused the fuck out of me. A few ticks ago, the aroma of her arousal had saturated the air, yet now a bitter, unsavory smell overpowered it.

"I will have to take both of you? At the same time? No, no way," she vehemently denied while struggling to break free from my arms. I let her go, and she scampered backward. "There must have been some mistake! I'm not kinky. I'm plain vanilla. Monogamous," she insisted, and even though some words were unfamiliar, I got the meaning.

The growl that left my lips was all mine. "I will not share you with anyone else other than Thora. You better not try to attract the attention of other males because I won't hesitate to punish you, Mate. And I promise it will hurt," I snapped at her. Thoughts of River with another male was more than I could bear.

My reaction seemed to pull her up short. She took a deep breath, then whispered, "But there are two of you and one of me."

"Yes. Forming a Sacred Union is a gift above all others. You will have the protection of two males. You will have the love of two males, and you'll be cared for by them. You will have two mates that will need you more than the air they breathe." Her lack of acceptance prodded me to add, "The faster you leave Earthly notions behind, the better it will be."

She bit her bottom lip, and then her tongue darted out to wet the swollen flesh. Curious, I touched her mind, needing to know what was running through it, and found fear clouding her thoughts.

She needed my arms, even though she might not realize it, my embrace would calm her. Her heart would follow the rhythm of mine, and her breathing would slow down. "Come here," I ordered.

She didn't move.

"Do not test my patience, psehimou, for you will find out what happens when you disobey," I snapped and was about to grab her, when she scooted closer.

I'd let it go this time. Next time, though, I'd put her over my knee and make sure her bottom turned red, and she learned her lesson—her well-being was my top priority. She stood rigidly in my arms for a moment before she relaxed in my embrace. I lifted my hand to her cheek, and she leaned into my touch.

"Okay," she whispered, her breath tickling my palm.

Just one word, but strong enough to settle my inner turmoil, to release the air that had been trapped in my lungs.

I had answered her questions, appeased her fears, and now the time for her reward had come. Taking a step backward, I put space between us so I could cup her heavy mounds and push them together, before I took one of her nipples in my mouth. I teased it with my tongue, then sucked hard, feeling the hard peak elongating. She arched her back, and more sounds of pleasure escaped her lips, spurring me on. Letting it go with a pop, I moved lower, tasting as much of her as I could on the way. The sweet flavor of her skin matched the alluring aroma wafting off her. The combination was addictive, and I knew once I tasted her cream I'd be a goner, addicted to her forevermore.

She so easily drove me to the edge of insanity with lust, but I had to stay in control—Humans broke easily. Hooking my thumbs inside her waistband and pulling downward, I took all of her garments and footwear off with one swift movement, baring her to me.

She startled and tried to crawl backward on the table but went nowhere.

"Don't," I ordered and tightened the hold on her ankles.

If she ran, the control I currently had over my predatory instincts would snap, and I'd end up chasing her. That would lead to Thora hearing her cries, and then he'd get involved—try to save her.

I wonder what seeing his mate naked would do to his rigidity.

I entertained the thought of letting her go briefly, but I was too selfish. I wanted her all to myself, so we'd play this game another time.

"What are you doing?" Her husky voice trembled.

I smirked, knowing no one had ever pleasured her this way. "I'm going to taste you."

"Why?" she asked, still trying to escape my grip and failing.

Spreading her legs wide, I couldn't take my eyes off the juices smeared on the inside of her thighs. The heady aroma raising my anticipation to intolerable levels. I licked my suddenly dry lips, thirsty for what only she could give me. "Because, Mate, your nectar is a gift from the Creator that I'd never allow to go to waste." The perplexed pout was adorable on her. "I will learn every part of your body more intimately than I know my own," I explained, and if she still didn't understand, I'd soon show her what I meant.

Her supple skin felt so soft under my fingertips. I lifted her foot to my mouth. She wiggled but subsided when I didn't let go. I kissed the bottom and she giggled. I kissed the other one too, and she tried to pull away once more.

"River," I admonished, her name rolling off my tongue easily, with familiarity, like we'd known each other for more than a few circles. "Do I need to tie you down?"

There was that rosy flush covering her cheeks again. "It tickles," she complained but stilled.

Fine, I'd accommodate her for now, but once we reached my dwelling, she wouldn't deny me the pleasure of discovering every erogenous nook and cranny of her, as was my right.

Placing her ankles over my shoulders, I slid my palms across her long legs feeling the clenched muscles hidden underneath. I didn't want her tense, though—I needed her to surrender control. So I followed the same path with my tongue. The rough texture—a contrast to the smoothness of her skin—added to the foreign sensations bombarding her, and I couldn't resist peppering the expanse with tiny bites that made her shiver and moan.

Slowly, she relaxed—opening up like the petals of a Wandalh bloom during the heat season—and presented the most precious treasure to me.

I nearly came in my armor at the sight of her hairless pussy. I squeezed the base of my cock and took a few breaths to regain control, lest I took her hard and fast, and ruined her first time.

She tried to cross her legs, but my wide shoulder inhibited her from succeeding. "Urien…" Her shaky voice trailed off.

When we visited her planet, I'd tear to pieces the males in her life that had come before me for making her feel insecure in her femininity. "You are the most beautiful creature I've ever seen. Feel what you're doing to me," I said, lifting her hand and placing it on top of my cock. "Why would you ever hide yourself from me?"

"It's unfair that you get to see me when I don't," she said boldly, and I much preferred this version of her.

"You're right." I straightened and removed my armor in record time.

Her eyes widened. "What is that?" she asked and gently probed my pectoral.

The Sirh, understanding my intent, retreated beneath my skin before she made contact.

She came closer and put both hands on my chest. Her touch ignited little fires, raising my temperature. "Does your skin change texture like an octopus?" Her tone was suddenly cooler, distant, and her gaze laser-focused on my skin.

I was coming to recognize when her Healer side was taking over. It was fascinating how easily she could switch her attention, and it'd be a challenge to keep her mind from straying. One I gladly accepted, and already, all kinds of ideas about how to distract her started forming. *Time to test some.* I lightly tapped her inner thigh and she pursed her lips in disapproval. I knew better, though, because the moment my palm connected to her smooth skin, her juices flowed.

Unable to resist her for a second longer, I bent and licked from the base of her slit to the top of her clit.

"Oh my God," she said.

Yes! Mission accomplished. Smiling, I raised a mental fist in the air.

"Not God, Urien," I corrected her, and she rolled her eyes at me.

I loved her small act of defiance, and I hoped she defied me many more times in the future, although that didn't mean she'd go unpunished.

Gently, but swiftly, I delivered a soft slap to her pussy, making my female moan in pleasure. My action got my fingers coated with her wetness.

Perfect.

Everything else in our quarters fell away, until only River remained. Her luscious body mine to do with as I pleased, and I longed to play. I circled her entrance with the tip of my pointer a few times before I slowly inserted it into her pussy. Her walls tried to block my digit, push it out, before relenting to my insistence. If my cock were to fit, I'd need to stretch her first.

Half-closed green eyes—surrounded by a hazy cloud of lust—tracked my every move as I flicked my tongue over her clit. Her moans became louder, the more the bead-like protrusion hardened under my ministrations. Sucking the little button in my mouth, I caught it between my lips and applied pressure as I inserted a second finger in her sheath.

"Ouch," she gasped, "it's too much."

I stilled my hand to allow her body to adjust, but I grazed the hard nub with my teeth, then laved it with my tongue to take the sting away, effectively distracting her once again. The alter-nating sensations—rough then soft—helped her relax. Her inner muscles loosened the death grip on my fingers, and soon she started whimpering with need, alerting me she was ready for the next step. So I started moving my digits in and out—mirroring what I'd soon be doing with my cock—then used a scissoring motion to stretch her enough to add another one of my fingers. She was all silk inside, smooth, but for a spot that felt bumpy. Curious, with a come-hither motion, I explored the raised flesh.

She arched high before her body slammed on the table as she screamed. The arm I had across her belly was the only thing that kept her in place. Her pussy convulsed, nearly breaking my fingers off while more of her nectar gushed out of her.

"Fuck!" In a heartbeat, I'd replaced my hand with my mouth, her sweetness exploding on my taste buds.

My whole body shivered, and thirst overpowered my other senses.

Finding the spot with my tongue that had driven her crazy was easy; and the more I played with it, the more she fed me her juices. Her moans rose to a crescendo, and she tried to close her thighs. So responsive, my female—her gasps and breathless pleas the perfect guide. Flattening my tongue and maintaining a fast rhythm, I pushed it in and out, never leaving her sheath entirely. She came apart a second time, and as ravenous as I was for her, I selfishly ate out her pussy.

She'd already become my addiction, but I didn't give a shit. She was mine, and I was hers.

Her hands found their way into my hair, which she bunched in her fists and used to push me away. I withdrew. The moment my tongue left her sheath, three of my fingers replaced it. She tried to push me away again, but the growl deep in my throat stopped her mid-action. Eyes that had been clenched shut in ecstasy, snapped open and focused on me.

"You can take all that I give you," I said with certainty, and her breath caught. "You were made for me, Mate."

She opened her mouth to argue.

There was no point, for I was right. And to emphasize my words, I withdrew my digits then pushed them back in, repeatedly, never breaking eye contact, not until she surrendered to the pleasure I was determined to give her.

So wet...

A hollow thud echoed in the room when she threw her head backward and groaned, "Oh, God."

A smile stretched my lips. This was only the beginning. I used scissoring motions to stretch her farther, and every time, her pussy fisted me tighter, as if it had a will of its own and it wanted to keep me inside her forever. "Come one more time, psehimou," I ordered, and ran the pads of my fingers across that special spot inside her that was rougher than the rest.

This time I recognized the signs. River was panting, and her heart was beating at a furious tempo. Her inner muscles had started twitching around my digits, and she was lifting her gorgeous ass off the table, matching the rhythm I'd set. It'd only take a few ticks before she came apart in my arms again.

"Urien, please." The whispered plea shattered the tentative hold I had on my primal urges—those that demanded I mark my mate with my seed.

In a swift move, I removed my digits and replaced them with the head of my cock. Her pretty green eyes widened in surprise, but I gave her no time to react. I bent and claimed her lips in a searing kiss at the same time I surged forward, burying myself to the hilt.

She screamed—the sound laced with pleasure and pain—and tears fell from the corners of her eyes while her body convulsed around mine.

Keeping my lower half still, I pressed my forehead against hers and breathed deeply in an effort to regain some semblance of control—an impossible feat when the exquisite walls of her pussy were squeezing the life out of my cock with her every heartbeat.

"Urien?"

Deep breath in...deep breath out..."I'm sorry, psehimou. I hurt you." I never wanted her to feel pain, yet that was exactly what I'd done.

She ran her fingers through my hair—the caress traveling to my toes. "Don't stop," she said, and pulled at the strands.

I let out a growl of frustration. What if we weren't as compatible as I'd initially thought. I lifted my eyes to hers, assessing my options, but she kept fidgeting underneath me, the friction nearly making me explode inside her.

Maybe she needed to climax a few more times before she was ready for penetration. *Damn it, why didn't I think of that earlier?*

"Don't you dare stop," she demanded; her voice, though, catching in the end, betraying how vulnerable she felt.

The trust that shone in her eyes had me pulling back until only the edge of my cock remained inside her, connecting us. "I won't," I said and pushed forward, gentler than before.

She winced, but arched her back, pushing her breasts onto my chest. Her lips sought mine, and I couldn't deny my courageous mate.

Lust...hunger...need...I put everything I felt into that kiss while I started moving, slowly pulling out just a couple of fingers before allowing her warmth to surround all of me again.

Soon, River's body relaxed under mine, and the gasps laced with pain turned to breathless moans asking for more.

And more I gave her—thrusting harder and faster. Pleasure coursed through my veins, making my blood boil. Emotions choked me. So many years of lusting after a mate, not knowing the shape of her, had come to an end. So many years of imagining the pleasure and the serenity she'd bring to me and Grim—never doubting she could handle us—and River had proved me right. So many years of despair, afraid we'd never meet in this lifetime, then the relief the moment she was finally in my arms.

Meeting me thrust for thrust—matching the rhythm I'd set, whatever pain she had felt was gone. The loud vocalizations coming out of her swollen lips guided me. Her tight pussy, now slick with her cream, felt divine. Her hands explored my body; her kitten claws that barely scratched my skin awoke a raging desire in me. I wanted her to mark me, but her bland nails and teeth would never be able to do so. A growl of frustration rumbled in my chest; the sound, though, only made her buck wilder underneath me.

I leaned on her—letting her take some of my weight—and brought my lips next to her ear. "Come for me, Mate," I murmured and sucked her earlobe in my mouth, then I grabbed her ass and lifted her higher, changing the angle allowed me to hit her sweet spot when I surged forward, making her cry out in pleasure as I impaled her with my cock. Once...twice...her movements faltered, and time seemed to stop, before she gasped, then she screamed my name while her body convulsed beneath mine. My groans joined River's as her inner walls formed the tightest silken fist I'd ever felt and violently drew my seed out of me.

Creator, she's magnificent.

Panting, hearts racing, I dropped my forehead on her chest, and inhaled the sweet, flowery scent that was now slightly altered by my own. My seed was already working to change her further in preparation for her sabertooth.

She was one step closer to becoming fully ours. Now to beat it into Thora's head that he couldn't avoid his destiny...

A RESOUNDING NO

RIVER

Holy moly, I was no longer a freaking virgin!

I had just lost my virginity to a fine specimen of a man—errr, male because he was definitely not human. Not with a cock like that. Let's be real, if babies came out of vaginas, then a thick cock shouldn't be an issue, but lacking actual personal experience in the matter, I was still amazed it had fit, although I was far from unscathed, if the soreness between my legs was anything to go by. Urien rested on top of me; his heavy torso acted like a weighted blanket, making me feel warm and fuzzy inside. Never in a million years had I imagined my first time being like that. How many times had I heard of horror stories of inattentive, selfish partners? How many times had supposed girlfriends cautioned me so I wouldn't get disappointed? Even Serina had suggested I should just get it over with because it'd be nothing special. How many times had Urien made me orgasm? I'd lost count, and the last thing he'd been was oblivious to my pleasure—

not only was he talented with his cock but with his fingers and tongue as well.

How would it be with two of them? Was Thora a considerate lover too?

My cheeks burned as shame filled me the moment the forbidden thought entered my mind. Normal people didn't lust after two men, and they didn't get intrigued by the idea of being shared. I was appalled at my train of thought, yet my core clenched around the thickness still in me, causing something wet to trickle down my butt.

My face, neck, and ears suddenly felt impossibly hot. *Oh my God, that's his seed. Should I ask him to get off me? Should I go clean myself or wait?* Darn it, I'd never bothered to learn the etiquette about proper behavior after sex, and not knowing how to act started freaking me out.

"Stop." His smoky voice was too sexy for me to object to his bossy tone. "Whatever we want to do, is what's appropriate, and right now I want nothing more than to hold you, joined as we are. Will you allow me this pleasure?"

Was Urien right? Maybe I should let any preconceived notions go, because based on the reverent way he spoke about Sacred Unions, if I didn't, I could end up missing something great. I was no longer on Earth, and what happened in space, stayed in space, right? Nobody had to know.

The little devil on my shoulder, though, was quick to butt in and remind me that if mates were rare, why had Thora rejected me? Was I less because I was human, or was it my appearance that put him off? Self-deprecating thoughts swirled like slow-moving poison in my mind.

A sharp nip had me nearly jumping out of my skin. "What

was that for?" I lifted my hand to rub the side of my breast, but Urien was already kissing the hurt away.

"I'm not going to let you torture yourself because Thora is a fool," he said. The tips of his lips lifted, and his eyes sparkled with mischief.

"Really? What are you going to do?"

A wide smile broke across his face the way the moon rose and illuminated the night sky. "I'll teach him a lesson."

"Strap in, we are about to enter Saber's atmosphere." Thora's authoritative voice echoed in the room, the deep tone snaking its way to my core, heating it, and making me yearn for his touch. How could he have such an effect on me when I was in Urien's embrace?

Speaking of the chivalrous male, I winced when he carefully pulled out of me, and he didn't miss it. Brows furrowed, he turned toward a bench and picked some type of cloth, along with my clothes.

I reached out to take them. "I can clean myself."

"I want to do it," he said and got on with the task.

Covering my face with my hands, I tried to hide my embarrassment. Yet, a few moments later, I was laughing out loud because the thought that he deserved five stars for being an attentive boyfriend struck me.

He did a thorough job, then proceeded to clean himself.

"Don't I get to clean you?" I asked while getting dressed.

Suddenly, images of me on my knees with his cock deep in my mouth infiltrated my mind. "You're projecting." I laughed.

Urien grinned like a Cheshire cat. "Next time, psehimou." His raspy voice held all kinds of promises, and I shivered in anticipation. Our first time had been explosive; would I survive the next one? Did I even care? He led me to a chair and made sure I was strapped in properly.

I was used to being the one tending to others, but since I had no idea how things worked in a spaceship, I didn't mind him taking care of me. The way he double-checked each strap, and then made sure it wasn't too tight that it'd leave a bruise, yet tight enough to be secure, showed me he cared. Had a man ever taken care of me that way besides my father? I couldn't think of anyone.

When he was done, he took the seat next to me then reached out and engulfed my hand in his huge one. Looking at our entwined fingers, a blush crept up my neck and across my cheeks.

Urien tilted his head sideways—the orange streaks in the green irises of his eyes reminding me of glowing embers... their warmth beckoning. "What are you thinking, beloved?"

"Of the landing," I replied quickly...too quickly, then ducked my chin, suddenly finding the floor interesting. From my periphery, I saw his lips form a thin line, but he didn't press the issue, and I was glad. I hadn't lied exactly, but I hadn't been forthcoming either, his considerate action had left me feeling too raw.

Without warning, a metal-scraping-on-metal sound blared through the room. I hunched my shoulders and slapped my palms on my ears. Next to me Urien roared in pain. His whole body quaking. Darn it, his hearing was more sensitive than mine. I didn't think, I just reacted by placing my hands on top of his, forming an extra barrier to protect his ears. Orange eyes—Grim's—locked on mine, and the roar turned into a growl. I counted that as a win.

Luckily, the sound only lasted a few seconds, but then the shaking began, and I let go to grab my seat. Before I could, though, Urien grabbed my palms and pressed gentle kisses on both of them.

"Thank you," he said in earnest.

I was planning to say you're welcome, but that wasn't what came out of my mouth. "I'm scared," I blurted, then snapped my lips and eyes shut.

He squeezed my hands. "Thora will get us onto the surface in one piece, psehimou. He'd never let anything happen to you...now me, on the other hand, he wouldn't mind making my life difficult." He chuckled, effectively distracting me and making me smile too.

Not long after we stopped talking, the shaking stopped and the ship powered down. We had arrived on Saber.

Urien unbuckled himself, and I'd been watching how he did it, so I didn't notice Thora appear in the entrance of the room, and his voice startled me.

"She is not to be seen till we reach the palace," he barked and left.

His words send a chill down my spine. I was under a contract, they knew I was coming. "Why shouldn't I be seen?" I asked and turned to Urien for an answer. He was still staring at where Thora had been standing a moment ago. A frown marring his face.

"Besides the Queen, you are the only other female on the planet," he said absentmindedly. "I'm sure it is a temporary measure. Until you see the Queen," he continued, but his tone had changed.

Did he just lie to me? I could not explain why I was suspicious, but I must have been affected by all the growling and snarling he'd been doing, cause I was hearing it in my head now too. I didn't question him, though, because what was the point? So we were the only two women on the planet. Not a big deal. Not weird at all.

Thora reappeared at the door carrying a huge cloak on his arm. "Wear this," he ordered and handed it to me. I folded my arms across my chest, refusing to take it. I'd had enough of his bossy manners.

Meanwhile, Urien sauntered into his personal space. "Remember who you are talking to." His words carried a warning, yet neither seemed willing to back down, and I bet the situation would escalate quickly, unless I diffused it.

So I wedged myself between the two males, grabbed the cloak, and faced Urien. "Will you please help me? It's too big, I can't put it on by myself." An innocent white lie, but it worked.

Thora took two steps back, and Urien focused on helping me. When he'd tied it around me, I was effectively hidden... and blind. No matter, as long as we got out of this spaceship and back on steady ground. I felt an arm behind my knees, and another touching my neck before the world tilted sideways, and I was secure in someone's arms.

Besides the rustling of the fabric covering me, I couldn't discern other sounds on our way to the palace until we stopped and a low voice said something indiscernible before a door opened, then closed, and I was lowered to my feet.

"Is this Earthling the Healer?" a male asked. His guttural tone did not sound friendly at all, and if I weren't hidden already, I'd have been searching for a spot to hole up.

"Yes. We are to transfer the Healer to the Queen," Thora declared in a voice that brooked no arguments.

I exhaled in a rush. They wouldn't be leaving me with someone I didn't know.

"Change of orders. The Kings are already waiting for you in the War room."

Nope, better the devil you knew, people said, and I agreed. Stepping backward, I bumped into a solid chest. Hands immediately squeezed my shoulders in an effort to reassure me.

'Shhh, psehimou, you are safe. I'll meet you as soon as I can.' I jumped upon hearing Urien's words loud and clear in my head, but before I could react, Thora spoke.

"If anything happens to the Healer, I'll hold you responsible, Saberian." Then he guided me forward to the other guard.

I was stumped. It wasn't Urien who'd consoled me with his touch but Thora, and he'd sounded like he cared for my well-being. *Frustrating man.* I didn't understand him. Two still bands dug into my bones when the stranger picked me up, and carried me away from the two males I'd become fond of. Cold seeped into my body, and the ride was jarring as he held me away from his body. When I heard the male sniffing near the top of my head, my heart began racing, and I started hyperventilating. I literally couldn't see where he was taking me, or do anything about it. What if he had nefarious—

His snarl interrupted my train of thought. "Settle, Healer," he ordered.

If my gut hadn't been screaming at me to stay quiet, I'd have given him a piece of my mind, thinking he could boss me around. I suddenly felt sorry for the Queen. She probably dealt with males acting like they knew better on a daily basis.

My carrier stopped, knocked on a door, and when a muffled answer came through, he entered a room and lowered me to my feet. I expected he'd uncover me, but he didn't. He stepped out of the room, and even though my relief was instantaneous, the quiet creeped me out. I had to see my surroundings and since the little voice inside my head was silent, I decided to take the cloak off.

It required quite an effort, and while I tugged and pulled, the floor came into view first. It was some kind of gray-toned rock, smooth and variegated with gold and black veins across its polished surface. Throw rugs and pillows were strewn around tactfully, adding a warm touch to the large living area. There were couches near the windows designating a cozy sitting space, but what took my breath away were the huge bay windows overlooking a turbulent violet-colored sea.

"Not that I mind the company, but who are you?"

"Doodles on a cracker," I squeaked and spun toward the voice, only then noticing the very human and heavily pregnant woman lying on a bed the size of two king mattresses put together. She seemed shocked to see me, and maybe kind of angry too.

How did I miss that another person was in the room with me, even if said room fit both floors of my townhouse in it? No matter, it was time to put my professional hat on and do the job I was hired for. "I'm sorry, your Majesty," I said and bowed my head respectfully.

"No need for formalities. Call me Kali." She braced her elbows against the mattress, pushed, and sat with her back on the headboard—a groan escaping her in the process. "I swear these kiddos are playing football with my bladder, but do tell. Who are you and who brought you here?" The growly undertone accompanying her question made my knees go weak, and the desire to run arose out of the blue.

But this wasn't the first time a patient had scared me, and I knew how to deal with them. It was just that they weren't usually the pregnant women who did so. "My name is Dr. River Margeaux. I was hired to oversee your pregnancy," I replied, hoping my soft and even tone would calm her, like it had done to so many others in the past.

She glanced around as if looking for something, then baffled, she repeated, "Hired?"

"Yes. One of your employees sent a job offer to Inova Fairfax Hospital. The administration accepted, and I was appointed the role. So until a little bit after your delivery, I'll be your personal doctor," I explained, hoping to further put her at ease, but my words had the opposite effect. She narrowed her eyes and pursed her lips.

I saw the evidence of her anger rising, but more so than that, I felt the thick, suffocating heaviness clouding the air. "Everything is legal, your Majesty," I added as an afterthought, doubting it'd help. The situation was weird, but then again, I was on an alien planet conversing with a human. What did I know?

"You can call me Kali, doc."

"Then I must insist you call me River." I smiled at her.

"Deal," she said and returned the gesture. "Please sit. I've called for the Kings."

Called the Kings? How? She hadn't used a phone, or any device for that matter.

"Once they get here we'll have a nice conversation to clear the situation. Help yourself if you're hungry." She pointed toward a long table filled with fruits and meat, then added, "The food is safe for humans."

At the sight of the rich buffet, I realized it had been a while since my last meal, but my appetite was gone. *Ha! A first for me.* Nonetheless, not wanting to offend her, I went and picked something that looked like grapes. I nibbled on the small orange bubbles, but with my mind racing a thousand miles a minute, their taste didn't even register. *Wasn't I supposed to be here?* I'd seen the contract, signed it, but was it even legit? Had I gone through all that to get here, only to be sent back to Earth again?

Suddenly faced with a dilemma of whether I would return to my comfortable and familiar life or stay and explore a new planet and an unexpected relationship with those who claimed to be my soulmates, I was surprised to realize the answer was a resounding no. I didn't want to go back so soon; I wanted to see where the connection with the two alien males would lead because this could be my only chance at true happiness. And I wouldn't miss it for the world.

"I haven't seen another human in forever," Kali said—a wide grin stretching her lips—interrupting my thoughts.

"How did you end up here?" I blurted out without thinking, then slapped a hand over my mouth.

She brushed my gaffe off with a laugh. "Oh, that's a story for another time." She evaded before posing a question of her own. "Won't your family miss you, if you stay here for so long?"

"Um, I don't have anyone. Well, that's not exactly true, I have my best friend, who is like a sister to me, but I told her I'd be on a work trip for the next year or so. She understands, she is quite the workaholic herself." Sharing came easy with her, when I usually kept everything close to my heart. What was it about this woman?

"I'm sorry about your parents," she murmured so very softly that I doubted it was meant for my ears.

How had she known? I hadn't mentioned they died. She could have assumed we were estranged, yet she hadn't. Before I could ask her about it, the door opened, and my mouth went slack as three imposing figures sauntered in the room.

SHOULD I BE WORRIED?

RIVER

The hulking males wore the same kind of armor Urien did. Nothing on them signified who the King was—at first glance, only their unusual skin tones set them apart from one another, though none of them had Urien's fiery tone or the color of a clear blue sky like Thora did.

The red guy bowed his head respectfully my way and headed straight to Kali. He knelt by the bed and placed his hand on top of her belly. A small smile played on her lips, and when she buried her fingers in his blond hair, her expression turned to one of contentment.

The purple one—and bulkiest of the three—stood by the entrance like a silent sentry and stared me down.

A bead of sweat trickled down between my breasts. The desire to fidget, and to check my clothes for anything out of place was strong; instead, I straightened my shoulders and stood still because I was being judged. I was one of the best obstetricians in the world, and I'd provide his Queen with the best of care, but no matter how confident I was in my abilities, I still averted my gaze, failing at this game of intimidation.

These two were far away from me and felt somewhat non-threatening, but when the silver male came toward me, I couldn't not retreat. He didn't walk, he prowled, and in my mind's eye an invisible sign above him indicating 'predator, run!' started flashing a warning, yet his tone was warm when he offered me his hand and said, "Welcome, Healer."

My eyes widened at the very human-like gesture, but I didn't keep him waiting, I grasped his palm and shook slightly. It took me a second to find my voice, and by the time I was about to speak, Kali called out his name, "Arana."

The alien flashed me a smile that reached his eyes, taking my breath away—*God, they were a handsome bunch*—before he schooled his features into the hard mask he wore a few moments earlier, and turned toward her.

The other two focused on her as well, giving me the opportunity to study them. Upon closer inspection, I noticed them fidgeting. They weren't moving per se it was more the nervous energy they were exuding, and the stolen looks they exchanged with each other.

I briefly wondered why I could discern their mood, but then another realization distracted me. These males seemed intimidated by the pregnant woman lying on the bed. It was an interesting puzzle. Kali was human and the Queen. Did she have ruling power over them? If these aliens were all Kings, who was the husband? What was going on here?

"Psehimou, you summoned us?" A giggle almost escaped me upon hearing his innocent tone, but I cupped my mouth with my palm, holding it in. He knew he was in trouble. He'd also used the same term Urien did, so he must have been the spouse, although the red guy was resting his hand on Kali's leg—the gesture too proprietary to be platonic.

She narrowed her eyes and asked, "Seriously? You want to play games?" The sound of waves crashing ashore reverberated through the room when no one spoke. "Urien, Thora, come in here."

How could I have possibly thought Arana was handsome? He and the other two had nothing compared to the aliens that accompanied me here from Earth, whose looks alone made my breath hitch and my heartbeat kick up a notch. Urien came in first, sparing only a quick glance at the room before his eyes locked on mine. Thora, on the other hand, who followed behind, looked everywhere else but at me. Darn it, I wanted to slap his face...maybe then he'd get off his high horse and actually see me as something other than an annoyance.

"Love, we had to do something," said the male sitting next to her softly, then reached out to brush a lock of stray hair from her face, only to have his hand slapped away.

"And you abducted a human," she screeched, flailing her hands around in frustration.

"We aren't going to stand by watching our mate wither away, Kali! We almost lost you twice." The purple male, who'd remained silent so far, growled menacingly at her.

Even though the balcony doors were wide open and fresh air circulated the room, suddenly something heavy permeated the space. I coughed once, but tried to suppress the urge, not wanting to interrupt now that the tension was tangible. Urien moved closer to me, his muscles strung tight, ready for action. I wouldn't mind a hug right about now, but I wasn't brave enough to ask for it. Was I in danger? From a pregnant woman? I was pretty sure she was slower than a turtle at this point of her pregnancy, the angrier she got, though, the heavier the air became.

I didn't believe I was in danger, but what was wrong with Kali that they'd almost lost her twice? My palms itched from the desire to examine her, to find out what was wrong and try to fix it. My sight blurred, all the colors dimmed until my vision changed to hues of black, white, and grays. I felt something exploding out of me, and instantly knew I'd just emitted sound waves because they reflected on some of the surfaces, deflected on others, or were absorbed. The people in the room disappeared, and in their positions stood ultrasound caricatures, whose bodies had turned into information maps I was able to read. Of their own accord, my eyes zeroed in on the pregnant woman and the three little babies moving in her belly.

I staggered backward, tripped on my own feet, and would have fallen if it weren't for Urien grabbing my elbow. The action jarred my shoulder and sent a jolt of pain across my arm that brought me out of whatever had just happened and back into the present situation.

"...smell her, Arana. Whose scents are on her?" Kali finished her question with a menacing growl that sounded scarily similar to one a big cat would make.

Ducking my chin, I let my hair fall and cover the side of my face, and sniffed myself without making any noise. I could detect hints of my perfume, but nothing else.

No matter how tall this woman was, she was still small compared to these gargantuan males. How was she not afraid of speaking to them like that? They could easily break her in half, they looked that strong. Looking at her standing her ground, chin high, not at all intimidated, turned Kali into one scary person. And the funny thing was, Arana did as she demanded. I heard him take a deep breath through the nose— the others did too.

Crap! Kill me now.

"The Healer smells like them." Arana pierced the male next to me with his gaze, and it was like I could see dark clouds blanketing his eyes.

"Because she has been traveling with us, my Queen," Urien said in a rush. "There was an incident, we got stranded on XT-145 and then attacked. We had to…"

He kept explaining, but I no longer heard the words. My heart was breaking into a million pieces, and it was all my fault—I'd fallen for his pretty words. At least Thora had been up front from the start, and even though his rejection had hurt, he'd clearly communicated his dislike for me. Hearing Urien trying to cover what had actually happened between us hurt, as in someone-had-thrust-a-knife-deep-in-my-gut-and-twisted-before-pulling-it kind of hurt. He didn't want his people to know about us, about me. Maybe he'd lied and there was another woman. What did he think? I'd be his side chick?

I felt my chest cave in. Rubbing the area with the heel of my palm, I tried to ease the ache, but then noticed Kali watching me. I switched everything off and put on a stoic mask like I'd done countless times before every time I'd had to deliver bad news to patients. Thora's voice reminded me I wasn't alone, so later on, when I'd finally be alone, I'd allow myself to process everything that happened and crumble, if need be, until I got everything out of my system.

"Urien mated her," he said, and his declaration was met with stunned silence.

A wave of fury, like fingers wrapped tightly around my neck, brought me to my knees and made breathing difficult. Growls and snarls mixed with words, but I couldn't understand through the rattling sound that filled my ears.

"My Queen. My Kings. Please!" Urien cried out, begging— for what, I had no idea—but soon, I was able to gulp sweet, sweet air into my lungs again.

Both of my males were on their knees too. They straightened before me, and Urien offered his hand to help me get up.

Darn it, River, they aren't yours. I reminded myself, scoffing at the gesture, and rising to my feet. His eyes widened, yet his brows furrowed. *Well, what did you expect buddy?* I thought, and his mouth opened, but the silver male spoke before Urien could.

"Explain," Arana ordered his men, but I beat them to it.

"Urien and I had sex. It won't happen again, and it won't affect my performance as the Queen's doctor," I said, voice steady and calm, yet the stupid organ in my chest crumbled further. Thank God it wasn't the one calling the shots.

"Yes, it will," the frustrating male next to me said, and while I wasn't a violent person, the urge to set the absurd alien ablaze struck me.

The smile that blossomed on Kali's face reached her ears. The woman confused me. She seemed angry before when she smelled the men on me whereas now that I admitted to having sex with one of them she was happy. *Go figure.*

"Warrior," the purple guy barked.

Urien turned to me, and when I refused to look at him, he hooked a finger under my chin and applied pressure till I did. "We didn't have sex," he said. "We mated." Then he dropped his hand and addressed his Kings, "We formed a Sacred Union, but we haven't completed the Mating Ritual. We can't. Not without Thora."

"You fucking stung her! You ruined her," he yelled from across the room, and in the blink of an eye he was on Urien.

They started fighting, in the room with a heavily pregnant woman, a super stressed human—namely me, and three other males who were observing them, seemingly unperturbed. They were so fast, they blurred, but the sound of flesh hitting flesh was unmistakable despite them being aliens. It seemed like they were oblivious to pain, but I felt every single blow, every single gash on their skin. My chest and neck were on fire, yet I wasn't the one bleeding.

"Stop," I cried out, catching Urien's attention.

He stepped backward, doing my bidding, when he suddenly fell in a heap.

The loud thunk of the impact had me scrambling to him, but Thora blocked the way.

"Move," I ordered.

He stood still. "It's only a little poison," he said, his tone unapologetic, "no need for you to cry over him."

Red hot fury, the kind that destroyed everything in its path, ferociously bubbled up to the surface, searing my insides until it exploded. My hand flew, and a loud crack echoed as his neck jerked to the side.

He slowly straightened, his tongue darting out to lick the drop of blood from where his teeth nicked his lip when my palm connected with his face. He pretended to be cool and collected, yet I could see the hurt in his eyes.

"You don't want me? Fine! You think a green line gives you the right to dictate to me? It. Doesn't. What kind of person hurts another without provocation? He did nothing to you." I rarely lost my temper, if ever, but yelling in his face felt good. He'd chosen, so now he had no rights over me.

He crossed his arms over his chest and stood his ground. "But he did to you." His voice, though, wasn't as sure and steady as it had previously been.

Good. Because he was mistaken. "Not. Against. My. Will." I emphasized each word so there'd be no doubt.

"I—"

"You rejected me, why do you suddenly care? Leave us alone," I interrupted him, raising my voice higher, in proportion to the growing sense of urgency filling me. Urien was still...too still, and my gut screamed at me that something was very wrong.

Thora grimaced, for once his expression was easy for me to read, but I couldn't deal with his hurt, even though I regretted causing it. He moved to the side, and I raced to the male that had already burrowed into my heart.

I placed my fingers on the side of his neck to check his pulse, but couldn't find it. I brought my hand under his nose hoping to feel a slight tickle from his exhale, but didn't. My own heart started racing, it seemed impartiality flew out the window when the patient was someone you cared about. But before I allowed myself to go into full-blown panic mode, I lowered my head over his face, trying to hear his breathing, and at last, I did. The quiet whoosh was barely audible, but it was there.

"Something's wrong, I can't get a pulse and he's barely breathing. Urien needs medical attention now." Dealing with crises was part of my job description, so my voice came out steady and strong, even though I was crumbling inside.

The red King knelt next to me, then hovered a small wand over the still body. "Thora, what was on your blade?"

"The Hunchgale's quilt," he answered, hovering closer.

"You fool," the Royal muttered under his breath and picked Urien up. "I'll take him to the Healers' Chamber."

"I'm coming with you," I declared, and saw his denial coming, so I didn't give him the chance to voice it. "I'm a doctor and I won't leave his side." Dissuading me was off the table. Urien might have tried to hide what'd happened, but I wouldn't let his rejection get in the way. Not yet. He'd fought our attackers and protected me, so I at least owed it to him to stay by his side and make sure he recovered.

The Queen, who had been conversing with the other two Kings, spoke up, "Mes, she needs to take care of her mate."

"He's not my mate." Each word uttered felt like the slice of a knife, but I needed to speak them out loud.

Once this was all over I'd return to Earth and I'd be fine. I would not let a fling with an alien stop me from living my life. Because what had happened on the ship was just a one-time thing, it wouldn't be happening again.

"Whatever you say, River," she singsonged, but I cared

none for that. What was important was that Mes had nodded his head to Kali, then hurried to the Healers' Chamber. I guess that's what passed for the doctors' office here, so without waiting for an invitation, I followed them out of the room.

The King picked up his pace, and I had to run to catch up with his long strides. The silence was suffocating because the male's distress was evident in his clenched jaw and pinched eyebrows. He also believed what was going on with Urien was serious, and that was harder to take than my own assessment.

We reached our destination in no time. A door to the left opened automatically, and we entered the infirmary, only for me to stop mid-track—momentarily stunned by what I was seeing. Equipment with uses and functions unknown to me was set across the length of two of the walls, whereas some kind of beds—similar to what I had sat on in the ship—lined the third side, and in the center of the room there were two operating tables with lights and screens surrounding them. Mes gently placed Urien on one.

I scanned the room for anything that might look familiar —I needed a stethoscope, a ventilator and an electrocardio-graph for starters—but didn't find anything that remotely resembled those devices. Needing to check on Urien, I turned and gasped. He no longer wore a uniform, but lay naked in all his glory, and a semitranslucent gel-like film had encased him. It was slowly shrinking, seemingly becoming a second skin. The King moved around the room, gathering more equipment I didn't recognize. "Are you a doctor?" I was ninety-nine percent sure that he was, but I needed confirmation.

His golden gaze would make anyone feel inferior if it weren't for the gentleness shining through. "I'm an Archhealer. Urien will be fine as soon as I give him the antidote," he said and pointed to the mixture he was preparing.

I moved closer to the unconscious male. He looked so pale, his green and orange coloring was fading, taking on a gray tint. *That can't be good.*

The King was quiet and efficient with his moves. Once he was done, he walked to the top of the bed and tapped on the translucent screen that, among other things, was showing Urien's cardiovascular system, then placed the small vial he'd been holding in a slot. The gel-like film covering the warrior's body expanded again, and a smoky brown-colored substance spread inside the film. Then as it shrunk again the antidote was pressed into Urien's skin.

Almost immediately, I could tell the difference. His skin was returning to its fiery tone, and his chest lifted higher than before with his every inhale. Reassured that he'd be all right, I allowed myself a reprieve. There were so many things I wanted to explore in the room, and being here with someone who knew what everything was could be an opportunity I wouldn't get again.

"Can I touch it, without harming him?" I asked, holding my breath, like a kid waiting for her mother's approval to enter a candy store.

"Yes. Nothing can harm the person inside a healing pod," he explained while he finished whatever he was typing on the bed's screen.

I bounced around the room, careful not to knock over the equipment.

He chuckled at my reactions as I explored the alien technology. "You must have questions. Feel free to ask what you wish. My name is Mes." His voice was calm and inviting, and it made me look over my shoulder to find him sitting on a stool, with his back leaning against a desk and his long legs spread in front of him. The picture of ease, yet warning bells were ringing in my ears, cautioning me that this facade was deceiving, and he was dangerous.

"I'm not a threat to you, Healer. I hope you'll save my mate."

I turned to face him fully. "Can you read my mind?" Nothing seemed impossible after what had happened so far.

"Not exactly. Just your emotions and a few snippets of your thoughts here and there," he admitted, flooring me.

Needing to sit because my knees were about to buckle, I picked the other stool, pulled it next to Urien's pod, and sat heavily on top of it when my legs gave out, and vertigo made the room spin. I closed my eyes and took a few moments to regulate my breathing and calm my body, for the desire to ease this fellow doctor's burden was stronger than my momentary panic, so I built the walls in my mind that would protect and allow me to help him.

His mouth fell open slightly, and he said, awed, "You're gifted too."

"I could always feel things differently. I learned to protect myself early on in my life," I explained. His stoic expression showed me he was expecting my questions. I debated for a second, whether I should talk to him or not, during which he didn't try to convince me either way, just waited patiently for me to decide.

Well, he'd given me permission, so I took the plunge, and I thought to better get the most inappropriate question out of the way first. "Kali is the Queen. You, Arana and the other Royal are the Kings." My voice trembled, and I felt the heat rise to my cheeks. "How does it work? She is pregnant, so who is her husband?"

He chuckled, and I was glad he found me funny. The alternative could be much worse. I imagined an offended King would have many ways to punish available to him. "The other Royal is Rorc. All three of us are her mates. We've formed a Sacred Union, the same way as you, Urien and Thora did."

I chose to ignore the bit about me and insisted on finding who'd impregnated her, as I didn't think they'd be as forgiving if I ended up messing up that fact. "But who is the father?"

"We all are."

"You're all what?"

A loud belly laugh followed my question, and once again I was glad he found my confusion amusing. "The fathers," he said, shocking me.

"How would that even..." my voice trailed off when an image of me and my two mates popped in my head, making me turn beetroot red. "Oh."

He chuckled again, then sobered up and added, "Thora will come around. Once a Sacred Union is formed, it cannot be denied. Similar to what Urien felt when he had no choice but to sting you and initiate your transformation—"

"He stung Thora too." I had no idea why I'd just blurted that out—and so rudely interrupted him—but it seemed important.

He leaned forward, his body tense ready to strike. "He

did?" he asked, and I nodded. "That's...interesting." His deep voice resonated with me. He was magic.

"Why so?"

"I don't think it has ever happened before, Arana or the Elders would know for certain. I'm not familiar with their history just yet. Until recently I was Wravukian, then Kali Changed me, the same way Urien is Changing you."

My jaw dropped to the floor, causing a mini earthquake. "But she's human," I blurted. The shock rendering my filter unusable.

He shook his head negatively, not taking offense at my words. "Arana was the one who Changed her. Like me, she's a hybrid, but also stronger than any Saberian male alive."

"Where are all the women?"

"More than a hundred rotations ago, Yenoctonia happened. The Saberian females were targeted in an attack that claimed them all. There aren't any left." He dropped his gaze to the floor, and his entire body sagged as if he were carrying the weight of the world. "We're a dying species. Too many males falling into Lethe, and unless we find more females, this will be the end.

My heart already was breaking for this species, and I was afraid to ask the question but could not stop myself. Mes was parting with important information. "What is Lethe?"

"It's a warrior's end. The logical part of the male dies, and they become mindless animals bent on destruction and carnage that have to be put down." He finished the sentence with a heavy sigh, which told me more than he'd intended. It said that he had already had to put someone or many some-ones down.

The peek into the Saberian future left a bitter taste in my mouth. It went against my every fiber to just give up on someone.

"There is nothing to be done. Not even their mates would be able to save them at that point," he said, startling me with how easily he could read me.

I chewed the inside of my cheek, then worried my bottom lip. I didn't want to ask, but at the same time, I couldn't not ask. "What will happen to Urien when I return to Earth?"

Please, let it be that he finds someone else, although darn it, I didn't like the thought of him with another either.

"You cannot sever a bond without killing your mates. He and his sabertooth will die. So will Thora." His piercing gaze was solely focused on me. It was as if he could glimpse my soul, and it made me uncomfortable. He canted his head sideways and asked, "Would you do that to your mates?"

"No. I don't want anyone to die because of me. But I have to go back. This isn't my home," I replied but could no longer hold his gaze, so I averted my eyes toward the injured male and found two narrowed green ones staring back at me.

He'd heard what I said.

I gasped at being caught red-handed and was about to apologize when I remembered he too had denied what was going on between us.

Mes was slower at getting up, which verified my suspicion that he'd known Urien had woken up. *Freaking men! Of course they support each other.* Once the Arch-healer read what I assumed was Urien's biometrics report and typed something on the screen, the transparent gel-like film receded and another substance, the same coloring as Urien's skin, covered him from neck to toe before he lifted off the bed.

It wasn't the first time I'd seen this on him, but it would have to wait for later. "How are you feeling?" I asked, my voice not as steady as I'd have liked.

He wrapped his arm around me and pulled me close in a tight hug. "I'm all right, psehimou. Thora cannot really hurt me," he assured me, and I relaxed in his embrace at the same time I breathed deeply. His scent was rich and masculine, and it reminded me of woods and nature, with a hint of fur.

"Why did you let him hurt you?" the King asked.

Let him, as in he could have avoided being hurt?

"So he could feel the pain he causes. He's still denying our bond, and it is hurting River," he stated simply, as if he were talking about giving the last bowl of cereal to Thora because he was being a brat.

His explanation made sense because I'd felt every blow they delivered to each other. But I didn't know if I wanted to punch or kiss the guy.

"What?" Urien growled at me.

His clipped tone was inexcusable. "Um, I didn't say anything."

"You felt our pain?" He persisted, and both males zeroed in on me.

"Yes," I stuttered.

Urien ran his hands through his hair, messing up the strands, and muttered a few curses under his breath. Then he opened his arms wide and waited for me to step into his embrace before he said, "I'm sorry. I didn't realize our bond is that strong, because I can barely feel your sabertooth." His apology was sincere, but should I be worried about the saber-tooth part?

"Should you feel…my sabertooth?" I asked, puzzled.

"We should both feel and hear her, but it's like she is not even there, not exactly." Upon hearing the King's words, a tremor raced down my spine.

Was something wrong with me? I felt fine and was about to say so when the door whooshed open and in burst King Arana with a pale-faced Kali in his arms.

I GUESS WE WERE DOING THIS

RIVER

"The bleeding isn't stopping," King Rorc, who was right behind them, said as he helped Arana place the Queen on the operating table.

Their expressions were cool, detached, but I knew it was only a facade—the same humans wore when trying to hold the pain and worry at bay. It seemed we weren't that different after all, and realizing this truth eliminated the fear I'd been feeling.

The Arch-healer exploded into action. With the press of a button, a fine mist spread across the room, covering everything and everyone. Its scent was slightly off-putting, and when it made contact with my skin it stung. Then he grabbed three units of liquids—one red, one clear, and one creamy white—and proceeded to insert a cannula into Kali's peripheral vein on the inside of her elbow. Once he'd connected those, he ripped the bottom half of the dress she was wearing, and placed his palms on top and below her pregnant belly—a soft light glowing under them. Instant relief washed over her body, alleviated its tension, and her breathing eased.

For a moment, I could do nothing but stare wide-eyed. He was magic.

"Healer, I need your help," Mes's voice broke the trance his actions had created. "This is not my expertise."

"Have you found the cause of bleeding? I need gloves, a vaginal speculum, a portable ultrasound machine, and gel," I requested but stopped short. "Do you even use these? I'm not familiar with your technology, and we don't have time for a lesson right now." Kali's bleeding had slowed down, but it hadn't stopped.

Rustling sounded from where Urien was, and I saw him fall back on the bed. "Noymus must have finished uploading the information we copied from Earth's databases to the main system. The matgen should be able to provide River with whatever she needs," he croaked then threw his arm over his eyes and groaned.

"Stand in front of that alcove," the silver Royal pointed, and I rushed to the spot.

He tapped a screen, and I was bathed in a pink light. A few seconds later, my request materialized next to me. I wasted no time moving everything next to my patient. "Kali, the gel will feel cold. Arch-healer, talk to me. Do you know what's causing the bleeding?"

"She has a fucking shrapnel fragment embedded in her cervix from when she was nearly killed on that mission," King Rorc barked, making me jump.

"You'll get used to him," Mes laughed.

I seriously doubted it. He was all kinds of intimidating. "Okay, let me see what's going on," I said, and placed the transducer on top of the gel. I started with small circles, then widened their diameter. "The babies are all right. They aren't very active at the moment, which is good, and their heartbeats are strong…" My voice trailed off while I focused on locating the sliver that was causing trouble. *Where are you, little bugger? …There you are!* "The fragment has moved, and it looks like it's loose. I need to palpate the area, Kali. The moment you feel the slightest pain let me know."

"Mes will have to tell you. He's shielding me," she said and my gaze snapped toward the Arch-healer.

He was the picture of serenity with his closed eyes and even breathing, but upon closer inspection, his skin was blotchy, and his muscles tense. "I'm ready when you are," he said.

I wiped off the gel first. "I'll be gentle," I promised and put my fingers above where the small piece seemed to be.

A wave of dizziness suddenly assailed me; I swayed on my feet, and if it weren't for the two hands grasping my arms, I would have lost my balance. Turning sideways, I looked over my shoulder to thank whoever held me, but when I didn't really see him, but saw inside him, my voice got stuck in my throat.

"Healer, are you okay?" The gruff voice belonged to the scary alien. He was the one holding me, yet I couldn't see the purple of his skin. Instead, similarly to earlier, my vision had changed into a black and white image, akin to what the ultrasound showed, but this time when I focused on a specific area, the image changed. It became colorful, and I could discern the muscles, the soft tissue, and the veins.

"Yes," I replied and placed my hands on top of Kali's belly. "I can see inside you. I can see the fragment, and the tear that's bleeding," I exclaimed.

"Can you remove it? Dawn insists that we must shift, and not letting her is killing me," she said.

If we'd been back on Earth, the answer would be yes because I had the needed equipment. But here? I wasn't so sure. "It can be removed, but it will require surgery," I told her, then turned to the Arch-healer. "I'm not familiar with your technology, it is vastly different from what we have. I can guide you, but you will have to perform the operation."

"Can you show me what you see?" he asked, and a loud growl had us turning toward its source.

"No, that's out of the question," Urien quipped.

No one was allowed to interfere between me and my patient. "Yes," I contradicted. "How can I show you?"

Mes answered without hesitation. "Put your hand on top of mine, and bring to the forefront of your mind what you see." Then he looked at the injured warrior. "If you keep trying to get up, you'll fall on your face. I give you my word, I won't pry into her privacy."

Urien settled, albeit a bit grumpily, and I did as the Arch-healer asked. I focused on the pregnant woman until my vision changed, and then I positioned my palms on top of his. Nothing seemed to happen at first, but suddenly images of Kali shifting invaded my mind, and they were followed by sheer terror.

The King pulled his hands abruptly and cursed at the same time Kali gasped.

"What happened?" asked Urien, but I was too busy trying to keep my heart from escaping my chest.

When I could form a sentence again, I said, "I saw Kali's first shift, I felt her terror...how is that possible? How could you stand it?"

"That was just the first time jitters," she said—but it certainly hadn't felt that way to me—then added, "I would choose that experience over a life without my mates and Dawn every single time."

"I'm sorry, Healer. I hadn't expected you'd be able to delve into my memories." Mes's sincere apology touched my heart. He carried a great burden.

"So what now?" King Rorc snarled impatiently, pacing back and forth across the other side of the room.

"We'll take the fragment out," the Arch-healer said. "Get out of here, Rorc, take a breather—"

"You fucking stop if you want to keep your head on your shoulders, Mes." He was pissed with a capital p.

Kali laughed. "Love, you cannot hurt Mes. You love him and you know it. But you know, once these two are done, the babies will be hungry. Will you pretty pleeease bring me some orakj? I've been craving it since I woke up."

The purple alien glared at her, then spun around and left the room.

"River, we cannot give sedatives to Kali. They aren't safe for the offspring," King Mes said, and I sucked in a deep breath.

I needed to perform surgery. How would she stand the procedure without anesthesia? "It will be very painful, and she won't be able to stand still, Arch-healer. Instead of helping, we might end up harming the babies."

"I will keep holding the pain at bay, and you'll operate." His tone brooked no argument, yet I had plenty.

Kali lifted her arm and caressed her husband's face. "You can do this, River. Mes won't let me feel a thing," she said, looking at me.

"But he will. There must be another way."

King Rorc entered the room holding a tray with a lot of food piled up on top of it. "He has us. We can stand the pain."

"Will you need anything else?" King Arana asked after he deposited a variety of tools—some of which I recognized—on a portable table next to the operating table.

"No, these will do," the Arch-healer answered.

I was being outnumbered, and desperation filled me. What they were asking of me was preposterous.

"Come here, psehimou." Urien's voice brought a breeze of fresh air with it, and my feet obeyed the command before I consciously chose to do so.

Urien was sitting on his bed, and he was still taller than me. When I was within reach, he enveloped me in his embrace. "They trust you with their mate's life, my one and only. That is a thousand times more difficult compared to the pain they might feel. Let them help her, the only way they can." He kissed the top of my head, then pushed me to arms' length. He waited until I met his eyes, then said, "Go save the Queen, and come back to me."

All righty then, I guess we were doing this.

I'd do my best to ensure Kali had three healthy babies in her arms by the end of this pregnancy, even if staying here meant putting myself on the line. I just had to remain vigilant and protect my heart from two handsome aliens who had the ability to shred it to pieces.

WHATEVER IT TAKES

THORA

'You don't want me? Fine! You think a green line gives you the right to dictate to me? It. Doesn't. What kind of person hurts another without provocation? He did nothing to you.' River's accusations were playing on a loop in my head. *'You rejected me, why do you suddenly care? Leave us alone.'* Worse, they were partially true. The moment the Sacred Line had formed, I'd been stunned. Then guilt filled me, for I hadn't avenged Sharifah's—my Chosen mate's—death yet. So I reacted without thinking about the consequences. I rejected River.

My cheek still stung. It wasn't her strength that'd caused the shock—I'd barely felt the slap—it was the violence of the act that had dazed me. It went against everything River represented—tranquility...healing...a safe haven. And a seemingly so out of character act meant I'd pushed her to the edge of her limits.

What have I done?

Bile burned the back of my throat. Poisoning my own

191

Pair-bond who hadn't actually wronged me...pushing away my female...I shook my head, ashamed for committing such disgraceful acts.

River had left without a backward glance. That's what I deserved, but I couldn't stand the pitiful looks the rest of the royal family threw my way, and I was about to leave when the Queen's words stopped me.

"You can still fix the damage you've done," she said.

"How do you know?" I snapped, my tone borderline rude. I hated feeling out of balance, and at the moment everything was up in the air.

The tips of her lips lifted. "Because I'm a female."

"I'd listen to her if I were you," Rorc said and clapped me on the shoulder. "Let's have a drink while we talk."

Rorc gestured toward the sitting area next to the balcony.

I cleared my throat. The chamber was spacious, modest, and uncluttered. Besides the bed, there was a sitting area, and a dining one, but it was clearly their personal space. "Maybe I should let you rest," I suggested, and stepped toward the door.

"No. We need to have a talk about the birds and the bees," the female said, and both males snickered.

"Birds and bees?"

King Arana carried three glasses to the table. "Sit down, Admiral. You're not getting out of this."

Resigned to my fate, I joined the two males. The herbal scent with a hint of spice was strong as I lifted the glass. Kupna was the only drink I occasionally indulged in. I took a small sip, the liquid burning as it trickled down my throat. It was the good stuff.

"You cannot reject a Sacred Union, Thora. Once the Line

is formed, it's unbreakable." Arana was straight to the point, and it made me hate his kind a little bit less.

I was starting to realize that myself. I'd tried to push River out of my mind. I'd tried to drown the desire I felt for her. I'd tried to deny her. I'd failed on all counts, and hurt both my mates in the process. "Your Pair-bond knows what the Saberians have cost me. How can I ever be in a Union with one?"

"Not all Saberians have harmed you, Thora. Just one. Are all Wravukians good? You know they aren't. How can you judge an entire species based on the actions of one?" Although Rorc's argument was solid, I had never been able to overcome the hatred for them that had become a stain on my soul. Especially when it resurfaced every time I thought of my Chosen Mate, Sharifah.

"Is it her demise that still hurts, or the wound to your pride for failing to protect her?" the Queen asked, delving straight into the heart of the problem.

I must have gaped my mouth open, for the males laughed at me. Their female was very powerful. She had put into words my thoughts exactly.

"Yes, I am," she replied to my thought, without boasting, only stating, and perhaps warning me—she cared for her warriors. "You need closure."

Arana stared at his mate, then took a sip of his drink. He furrowed his brows and a soft rumble in his chest went deeper, rougher, and changed into a low growl. Something I wasn't privy to, passed between them. It put me on edge. "Relax, warrior," he ordered. "You will get the chance to avenge your chosen mate. Is the past so important, though, that you'll allow it to cost you your future? Are you willing to lose your Sacred Mates?"

Was I? Definitely not. Fuck, I had to find a way to make things right. "I may have handled the whole situation poorly," I admitted out loud.

"If by situation, you mean your female," Rorc, who was sitting near me, said and slapped me in the back, managing to rock me forward. "Welcome to the club, Admiral. Just a word to the wise, the way to a happy life is a happy female."

These beings had already seen me at my worst, what was one more blemish on my character? "I wanted to kill Urien for taking her," I admitted, disgusted with myself.

Arana laughed—the sound void of amusement. "You think a Wravukian is strong enough to kill a Saberian? Ask your people," he ordered, and I felt compelled to obey. My dealings with King Arana were few and far between, and I realized with a sinking feeling that he was very good at concealing the true magnitude of his power.

"I always believed we were equals in battle. Aren't we?" I asked Rorc, momentarily forgetting that he and Mes were no longer Wravukians, but hybrids.

"You are a fool, Thora, if you believe so. You cannot ever hurt him, not unless he lets you," the Third King of Saber said, and I winced.

So Urien had purposefully let me injure him. *Why?*

"You don't understand the importance of the Sacred Union yet, Thora." Kali's advice startled me. For this was the second time she'd replied to my thoughts. "But Urien does, and he's forgiven you already. He's the way to win your female's acceptance. Go talk to him. Fix what you've broken," she said while rubbing her belly gently. Her voice had been taut and her face a mask of concentration.

Suddenly, both of her mates flew out of their seats and raced to her side.

A grief-choked cry had me jumping up like a spring strung too tight.

"Fuck, you're bleeding again," Rorc said in a shaky voice.

"How can I help?" I asked them, but King Arana had already picked up their female and stormed out the chamber.

I tried to follow behind them but I was stopped by two snarling sabertooths. There was no way I could take two of them on. So when the one on my right nudged me to move, I gave up and followed them to a different chamber. I guess that was where I'd be staying.

Since my help is of no use to the Royals at the moment, I might as well take the time to decide on a course of action. Because Kali's words had been wise, and I'd truly be a fool if I didn't heed her advice.

Stepping into the chamber, I lost my train of thought. It was even bigger than the Royals'. The sprawling bed, big enough for three warriors not just one, was the centerpiece; there were futons and a big table with a buffet for a small fleet set on top. Throw rugs and pillows were placed near the long and narrow pool running along the length of one of the walls.

The knot in my stomach wouldn't let me eat, even though it had been more than a circle since I had last eaten.

With all those thoughts running inside my head, I wouldn't be able to relax enough to sleep.

A swim it was, then. Maybe the exercise would help me form a plan, so I took my armor off and dove in. Focusing on making sure my movements were rhythmic and coordinated, I pushed every major body part. I felt the burn as my muscles bunched and released at a punishing pace.

I tried to clear my mind, to find my center, but every time I closed my eyes, the pain etched on River's haggard face was all I saw.

Submerging myself, I yelled in frustration and watched the bubbles of oxygen rush to the surface. I remained at the bottom where the world was quiet until my lungs screamed for air, and when I resurfaced, I didn't feel an iota better.

I grabbed the edge of the pool and pulled myself out of the sanctuary the water had offered. As the cool air hit my warm flesh, I got the chills, but they barely registered. My mind was stuck on what had happened after I rejected the Sacred Union. I'd been standing on the ship's bridge, unable to resist checking up on River, and hating myself for being so weak.

The sight that greeted me, though, had taken me by surprise. Anger had turned into jealousy upon witnessing Urien waking up our female's body, upon pleasuring her. Then jealousy morphed into betrayal, for they were starting without me. Guilt however, was the strongest emotion of all and had rooted me to the spot, for how could I claim another, when I'd already had a mate I failed to protect? What if history repeated itself?

I'll protect our mate.

The gravelly voice startled me into action. I dove for my blaster, grabbed it, knelt, and scanned the room. "Show yourself," I demanded, expecting a Saberian to pop up and jump on me.

A chuff rattled in my head that I somehow knew was

laughter. *To come out now would be to reap you apart.*

"Who are you?"

I'm Reaper, your sabertooth, he said and withdrew to a place where I couldn't feel his presence anymore, leaving me alone with my thoughts...thoughts of a naked River, sprawled on the pod like an offering. I could still hear her moans and picture the blush that had covered her lush body.

I plumped down on the sofa and let my head drop forward, only then noticing my erect cock, and the string of pre-cum hanging from the tip. Fisting it, I pumped once... twice. Creator, I needed my mate. My soul had already been tethered to hers and Urien's. No matter the distance I put between myself and her—emotional or physical—I'd still end up crawling back to her. There was no point in resisting our Union anymore, my fate was sealed.

River, though, didn't want two mates. I'd heard her objections on our way here. Her customs were different. Dammit, mine were too, but I had a nagging suspicion that I needed her more than she did me. *I'll do whatever it takes to win a place in her heart,* I thought, and it was time I made that crystal clear.

Acceptance brought clarity, which allowed me to form a plan. And that plan didn't include me spilling my seed on the floor, but inside her, so I squeezed the base of my cock until the pain distracted me, and it softened. Not bothering to cover up—I was alone after all—my eyes drifted shut, my muscles relaxed, and my breathing eased as I was finally able to shed some of the weight I'd been carrying on my shoulders. The noises slowly quieted and I could feel a blanket of serenity covering me whole.

"They changed your room to accommodate our Sacred Union, psehimou. Do you know what that means?"

I leaped to my feet and did a double take when I saw Urien guiding River backward, farther into the room, his eyes momentarily meeting mine. So he was aware I was here; was she? Like a puppet whose strings had been pulled, I stepped closer before realizing what I was doing. Freezing in place, I scraped my hand through my hair. Doubting that my presence, especially in my naked state, was welcome. *What should I do?*

Get dressed. Yes! Now, where did I leave my fucking uniform?

"You did good, River. You saved our Queen, and I believe you deserve to be rewarded." Reverence colored the Saberian's voice; his deep timbre, though, implied all kinds of wicked things and was full of promise.

"Oh my God," our female gasped, and my eyes snapped to her—nearly bulging out of my head at the sight.

Urien had removed her top and gathered it at her wrists, binding them behind her. His other hand gathered her hair at the nape of her neck, and pulled, making her tilt her head back, and moan softly before his lips were on her delicate neck.

The light breeze that circulated the room carried her arousal. I took River's scent into my lungs, and it was like pouring oil onto a fire that awakened my hunger for her anew.

The warrior's hands didn't remain idle. He caressed her back, then slid his palms to her sides, eliciting another gasp from her before he grabbed her pants and pulled them down. "It's time you experience," he said as he kneeled and helped her out of the garment, "what having two mates entails." I couldn't see what he was doing, but it wasn't hard to imagine while witnessing a full-body quiver rocking her beautiful, lush form.

Urien unwrapped her like the precious gift she was, showing her off to me, trying to entice me. He needn't worry, for the decision had already been made. I wouldn't resist her...us anymore. Our bond was very strong. Their arousal was magnifying mine. I was burning up inside, and all the blood had drained from my head and pooled in my cock. I was certain he was feeling my hunger, too.

"But Thora doesn't want me." The hitch in her voice sliced my hearts open.

He didn't address her worry. Instead, he spread her legs apart, and dipped two fingers in her pussy, torturing us all. "Open," he ordered, and brought them to her lips.

Fuck! Was that her cream coating his fingers?

"Taste yourself," he added, voice low as he rose to his feet.

So far she'd been responsive to Urien's dominance, allowing us to witness her submissive side. She was magnificent, but her hesitation wouldn't do at all.

I growled, revealing my presence, startling her into the warrior's arms.

"He's here," her words were muffled by my Pair-bond's chest.

In three strides I was there, behind her. "Yes, and I'm done fighting our Union," I said, and plunged my fingers into her thick mane, then turned her head to the side, and fused her lips with mine.

River tensed under my hold, proving to me she didn't

believe my words just yet, and that was all right. What I couldn't allow her to do, though, was keep me at arm's length.

My hunger for her was a blaze I'd easily contained before, but now it raged and morphed into an uncontrollable inferno with one touch, and one point of contact was no longer enough.

The feel of my damp skin as I molded my body behind hers, made her gasp, and I seized the opportunity to slide my tongue into her mouth, to explore and learn how she tasted.

"Enough," Urien interrupted us, and while I bristled at the command, I pulled back. "It's time for your punishment," he added.

Being in a Sacred Union meant sharing. Yet satisfaction filled me when she lowered her eyebrows over dilated eyes and bit her swollen bottom lip.

"Punishment? Are you serious?" she asked, slurring the words.

Knowing I had caused the haze muddling her thoughts warmed my hearts. "You hesitated earlier, Mate," I explained before dipping my head and nipping the spot at the side, close to the base of her neck, making her shiver.

"When it comes to your pleasure and your safety, we need instant obedience, River. Trust us to know what is best for you." The warrior's voice was solemn. It was important she understood what he was trying to convey.

Upon hearing his words, her heart rate kicked up, and a slight tremor raced down her limbs. I didn't want her scared. "We'll go easy on you because this is your first lesson," I told her, needing to reassure her. "And if you're good, we'll reward you afterward."

"Have you ever been spanked?" He asked her, but she remained silent. "I'll take that as a no, psehimou, so we'll start there."

Her face turned a rosy hue before she got her hands free and tried to escape.

"Tsk, tsk. Where do you think you're going?" I chuckled.

"I'm not a child to have my butt spanked."

Urien led her to the table, then with a hand applying steady pressure on her back, he guided her to bend over it, diagonally near the corner. He peppered kisses across her spine before he nipped the plump flesh of her cheek, making her lift on her toes. "No, you aren't. Count to five."

Instead of lying still, River kicked her feet, and tried to escape his grip.

"Beloved, be still." The term of endearment rolled off my tongue, taking both of us by surprise. She stopped moving, but what was more? I meant it, and at that moment a little more weight lifted off my shoulders. I'd made the right choice. Taking her hands in mine, I stretched them in front of her, making sure she was immobilized but not uncomfortable, then lowered to her height, so she could see the sincerity in my eyes. "I promise everything we do will bring you pleasure."

"If at any point you don't like something, you say so, and we stop," Urien added, reassuring her further.

"Okay," she acquiesced, making a smile break across my face.

I kissed the top of her head and got up. The action brought my cock right in front of her mouth. The tip of her tongue touched me, when it darted to wet her lips. The featherlight touch packed a punch, and it made me groan and hunger for more. "Get on with it, Pair-bond."

The cur smirked, but soon enough he raised his palm, then brought it down on her delectable bottom, making the flesh jiggle and flush a soft pink.

"One," she gasped, and bit her lip.

He delivered the next two consecutively.

"Two, three," she said, and sighed as her body lost its rigidity, and she relaxed on the surface. Her breath caressed my length, and the sensation spread to my toes.

Suddenly, she pushed forward, her face bumping into my cock—the drops that had gathered on the tip smearing her lips. "Fuck," I growled at the sexy temptress.

Urien laughed. "You're enjoying this, Mate. Your pussy has creamed all over my hand. Is the punishment turning you on? Or is it Thora's cock?" When she didn't answer, a loud crack echoed in the chamber.

"Four," River cried out, panting.

"One more to go, psehimou, but I can feel your desire to discover your mate's taste. He's been tempting you since the moment you saw him, hasn't he? His scent is driving you wild with lust, isn't it?" he asked at the same time he brought his palm down on her ass, reddening it good.

"Yes," she screamed.

"Then open your mouth and take him in your haven. It's time for your reward." His voice dropped lower than before. He wasn't as unaffected as he'd pretended to be.

I closed the gap between us, half-expecting her to reject me, but she obeyed his simple command. Her lips wrapped around me, and her tongue massaged the sensitive head. My eyes drifted closed, and my breath caught in my lungs. She withdrew, and my hearts stuttered, but then sweet Vaults, she took me in her mouth again. The warmth surrounding me and the tight suction on my length had me almost blowing my load like a youngling. I froze and took a moment to regulate my breathing. Then I took control, slowly pushing deeper with every thrust, giving her less room to explore because I didn't want this wondrous experience to be over too soon.

Through hooded eyes, I watched her mouth stretch around my girth. She'd taken half of my length in, when she suddenly gasped, and opened wider, allowing the rest of my cock to slip inside. She gagged, but didn't pull away, and I felt her throat constrict around my cock. The liquid warmth and increased pleasure nearly drove me to my knees. I gently pulled out, and a string of her saliva ran from her luscious lips to the tip of my cock. The wicked image had my seed gathering in my balls as they lifted closer to my body. "Are you all right, beloved?"

Reverently, I caressed her cheek, then slid the pad of my thumb across her lips, before I pushed it in her mouth. She sucked the digit in, curled her tongue around it, and nodded, answering my question at the same time her eyes rolled back in pleasure.

Urien had started pounding her in earnest, turning her moans into cries of ecstasy. A sheen of sweat covered her golden skin while her body rocked back and forth.

None of us was going to last much longer, so I guided my cock to her lips again, and she took me in without hesitation.

Thrusting in tandem in and out, I matched my Pair-bond's rhythm, up until our self-control faltered, our moves turned jerkier, and holding my seed became an impossible task. "Come, Mate," I ordered, needing to witness her climax first.

At the sound of my voice, her muscles spasmed—her back arched, and her throat constricted around my length.

A welling pressure started somewhere deep within, causing a tingling to radiate outward. Contractions built as the orgasmic wave threatened to crash over me. Electricity shot through my body, short-circuiting all other functions— muting sound, and giving me tunnel vision. But the tension built to intolerable levels, until the wave crashed, leaving me with no choice but to release down her throat.

River's orgasm was still rocking her body, yet she swallowed as much as she could, the rest leaking from the sides of her lips, down her chin.

"Beloved Mate, you did good," I praised her, and reluctantly withdrew from her mouth.

She plopped her head on the table, her hair falling to the sides and covering her face. I stroked the soft strands, then cupped her neck and started massaging the knots of tension, until I felt her shudder and heard a sniffle.

I was still riding our post-orgasmic bliss, when the sound of her whimpers pierced my hearts and forced me back to solid ground. "River?" I asked, but she didn't reply. She didn't even lift her head. If she thought she could hide from me, she was sorely mistaken. I kneeled, then reached for her chin, and lifted her head to find her eyes filled to the brim with tears. "What is it, beloved?"

"What made you change your mind, Thora? Or was it all a trick to use my body? Will you reject me again now that you've had your fill?"

ALONE WITH MY THOUGHTS
RIVER

I should have been soaring high in the sky; with the wind under my spread wings helping me float through my climax's euphoria as I slowly came down, back to solid ground. I had set my inhibitions aside, and made myself vulnerable.

Sharing such an intimate act with both my mates should have been the best experience of my life, I should have felt blissful—one male was peppering kisses across my back, massaging my sore muscles, and the other was stroking my hair—yet I felt conflicted; Thora's words—*I'm done fighting our Union*—on replay in my mind, sowing seeds of doubt because that statement didn't mean he wanted me, it meant he couldn't resist what Urien called a Sacred Union.

The smooth, marble-like table felt cool beneath my heated skin as I rested my forehead on its surface and fought to keep the door blocking my insecurities shut. It seemed I wasn't good enough for men on Earth, or for a certain alien mate in space.

It was a hard pill to swallow, but I'd have preferred to have gotten hurt sooner, rather than later when he'd be firmly entrenched in my heart. *Don't cry, River...don't cry...* I repeated the mantra incessantly, hoping it'd come true.

No. Such. Luck. My breath hitched, and I pressed my lips tight to keep the sound from escaping. I was too late, though, for he hooked a finger under my chin, and didn't relent until I raised my head.

"What is it, beloved?" Thora's low baritone made the question sound like a caress as it slid from between his lips.

Just like the sudden, rapid, and uncontrolled release of impounded water from a dam that just broke, the words poured from my mouth in a rush. "What made you change your mind, Thora?"

With a heavy sigh, he let go of my chin and cupped the side of my face. His thumb glided over my cheekbone, and I found myself leaning into his tender touch. "I made a mistake, and I'm sure I'll make more. You need to be patient with me."

A warning for an explanation was not enough, not if we wanted to have a future together. They had different customs and lived by different rules. We needed to be able to communicate and find common ground.

I wasn't going to repeat the same mistake I'd made with William.

To anyone looking from the outside in, he'd been the perfect boyfriend with gentlemanly manners and a caring personality—always opening doors for me, touching my knee respectfully, or squeezing my hand whenever he'd sit close to me.

He'd fooled me too; and when I found out that he'd been

cheating on me because I wasn't putting out, and he had needs—his words not mine—I'd felt disgusted with myself, partially because when he'd readily accepted my request to wait until we were further into the relationship to have sex, I'd fallen for his good guy act, and partially because his excuse made sense to me—he had needs I hadn't fulfilled.

I hadn't satisfied one man's needs, how would I manage with two unless we talked?

So this time I'd ask questions and set my boundaries.

Looking around the room, I spotted the thin covers on the bed. They would do. I picked one up and wrapped it around my body into a makeshift dress…into a piece of armor. Then I faced the two—still naked—males looking at me with mirth in their eyes.

They could laugh all they wanted, but even though both of them had seen my bare body, I wasn't having this conversation naked.

"What made you change your mind, Thora?" I insisted, knowing the answer would either heal us or break us apart.

It looked like they both sensed the change in my demeanor because Thora donned his pants, whereas Urien manifested, seemingly out of thin air, a suit that looked like second skin—it had the same coloring, orange with green spots and stripes—with the exception the fact that it covered his male organs from view completely.

What a shame…River! Mind out of the gutter, I admonished myself, but I couldn't help but check out their cut physiques. I hadn't gotten a good look earlier and I regretted it.

"Let's sit, shall we?" my Saberian mate suggested, and I watched the powerful muscles in his body contract, giving the illusion of flames moving seductively across his skin, setting it on fire as he proceeded toward the sitting area near the balcony doors.

The space was bathed in a cool-white light, but the rest of the room was darker. Was the sun rising? I hadn't seen outside yet, and suddenly I was itching to do exactly that. A small detour for a quick glimpse wouldn't hurt.

The males sat on the big couch at opposite ends, leaving a gap in the middle for me. Instead of sitting, though, I walked past them to the balcony door.

The sight that met my eyes had goosebumps erupting all over my skin, and it had nothing to do with the cool touch of the sunrays of the sun, and everything with the fact that it was much smaller and blueish, instead of the big yellow-orange star I was used to.

I wasn't on Earth anymore, and the rest of the view attested to that too.

A violet ocean stretched as far as the eye could see. Lilac foam formed as the turbulent waves raged and crashed on its surface. The booming sounds seemed to follow the beat of my heart, and for a moment there, I transcended space and time; I became one with the sea...I became the conductor of a tumultuous symphony that expressed all the roiling emotions bubbling inside me.

Arms wrapped around my tummy, startling me, then pulled me into a warm chest. "Psehimou, please come sit with us." The pet name Urien called me by gave me butterflies every time it rolled off his tongue. He guided me to the sofa they were occupying, and I tried to gently disengage and move to the one across from them, when a second pair of arms pulled me down and made me lose my balance. Warmth crawled up my neck as I plopped on the couch with less grace than I would have liked.

"Beloved, you have the right to get mad at one or both of us when we get into an argument, but you don't get to keep us at arm's length." Thora's gravelly voice was filled with conviction, and the tattoo-like markings that were a few shades darker than the rest of his skin became more prominent as they darkened.

I lifted my hand to touch them, but then stopped myself. It was time to talk, not explore. "Okay, I'll try not to," I said and straightened my shoulders. "Your turn."

He angled his body toward me, then pulled at his uniform a few times till the pant legs were straightened, before he stopped and rested his torso against the back of the sofa.

The gesture immediately struck me as odd because I didn't think he was the type to fidget. Why was he suddenly agitated?

"I didn't change my mind," Thora said, and my hands clutched at the sheet covering my legs, trying to hold onto something, for I was about to fall off a precipice and into an endless void. His eyes followed my movement and he rushed to say more. "The moment I saw you step out of that vehicle on Earth, you rocked the foundation of my existence. You got under my skin, when no other female had done so."

Butterflies fluttered in my stomach, and I pressed a hand to quiet them. It was too soon to get my hopes up. "Then why did you push me away?" I asked.

He dragged his hand through his hair and cleared his throat a couple of times before he said, "You would swiftly become the center of my existence, and I wasn't ready to let go of my past yet."

God, he's insufferable. Getting him to explain was like pulling out teeth...slowly...one at a time.

"Your past? I need more, Thora." I wasn't willing to back down. This was too important, and the stakes too high—I wouldn't be moving to another state for my men, I'd be moving to a different planet.

His chest caved in, and he turned away, but then he sighed and looked Urien in the eyes.

Suddenly, I got chills and was overcome by the desire to stop him.

"I never wanted to be in a Union with a Saberian," he started, his voice tight, "not after one of them killed my Chosen Mate, and my parents."

"Your mate," I echoed, the sound hollow in my ears as a big quake shook the ground, and its surface ruptured. Ripped apart like a paper torn in two—deep, dark chasms forming. I grabbed the arms of both my mates—my fingers digging into their skin—terrified we'd soon be swallowed.

"River, open your eyes," they said in unison, worry tingeing their voices.

When did I close them? I blinked a few times, and the room came into focus. As it did, I realized it was my heart that was shaking, not the ground. I jumped into Thora's arms, and hugged him tight—needing to alleviate his pain more than I needed to breathe.

After a minute or two, he pulled me sideways and positioned me on his lap.

"Thora, we can't have a conversation like this." I giggled

while Urien scooted closer and placed my legs on top of his. "Is someone feeling left out?" I teased him, and he tickled my most ticklish spot, my feet. "I surrender," I cried out between belly laughs.

"Why not?" the blue alien asked, and his arms formed a bar around my waist as if he were expecting me to try to flee at any moment. "I need to hold you while I share this particular memory."

To show him I wasn't going anywhere, I wiggled my butt, trying to get more comfortable when a low groan vibrated in his chest. *Oopsie!* "Sorry...not sorry?" I stuttered, and he shook his head at me like a parent chiding a child, but I'd seen the tips of his lips lift. Still, I played along. "I'll be good, I promise."

If I hadn't been focused on his face, I'd have missed the transformation as his eyes lost their brightness, and a faraway look glazed over them. "I'd been mated once...a lifetime ago, when I was still a youngling and a blacksmith's apprentice."

My heart ached because I knew this story didn't have a happy ending and there was nothing I could do to change the outcome and spare him from the pain.

"Sharifah had lost her parents when she was an offspring, and she loved spending time with mine. So one evening, I had returned home from the smithy early, to one of her notes saying to meet her there." He dropped his forehead on my shoulder. His shaky exhale warmed my arm, and it brought to my attention that his temperature had fallen drastically as his too warm skin was now cool to the touch. I threaded my fingers through his hair, petting him, trying to convey he was no longer alone. "Their house wasn't far, and I'd chosen to walk. I'd even stopped to gather blossoms for the two females in my life."

His muscles bunched, his body coiling as if preparing for a fight, and his hands curled into fists before he lifted eyes that were drenched in anguish to mine. "I'll forever live wondering whether I could have saved them if I hadn't wasted time."

He was putting the blame on himself, but how could he have known, or even anticipated what was to come? He was wrestling with survivor's guilt, and I doubted he knew it. Not wanting to interrupt, I kept my mouth closed; he wouldn't accept my words that he wasn't at fault anyway, but I vowed to help him heal the first chance I got.

"A rattling sound was coming from the garden bed outside my parent's house, and I had thought it was a serpent I needed to chase away." A powerful tremor rocked his body and a tortured hiss slipped through his pinched lips. "Only it was her, lying there...gasping for air." His voice broke, but gritting his teeth, he continued, "I called out for help, but it was too late, and right before her hearts stopped beating she croaked out a name, Ivar Al-Jurjani the Saberian."

My own heart was bleeding. I wanted to hug him, but his perfectly still posture screamed a warning at me to stay away.

"When my parents didn't rush outside, the rustling sounds from inside their home registered. I stormed inside, and was greeted by my mother nearly torn to pieces on the floor in a pool of her own blood." His body was shivering uncontrollably, and his hands around me were shaking, yet he didn't seem to be aware. "My father was fighting a losing battle against a sabertooth."

A whimper sounded loud in the room, and I furrowed my brows in confusion.

Urien squeezed my legs, and his warmth seeped into my skin, silently comforting me. But I wasn't the one in need of comfort, Thora was.

My blue alien brought his hand to my face and...wiped the tears I hadn't realized I was shedding, then he kissed my eyelids. His gentleness was a soothing balm to my sorrowful heart.

"The rest is just a haze, but I remember slicing the beast and taking his left eye, before I shoved my dagger in the right side of his throat. He fled after that. I would have chased him, but I didn't come out of our altercation unscathed, and my body just gave out. But I'm stronger now, and I'll make him pay for his crime," he finished in a rush, and I knew it was for my benefit.

Sweet, considerate Thora. I shifted in his arms and enveloped him in a tight hug, which he returned.

Urien placed a hand on Thora's shoulder, in a gesture of solidarity. "I'm sorry for your loss, Pair-bond. I know how it feels to lose a mate and your parents at the same time." His voice was lower than usual, and its gravelly timbre was laced with pain. "Yenoctonia claimed mine, and I yearn to bathe in the blood of those responsible," he growled, making me freeze.

He had a mate, too? My muscles stiffened without permission upon hearing the news, and I had to forcibly relax because I didn't want Thora to know. I had to swallow a few times to dispel the thick ache in my throat. But I managed, and then turned to hug Urien too.

Both of them had survived such tragic losses, and they didn't know it was something we had in common. I'd experienced loss too—not that of a partner, but that of a parent.

And I knew grief could alter a person. It had made Urien overprotective, whereas Thora was afraid to let people in his heart—the fear of losing me was the reason he'd pushed me away.

It all made sense now, and it was only fair I let them know. I straightened, ending the hug, and Urien dropped his arms. "You both lost those you loved in the past, but you protected me when we crashed on that planet." It was important they understood. "You kept our attackers from hurting me. You kept me safe," I said in a steady and calm voice.

"Why do I hear a but in there, Mate?" Urien asked.

I'd expected I wouldn't have been the only woman they'd been with, but to hear they both had mates when Urien had said mates were rare was...unexpected, and it created conflicting emotions inside me. On the one hand, seeing proof of them having the capacity to love so deeply warmed my heart and made me yearn for what we could have. On the other, it filled me with trepidation because what if there wasn't any room left in their hearts for me.

My Saberian was waiting for an answer, though, and I gave him an honest one. "I heard the warmth in your voices when you talked about your females. I felt the pain their losses caused, and you're both still bent on avenging them— rightfully so." Feeling their limbs tense under mine, I halted, and lowered my gaze to the floor.

Biting the inside of my cheek, I tried to gather courage to express the rest of what I wanted to say. "They clearly hold special places in your hearts, and that's fine, but I'm not sure I can compete with their ghosts."

Eyes widened, and mouths slackened. The sight was comical, but I didn't have it in me to laugh right at that second. The next instant, though, was as if my words lit them on fire, and they started talking at the same time, when rapid knocking on the door made us freeze.

"Go away," Urien growled.

I slapped his arm. "It might be important, what if something happened to the Queen?"

"I would have felt it," he said, and it was my turn to look flabbergasted. "Come in," he called out while I picked my jaw off the floor.

At the door stood a Saberian with midnight blue skin and silver spots and stripes across his huge frame. He wasn't moving, yet the silver markings gave the illusion of constant motion. He was striking. "Urien, the Queen requested to see both you and Thora now."

"We're in the midd—" my Wravukian mate started, and I interrupted him at the same time the warrior growled a warning loudly.

"It's okay, go." There was no need for a fight. "We'll pick up this conversation later," I promised, but I could really use some "me" time in between to digest everything and come to a conclusion.

Eyebrows squeezed together, and lips pressed tight conveyed their reluctance, but both of them made sure to kiss me thoroughly—even though another was watching us— before they got up and walked out of the room, leaving me flustered and alone with my thoughts.

MAY REAPER BE BORN
URIEN

Djoser gripped my arms in greeting, and I returned the gesture. His eyes were lit with mirth. "I guess congratulations are in order, since the Wravukian is standing and all," he said once my Pair-bond had closed the chamber's door behind us.

Thora's anger felt like a sharp spike in temperature, and even though I was used to Grim's moods being different from mine at times, the sudden intrusion of the foreign emotion made the world around me spin, before it settled on its axis again.

Earlier, when we mated River, we'd given her our seed at the same time. We'd taken the second step that would lead to her sabertooth's emergence.

Elation had joined my climax's euphoria, and I felt the happiest I'd ever been. Lost in bliss, it took me a moment to realize my emotions were amplified by another's...by Thora's.

And as we locked eyes, I saw the recognition in his too.

The mental link that would give us access to one another's mind and allow us to communicate had strengthened to the point we sensed each other's emotions, although I couldn't detect River's yet.

So when the Wravukian tried to sidestep around me, I anticipated the move and blocked his way because Djoser had spoken in jest; he hadn't meant anything by it.

"Why, thank you, honorable warrior." I chuckled at the same time Thora growled. *Better not test his patience just yet.*

Why not? I'd love to teach him a lesson, Grim suggested, and I mentally rolled my eyes at my sabertooth.

Djoser frowned and said in a tight voice, "The Queen sounded distressed, you better get going. They're still in the Healers' Chamber."

I saluted the Elite, and we parted ways.

"Next time you get in my way, I won't hold back," my Pair-bond said in a carefully controlled tone on our way to the Royals.

Shaking my head, I managed to keep a straight face. "And you need to learn not to take everything seriously. The warrior was joking."

"At my expense," he mumbled angrily while grinding his teeth, and I couldn't hold back—I burst out laughing. He still had a lot to learn, and I was looking forward to his sabertooth coming out to play.

It would be fun watching the icy cur thaw.

We remained silent the rest of the way, and by the time we reached our destination, he'd calmed down.

Before I could knock, the door opened and the Second

King of Wravuk gestured for us to get in. I bowed my head respectfully and entered, only to be met with a dreadful sight.

The Queen was sitting on the med-pod with tears pooling in her red-rimmed eyes, and her face was paler than usual. Seeing her like this after we'd almost lost her sent me into a tailspin, and I rushed to her side without taking into consideration the distressed mate hovering near her.

An obstacle of purple muscle blocked my way, and a low, threatening growl warned me of my infraction, letting me know he was ready to tear off body parts that were definitely essential for me to keep breathing.

Grim's answering snarl rose in my chest, but I swallowed the sound and immediately tilted my head to the side, revealing my neck in submission.

Arana knew I'd sooner end my life than hurt his mate.

Mes was generally very difficult to rattle.

But Rorc?

My muscles tensed, remembering the hierarchy challenges that took place a few circles after the Queen's fight.

Fuck, I was screwed, and this was going to hurt.

"Move over," Kali demanded as she pushed her mate out of the way. Then, ignoring his answering snarl, she wrapped her arms around my waist, turned sideways to fit the bulge of her belly, and hugged me tight.

I stiffened—all my limbs locking in place—unsure of the protocol. Saberian Queens were never this forthcoming with anyone outside of their families.

But then her silent tears wet my Sirh, and it let the moisture through, analyzing it before shooting a distress signal straight to my brain.

My arms, of their own accord, lifted and enveloped her smaller frame—my protective instincts going haywire. "What's wrong?" I asked softly.

"Kali, you're freaking Urien out, and I won't be the one kissing him better once he breaks down in tears. Rorc can do that." Arana, who didn't want his mate upset over anything, tried to lighten the mood.

It worked because she laughed softly, and pulled back.

I dropped my hands and waited. In the short time I'd known her, I learned she wasn't one to talk in circles. "I had a vision," she said, and sought her purple mate as if needing to draw from his strength.

He caressed her cheek, then led her back to the med-pod and lifted her on it. "What you saw is not set in stone, little one."

A weight settled in the pit of my stomach, and through our bond, I could tell Thora shared the feeling.

"You bit River to complete the union, but her sabertooth wouldn't come out." Her voice was barely above a whisper, but it felt like a sucker punch, rocking me backward

My insides twisted painfully. *How is that possible?*

"She died, and soon after, I and the cubs died too," she finished in a rush, confirming my greatest fear.

Blinking to clear my blurry vision, I looked around, searching for something…anything that would help. There was nothing. "What do I do?" I croaked, then turned to Thora. "What do we do?"

Our bond radiated with pain, and he placed his hand on my shoulder in solidarity. "We'll find a way to save her."

"You need to turn Thora first," the Queen said, startling us all with a solution that was unheard of. "With him you might be able to bring her sabertooth out before it's too late."

"Psehimou, that's…dangerous…" Arana hesitated, probably not wanting to upset his pregnant mate further.

"Dawn tells me it was done in the past," she insisted, and a sliver of hope sparked and shed its flickering light on the darkness threatening to swallow my soul.

Her words also jogged my sabertooth's memory. *I know what needs to be done…He can survive it,* he said with determination.

Were there any who didn't? I asked him, and instead of words, he shared in my mind's eye images of mangled bodies in half-shifted forms. Fuck.

"Grim knows what we must do. But there's a chance that you might not make it." The restless energy coursing through my body made standing still nearly impossible. We needed to act now, but we had to explain first. "There are three steps to Changing a male. We took the first, I've already stung my Pair-bond. The second is a blood exchange—"

"Let's do it now," Thora interrupted. "We need a scalpel," he added and stomped toward the cupboards in search of one.

But that wouldn't do. "No," I corrected. "We need one of the ceremonial knives that's stored along with the Sacred Weapons." I needed permission to access that chamber so I turned to the First King of Saber.

"Whatever you need, brother," Arana said.

Thora's emotions bled through our bond to me, and my skin started to itch painfully, barely able to contain me. "Lead the way, Pair-bond," he ordered.

It was the first time he used the honorific title, and I hadn't realized how much I needed to feel his acceptance of us until this moment when another piece fell into place, further solidifying our Sacred Bond.

"Thora," Arana stopped him at the door. "I met with Ivar." His lip curled in displeasure. "His recount of the events is different, but he mixed lies with the truth, and I don't trust his words."

My Pair-bond didn't move, didn't blink, didn't even breathe.

"Your challenge request is accepted. Dagoner will arrange the fight and let both of you know."

A tight-lipped thank you and a nod was the only response Thora was capable of forming with the onslaught of rage coursing through his veins.

It was enough, though, and we hurried out of the Healers' Chamber and headed toward the Sacred Weapons repository.

Thora kept pace next to me, his steps as silent as mine.

"What is the third step?" he blurted.

That question had an easy answer. "I bite you to release your sabertooth." Then I pointed out something he hadn't noticed in the midst of everything that was going on. "He's already reaching for the surface. Look at your arm."

He did as asked, and I heard him gulp. He had every right to be apprehensive. What we were doing was dangerous because at the least, it would cost him his identity, as he'd turn into a hybrid, and at the most...it would cost him his life.

I hoped he'd survive the transformation. *Creator, let him survive this*, I prayed, because any other outcome would wreck our mate, and according to the Queen's vision, it would mean her death as well.

Grim released a sorrowful chuffing sound that matched the desperation that—like quicksand—was slowly sucking me into its depths, ensnaring my body in an inescapable trap.

Until at last, we'd reached our destination.

The two elite warriors guarding the entrance to the chamber with the Sacred Weapons had already been notified, and they let us pass. As the doors closed behind us, we were enveloped in an eerie silence that breathed and had its own pulse.

I let my sabertooth take the lead since he knew what we needed. Thora remained close at my heels. We walked to the farthest end of the chamber before we stopped in front of the ancient Altar of Brotherhood. It was made of big shiny black stones, and I'd never questioned the origin of its name before, but now it made sense. It vibrated with power, and it made the hairs on the nape of my neck stand up.

Thora walked to the other side and stood across from me. His expression was sober, focused on what lay in front of us.

Spread on the Altar's surface were nine ceremonial knives. The hilts were made out of the same material as the stones, but the blades attached had different shapes and colors.

Grim insisted we use the kris knife with the orange-hued, wavy blade that reminded me of flames. So I hovered my hand over it, wanting to get a feel for the object before I picked it up.

Power vibrated under my flesh, and arcs of electricity crackled in the air before they connected with my palm, jolting but not hurting me.

A chill raced down my spine the moment I grasped the hilt. The chanting voices of warriors long gone echoed in my mind, encouraging me to join. "Venom that's been injected, the future realigned," I murmured, and wisps of fog swirled around our feet, swallowing everything in their path as they drifted higher and higher, until we were enveloped completely in a cool cocoon.

"Blood that's been mixed..." I said, and slid the sharp edge of the knife across my palm. We watched my blood sizzle on the blade before it evaporated in a puff of smoke. Then Thora offered his hand to me, and I sliced his flesh.

Both of our wounds were still bleeding, and I knew ancient magic was at work, keeping our regenerative abilities dormant.

I laid the knife on the Altar and clasped his hand. Feeling our blood mix, I recited the rest of the words that were altering my Pair-bond. "...will forever bind."

Taking a deep breath, I tried to calm my racing heart. The next step would change everything.

Thora squeezed my hand in encouragement. "I accept the honor." His reverent voice reverberated around us, pushing away my trepidation.

Without breaking the hold, I lifted his wrist close to my mouth. My canines elongated of their own accord, making forming words difficult, but I managed to say, "Bite will free the sabertooth that's been confined." The need to sink my teeth into his flesh hit me, and I couldn't resist anymore.

Suddenly, we were transported to another place, where an assent of unintelligible voices rose from the thick veil that surrounded us. I looked wildly around trying to get my bearings, and as the fog slowly dissipated, figures started coming into view.

Figures whose faces were familiar to me.

We were surrounded by my ancestors, and as the crowd parted, my father emerged, looking upon us with pride.

"Son—" he choked, and I opened my mouth to speak, but nothing came out. Next to him were my mother and sisters.

'Where are we?' Thora asked through our bond, and it was like a dam had been broken, letting everyone's emotions rush in my direction, flooding me.

We both fell to our knees, still grasping each other's hands, and I instinctively knew we shouldn't break the connection.

An Elder I didn't recognize approached us and placed his palms on our shoulders, and strength seeped back into our bodies. "Welcome, warriors. Blessed be," he said in his otherworldly voice.

Feeling rejuvenated, we got up on our feet, and beaming smiles met us everywhere I looked.

One by one each Saberian approached us and touched either our shoulders or our united hands before repeating what the Elder had said.

Having lost my sense of time, it could have been an eternity that passed or just a few moments before my family finally approached us.

They formed a circle around us and they started chanting the ritual words I had recited not too long ago. And as the chant came to an end, they stepped closer, tightening the circle until they held us as one in their embrace.

The pain of their loss flared with a vengeance, and Grim roared in agony. My throat felt thick, and their faces became blurry as moisture gathered in my eyes. I'd missed them so much.

"My son, my warrior, do not let sadness linger in your heart, for we will meet once more when the time is right, but never again until then." The sweet cadence of my mother's voice rang softly in my ears. But then her demeanor changed, for she had a purpose to fulfill. "May the Creator bless your Sacred Union," she said, and kissed my forehead. "May your brother always watch your back," she added, along with a kiss on my right cheek. "May your mate give you many cubs and fill your soul with light." She finished with a kiss on my left cheek.

Once again I tried to speak but was unable to do so, but before panic could sink its claws in, I felt a warmth expanding in my chest. Slowly all my concerns and worries fell away, and I watched, enthralled, as my mother turned to Thora and said, "Honored warrior, new son, welcome," taking him by surprise. She then repeated the soft spoken words she'd given me, along with her kisses.

By the end, my Pair-bond's body was shaking, and his thoughts were a mess. But everything stilled when my mother's voice rang clear and strong. "May Reaper be born."

"May Reaper be born." The other Saberians that were no longer visible echoed her statement.

My father, who'd been standing silently next to my mother the whole time, stirred. "Do not be afraid of your sabertooths, they are your greatest strength," he said while misty tendrils wrapped around my and Thora's bodies, blocking everything from view. "They are what your mate needs...what your Royals need. Be safe. Be strong." His deep timbre accompanied us as we were transported back to the repository.

As our feet were placed on solid ground again, I knew that the ritual was almost complete, so I uttered the words that would irrevocably change Thora's life, "Brothers by blood-right now forever intertwined."

NEITHER OF YOU WILL SURVIVE
RIVER

I hadn't meant to fall asleep, but exhaustion had set in, and I hadn't been able to resist the allure of the heavenly bed that'd been calling out my name. Based on the brightness of the suns, I'd had a few hours of rest. Urien and Thora hadn't returned yet, so after taking care of business, I decided to check on the Queen.

Thankfully, the Healers' Chamber wasn't that far from my room. I was there in no time and knocked on the door. When I got no answer, I twisted the handle and peeked inside.

Two males were hunched over some kind of device, but they jerked their heads toward me the moment I leaned in. Their mouths fell open, and their eyes widened in surprise.

It was funny, but I refrained from laughing in case I offended them. "Is the Queen here?" I asked, although a cursory glance showed she wasn't.

They shook their heads at the same time, and I slapped my hand over my mouth to hold in my laugh. "I'm sorry for interrupting you. Bye now," I said, and closed the door before I erupted in a fit of giggles. They acted as if they hadn't seen another woman in their life.

Then I remembered what Urien had shared with me last night, the memory sobering me up. *Oh my God, they probably haven't,* I thought, feeling sad for them.

Out of the blue, a sharp pain nearly had me doubling over. I clutched my abdomen, and tried to breathe through the uncomfortable sensation.

Food had been the last thing on my mind when I got up, but I should have eaten. Well, first things first, I'd make sure Kali was all right, and then I would hunt down something to eat.

As soon as I could stand straight again, I started toward the Queen's room. I was about to go in when a girly voice with a strange accent had me looking up. The sight stopped me in my tracks as fear raced down my spine.

A face that was a mix between humanoid and reptilian was attached to a body covered in dark-green scales and a tail that trailed behind the biped creature.

My heartbeat started racing and the pain returned, this time, though, in my chest. I pressed the heel of my palm between my breasts, and it helped a little bit.

"Look, mommy! This female is the Healer Kali mentioned. Can I hug her?" the smaller of the two spoke with exuberance only children possessed.

"Kas," her mother admonished. "Come here, sweetheart. I don't think she has a translator, and you're scaring her because she can't understand you."

The adorable child scrunched up her almost non-existent

nose. "Why would I scare her?" she asked—her tone subdued
—before she sniffled loudly, breaking my heart.

It wasn't her fault. I wasn't on Earth anymore, and I better
get used to seeing alien creatures fast. "I'm sorry, you just
caught me by surprise. I can understand you and I wouldn't
mind a hug," I said, and before I had uttered the last word, the
little ball of energy barreled into me. "Umph!" Dang it, she
was very strong.

"Please excuse my daughter," the bigger of the two said
while approaching us. "Restraint is hard when everything is
still brand new."

"All good," I wheezed, and the mother gently unwrapped
her daughter's arms from around me.

Then I remembered her earlier comment. "Um. Why can I
understand you?"

"You must have a translator embedded somewhere behind
your ear. That's how it's usually done."

I felt like hitting something...preferably two someones
who were absent at the moment, and this said a lot, because I
wasn't a violent person. "Oh, insufferable males! I'm definitely
having a conversation with them about sticking things in me
without permission," I pushed the words through clenched
teeth, and finished with a growl—accomplishing a perfect
mimicry of one of Grim's snarls.

The Queen, who opened the doors to her room just as I
finished speaking, burst into laughter. "Oh doc, you're going
to make me pee myself."

"Oh my God, Kali! You shouldn't be up," I chastised, and
immediately wrapped my arm around her waist, nudging her
back to bed. "What are you doing up?"

Instead of walking backward, though, she embraced me. "I'm good. Thank you for saving my babies." Emotion overflowed from her voice, and it brought tears to my eyes.

"You're more than welcome, but how can you be on your feet? I operated on you a few hours ago."

She pulled back and quickly swiped the area under her eyes with the back of her hands. "The benefits of having a Healer for a mate, I guess." She chuckled, then continued, "Plus my sabertooth's regenerative abilities helped as well. Once you removed the foreign object, Dawn made sure we were completely healed."

"Is it my turn for a hug now, Kali?" the girl asked, and put a smile on all of our faces.

"Of course it is, Kas," the Queen said, then opened her arms wide, and the little one didn't need to be asked twice. "River, I want you to meet my friends. This is Tris, and her daughter, Kas. They moved here recently, and let me tell you, we need as much girl power as we can get if we want to stand a chance against all the testosterone on the planet." She strutted to the dinner table—back straight, head held high— and if one looked at her from behind they wouldn't be able to tell she was pregnant. Authority clung to her like an expensive perfume. "The males have been alone for too long, and they've become complacent," she finished and gestured for us to join her.

The reptilian woman paled, her green skin losing its vibrancy. "Kali, if the males catch us scheming against them"—a shudder rocked her frame—"no, they should be served."

"You're not on Mardon any more, honey...nor must you

serve anyone." The Queen squeezed Tris's arm and kept her voice soft. "If any male dares to even suggest such a thing, I promise you he'll be dealt with immediately. No, we'll shake things up here."

And I believed her; so did Tris, who was nodding her assent.

Kali emanated power; the energy was subtle, but a force to be reckoned with. And I'd never met anyone like her.

Suddenly, chills raced down my arms, raising goosebumps along the way, and it wasn't a pleasant feeling. Maybe later I'd visit the Healers for a checkup, but there was nothing I could do now, so I put it in the back of my mind. "I don't know if I'm your girl either," I confessed. "Serina, my best friend, though, is exactly who you need," I said, already missing her so much. We always found time to talk on a daily basis—be it messages or on the phone.

She'd be worried sick by now. I had to find a way to contact her.

"That's an awesome idea, River. Do you think she'd be up for a trip?"

With Serina here, my family would be complete. "Yes, she'd love to come here," I agreed readily, and if my best friend wasn't up for it, I'd find a way to convince her.

Kali didn't miss a beat. "I'll have Mok set up a communication's channel asap."

My jaw dropped. I hadn't really believed she meant it, but I could sense her determination. "You would do that?"

Gray eyes gave me all their attention. It felt like she was looking into my soul. "River, we possess the technology to travel back and forth to Earth as often as we like," she said carefully, then as if coming to a decision, she rushed the rest. "I can tell she's important to you. You've become important to me, and I want you to be happy here. We will figure this out."

I didn't think, I just reacted. Leaning in, I hugged her tight, and whispered my heartfelt thank you. When I pulled back, her smile lit the room until her eyes met mine.

Then her eyebrows drew together and her gaze darkened. "River, you're bleeding," she said, but her voice was unintelligible, as if she were talking from somewhere deep in a cave.

Something wet trickled down my ear, and I wiped it away, only to realize as I brought my hand in front of me that it was blood.

That can't be good. Fear skittered down my spine.

Had the temperature dropped? I was cold.

Where are my mates?

Suddenly, a scream burst from my lips as my body was racked by excruciating pain. A hundred scalpels were slicing me from the inside out. Every incision precise, methodical, and inflicting maximum damage.

The women blurred, the room spun, and I hit something hard. I tried to curl into the fetal position but my muscles weren't cooperating. My limbs flailed and writhed on their own; I was no longer the driver of my body, and nothing I tried helped.

Am I having a nightmare?

Adrenaline shot through my system, energizing me, but I couldn't wake up. My heart was screaming in my chest, and my lungs screamed for oxygen. The agony lasted an eternity, until finally my brain couldn't take it anymore, and I lost consciousness.

I was trailing through the mists, trying to find my way out, but the smoky tendrils kept grabbing my clothes, slowing me down...but I had to find the way out of here.

A deep masculine voice penetrated the haze. It felt familiar, but I couldn't place it, nor could I put a face on it.

What if it was another trap of this place to keep me here forever?

"Psehimou, we got you. You're okay now," it said, and something in me stirred.

Oh my God, something was growing inside me. Dread filled me. I was going to die.

"River, open your eyes, beloved." A second voice joined the first, but it was too authoritative—I didn't like it.

The thing inside my body tried to get out, and I screamed as fur sprouted from my skin and I was destroyed from the inside.

A featherlight touch caressed my face, beckoning me to open my eyes.

After a few failed efforts, low red lighting filled my sight. Two figures were sitting next to me. Both caressing my face and my hair lovingly.

My mates...

"What happened?" I croaked, my throat too parched from the ordeal.

Thora brought a cup of water to my lips while Urien lifted me and supported my back so I could drink.

When I had enough and Urien lowered me to a pod, I realized I still had no control over my limbs, and even though panic was setting in once again, my body was relaxed. "Why can't I move?"

"You're in the Healers' Chamber. They gave you a sedative, but it's wearing off, and you will regain mobility soon," Urien explained in a calm tone, yet his face was etched with worry. The smile that usually graced his lips was replaced by a scowl.

I glanced at Thora. Worry lines marred his forehead, and his yellow-amber eyes were peppered with dark-green flakes that made them look grimmer than before.

"What happened?" I repeated.

They shared a look. The kind of look you gave someone when you had to tell them bad news.

I inhaled sharply and braced myself.

"Your Sabertooth is different, and your body is fighting the Change. We need to complete the union, my love," Urien explained, but I could tell he was holding something back.

"Or?" I prompted, needing to know the rest. I was a big girl, I'd handle it.

Thora stroked my cheek while his thumb slid slowly over my lips—the intimate action was full of love...I could feel it deep in my bones. His words, though, were full of anguish when he said, "Otherwise, neither of you will survive."

WHAT CAN WE DO?
THORA

White clouds obscured my vision, but I knew we were back on Saber because the sensation of weightlessness was gone.

A riot of emotions—awe, acceptance, connectedness—racked my insides and cracked the cool exterior I'd carefully cultivated after the massacre of my family. For this ritual Urien was performing would not just grant me a sabertooth, but a blood brother as well.

And that realization softened the pain that came with my decision to forsake everything familiar and all that I had fought for to become a hybrid.

The mist dispersed as quickly as it had appeared, revealing Urien and our clasped hands on top of the altar between us.

"Brothers by bloodright now forever intertwined," he said, sealing our fate and making the room spin.

Fire seared my palm as an invisible branding iron marked my skin.

Agony raced through my veins and brought me to my knees.

Urien's cries matched my own until his feet no longer held him, and he fell beside me, breaking our hold.

Slowly, the torment subsided, my hearts calmed, and I was able to draw air into my lungs.

What just happened?

"Urien, are you all right?" I asked, and lifted my palm to my face.

I'd been so absorbed by the thick shimmery lines forming an internal vine around and on the cut—that looked as if it had been healed a long time ago, and not just moments earlier —that I didn't immediately notice the spots and stripes inter-twining with the markings of my Wravukian ancestral line.

But when I did, my eyes nearly bulged out of my skull because there was no hiding the fact that I was a hybrid now. I shouldn't have assumed I'd remain the same on the outside like Rorc and Mes had. Gulping the lump that'd formed in my throat, I thought, *It's all right, my mates were worthy of the price.*

"Yes," he croaked, then grabbed the altar to help himself get up.

Following suit, I rose, then scanned him from top to bottom—the need to ensure he was uninjured beating at me. "Fuck! That was intense," I admitted.

"How are you feeling?" he asked while examining his own hand, which had the same mark as mine—the rest of his skin had remained unchanged.

Glancing behind me to check whether I had suddenly sprouted a tail or something I wasn't aware of yet, I blurted, "I don't feel any different." Tentatively, I slid my finger over the mark, and when I wasn't zapped with pain, I applied more pressure to feel its raised ridges. "I'm drained, but still me...I think."

My Pair-bond's sharp eyes lifted to mine—only, they were no longer green, but orange. "You are different. Grim is itching for a fight, and I'm sure Reaper feels the same. Hierarchy is very important to them, and that's how they establish their dominance."

I appreciated the lesson in societal norms, but I cared more about why I couldn't sense my sabertooth yet. Had something gone wrong? I opened my mouth to ask when I felt something unfurling inside me, taking more and more space while pushing me out.

The burning sensation from before returned, albeit more bearable this time as it started spreading from my chest outward to my limbs.

"Don't resist, let him take the reins," Urien guided me, but it was so fucking hard to let go when it felt like I was being kicked out of my own body as it started breaking and reshaping.

I opened my mouth to let my Pair-bond know exactly who would be taking the reins, when a guttural roar erupted from within me.

In an instant, Grim was standing in Urien's place, letting loose an answering growl of his own, which seemed to goad Reaper on, and I suddenly found myself on the floor. Only, it wasn't really me, and I had no control over this body.

Our senses were sharper—recognizing, analyzing, and cataloging a myriad of information from our immediate environment faster than the speed of light. Dark-blue fur covered us, and we stood on four paws nearly the size of my head.

I'm stronger than you, Reaper said, his voice unfamiliar, yet...not. *I'm in charge now.*

'The alpha gets to control both of your bodies. You have to fight him, Thora, establish your dominance.' Urien's voice drifted through our bond to my mind, sounding clear and loud, unlike before.

'Now you tell me!' I growled at him. How was I supposed to do that since I didn't have a form, and neither had my opponent? I just sensed he was in front of me.

Iron bars started appearing one by one around me, caging me in. The hairs on the nape of my neck lifted, as fear skittered through me. The sensation, though, was jolting because I didn't have hair at the moment but fur.

Okay, I needed to establish my dominance...but how the fuck was I supposed to do that? Especially when the cur had almost succeeded in building a cage around me.

'Push him back. Lead him to the recesses of your mind, where you let him come out only when you both agree.' Urien answered the question I hadn't asked, proving he was there watching over me like a brother would, interfering when needed, but otherwise, just keeping a watchful eye.

Reaper growled menacingly at our Pair-bond. He didn't like him sharing his knowledge with me. He had the reins for the first time and he wanted to explore, but first he needed to prove that he was stronger than the sabertooth standing in front of us.

Weird didn't even begin to explain what I was experiencing.

The power running through our limbs.

The energy crinkling and cracking.

The muscles bunching and releasing.

It was all surreal, disorienting.

Grim swatted our muzzle—claws retracted—trying to instill some sense into Reaper, who hadn't stopped snarling at him, and to give me time to get my bearings.

So I let my senses expand and reached out with my spirit to touch Reaper.

Like leaves blown away by a strong wind, the bars he'd formed around me fell.

A plethora of scents assaulted my sense of smell, and bright colors blinded my eyes.

My breathing became labored, yet the movement of our lungs didn't reflect that; it was slow and steady following Reaper's exhalations.

'*You can do it, brother.*' Urien's firm tone and continued belief helped me center myself.

I focused on the life force I now shared a body with.

Reaper had his sights on Grim, dismissing me already as weak, and that was his first mistake. As I neared, I noticed his energy was a darker shade of blue then mine, and the menace emanating from him was palpable. Wherever our lights touched, it felt as if I were standing too close to a fire.

Steeling myself for impact, I hurled my energy at his. The colors clashed, and he howled—the sound piercing our sensitive ears. But I didn't relent I enveloped his light with mine. Reaper thrashed and tried to evade my hold, unsuccessfully. He wasn't deterred, though, as he changed tactics. Out of nowhere tentacles slithered and tightened painfully around me.

In the middle of everything going on, through our new bond, I could feel Urien's sabertooth riding him hard. He could sense our weakness and needed to establish his dominance.

Reaper had the same access I did, and he realized a tick too late that if he wanted to win the fight against Grim, he'd have to lose the one against me.

We both knew the moment Urien relented and Grim won. They attacked without hesitation, forcing Reaper to divide his attention, and that was my chance.

I encircled his dark aura down, then constricted it to the point the light of his soul started flickering. Doing so caused both of us a world of hurt, but it had to be done—he had to yield.

Surrender, Urien and I ordered at the same time, before a new voice, too guttural and deep added, *'You need to learn when to give in to live another day, brother.'*

And it was Grim's words that had Reaper surrendering our body to me, and then retreating from the forefront of our consciousness.

The shift back to two legs was painless and fast, and I knew it was because it'd been voluntary.

Urien shifted too and clapped my back. "Brother," he said, his tone warm and full of emotion.

"Brother," I replied, because I got it, and I felt the same.

"You seem to have a little bit of an issue there..."

I jerked this way and that, checking to see if I'd forgotten to shift any body parts when he chuckled dryly.

"I'm talking about your uniform," he clarified—a smile stretching his lips wide.

'Fucker.'

"I heard that." He laughed heartily, then offered me a black garment I hadn't noticed he'd brought with us. "Step into it, and it will adjust to your size."

Thinking it was nanotechnology, I did so without asking questions. But as it shrunk to my size, a myriad of tiny little creatures came to life and started crawling on my skin. I slapped my torso, trying to get them off me without success. "What the fuck, Saberian!" I cried out when they disappeared into my body.

"Calm down," Urien implored me, but I was fuming and considered punching him in the face when the creatures resurfaced.

They were no longer black, but the exact color of my skin —markings and all. I tried to lift the material off me, but it felt like I was pinching my own skin.

"If you want it off, you have to tell it so," he said, and I arched an eyebrow, not trusting he was serious. "It's made out of a local plant," he continued, "the Sirh is semi-sentient, and it shifts with you. It also offers another layer of protection; but whenever you don't need it, it will retreat under your skin."

His demonstration along with the explanation put me at ease because I'd heard of it, just never seen it in action.

It took me a few ticks to calm down. "You could have warned me," I grumbled.

"Where's the fun in that?" He laughed, and I lightly jabbed his ribs. He sobered, though, and added in a more serious tone, "Your sabertooth is nearly indestructible, but he has one weak spot—the trachea. Always keep the protection of the vulnerable area at the forefront of your mind, especially during battles when our predatory instincts are at their peak, because our other halves tend to get carried away."

"This knowledge would have been useful…" I trailed off—what's done was done, and now I finally had a chance to exact revenge.

Urien's nostrils flared, and his eyes narrowed while anger rolled off of him in waves. "I saw what the cur did to your family. He'll pay for his crime soon enough."

Initially, he hadn't believed that a Saberian had committed such an atrocity. Now, though, he'd seen the proof in my memories, and this visceral reaction to something that had been done to me broke down the last of the walls I kept up because of what species he was.

It was time I shared my plans with my new brother. "I don't want us to complete the Sacred Union yet." His eyes widened in surprise, and I rushed to say the rest. "I want the challenge to be over first, so I can put my past securely where it belongs…in the past. River deserves the worlds, and I want to go to her with a clean slate. I need to be able to show her there are no ghosts in my hearts…only her."

He didn't comment immediately, and I was glad because that meant he took my words seriously. "It's the best way to put our mate's worries at rest. So we wait until after the chal—"

His voice was cut off abruptly and he doubled over.

My lungs seized and black spots filled my vision.

The painful sensations were there and gone in a flash.

I felt Reaper's protective instincts rise, and his desire to act became mine.

Mate! he cried out. *Something's wrong with her.* Dread settled in my stomach, setting my insides on fire.

"River," both Urien and I exclaimed at the same time and stormed out of the repository—for it was not our pain we'd felt, but hers.

Everything else faded but the need to get to our mate.

All the trials I'd been through so far would be in vain if something happened to her.

Creator, life without her isn't worth living. Please let her be all right, I prayed while my feet barely touched the ground in the race toward our female.

We were nearing the personal chambers. They were right around the corner, and we took the turn at a full-blown run.

A warrior jumped out of Urien's way and crashed into mine. His hands grabbed my forearms, and we both managed to stay upright. As I blinked and focused on the male—the one-eyed male—time stopped, and even though I'd never seen him in his biped form, I recognized him immediately.

In front of me was the being who'd been my nemesis for more than a hundred rotations.

His eye flashed with instant recognition, and his lips tipped in a self-assured smirk. "What's the rush, Wravukian?" he asked and leaned closer. "Are you worried I'll take this female from you, too?" he drawled. And the only thing keeping me from shifting and shredding him to pieces there and then was the scent of River's blood in the air.

But then he sniffed loudly before bringing his mouth close

to my ear. "She smells delicious...don't you agree, hybrid? I think I'll keep this one alive until she gives me a cub."

Before he could finish that sentence, I grabbed him by the neck, and slammed him into the wall.

Red bled into my vision until it was all I saw.

Reaper—having heard the Saberian's comments—surged to the surface, furious at the male threatening our family.

"Guards," the coward yelled.

"No one's going to save you this time," I threatened, feeling fur sprouting on me.

Someone—sounding far away—called out my name, but I paid no mind to him. The one I'd been looking for all this time was finally in my grasp. My teeth elongated, and I smiled with malice, needing Ivar to see his end coming.

I squeezed my fingers tighter, cutting off his air supply. Euphoria filled me as my arch-enemy started thrashing and clawing at my arms, trying to break my hold.

That was not happening.

Suddenly, another male barreled into me from the side, and we both tumbled to the floor, but he landed on top of me.

"Get off me," I growled, and punched him in the ribs in an effort to dislodge him.

"What the fuck, Thora!" Urien shouted, "Our mate needs us. Snap out of it."

His words were like someone doused me with ice-cold water. They dispersed the red haze and brought me to my senses.

'River...' I reached out through our Sacred Bond, but she wasn't there.

My Pair-bond, though, heard me all right. "Mes took her

to the Healers' Chamber. We have to go there now," he said and got up, then offered me his hand.

I grabbed it and hoisted myself upward. A quick glance around showed me that the coward had fled. No matter. He'd pay for his crime soon.

The blood drained from my face upon seeing River lying unnaturally still in the med-pod. Her once golden skin was now a dull parody of how bright it was. Her chest barely lifted, but the gasping sound when she inhaled was too loud in the chamber.

Was I too late? Fear rooted my feet to the spot, and I couldn't go any farther. Tremors rocked my frame, and it felt like I was a touch away from my body shattering into a thousand pieces.

The only consolation was that the Prince of Wravuk—and now Second King of Saber—was attending to my mate. He was a renowned Healer, and if anyone could help her, it was him.

Urien stepped closer, and I found the courage to do so too.

Up close I saw that Mes was scowling at the data on the med-pod's screen. He mumbled something to the other Healer in the chamber, and the Saberian handed him a syringe filled with some kind of red liquid. Then the Royal searched for River's veins and carefully injected her.

The moment the liquid flowed into her system, the difference was apparent. Her labored breathing calmed, and her heartbeat picked up its pace.

The extra senses that came along with having a sabertooth were quite useful. Sensing the change in her condition, I felt Reaper settle inside me too. But that only lasted until the two healers approached us, when an involuntary growl escaped from my lips.

Reaper was suddenly snarling and pushing to get control of our body from me so he could fight these two males. I fought back with teeth and nails to keep him contained. This was not the place for what he wanted.

"I would ask you if you Changed him, Urien, but I can see it," King Mes commented good-naturedly. Then added, "Your sabertooth will have his chance to find his place in the hierarchy in the Pitt. Later."

I inclined my head respectfully, happy that my animal hadn't offended our future King.

"What's wrong with our mate?" Urien asked, and the pain in his voice mirrored my own.

He answered our question with one of his own. "Can you feel her sabertooth?"

Reaper?

Barely, he growled, *I think she's hiding from us.*

Urien was the first to answer, "Grim said she has retreated deep in River."

"Reaper agrees. He said that she's hiding from us." Although I couldn't fathom the reason why. We would never hurt her.

The Arch-healer seemed deep in thought, but then he spoke, "Her sabertooth should be present, ready to surface, but I can barely sense her..." his voice trailed off, and the hesitation scared me.

"The transformation should be reshaping and simultaneously healing River's organs. At least that's what I'd observed
during Kali's Change," he said, and suddenly I wanted to grab
my mates and flee the impending doom that was fast
approaching—alas, I remained where I was. "But your
female's organs are being healed. Her body can't stand the
painful process much longer," the King finished, blasting my
world to smithereens.

No...no, we can't lose her, I thought, and Reaper echoed my
sentiment. "What can we do?" I croaked and held my breath at
the same time my Pair-bond said, "there must be something
we can do."

"We've given her a suppressant for the pain, but it won't
last forever. You must complete the Union, and bring her
sabertooth forth."

I walked to my mate's side and started stroking her silky
hair. She felt so fragile...so breakable under my fingers. "We
will make sure she surfaces," I said, determined to succeed in
the most important task of my entire life.

Urien stepped to her other side, and caressed her face.
"Psehimou, we got you. You're okay now."

Her eyelids fluttered when she heard his voice, and hope
blossomed in my hearts.

"River, open your eyes, beloved," I implored her and
waited.

Her heartbeat spiked, and her breathing turned erratic for
just a few ticks, before both returned to their previous relaxed
state.

The next few spires passed torturously slow when at last she opened her eyes.

"What happened?" she asked, and I immediately offered her water. Her voice was so scratchy; I could only imagine how painful it must have been to speak.

Urien lifted me and she gulped down the liquid.

Having satisfied her thirst, she seemed to take stock of her situation because she started panicking. "Why can't I move?"

"You're in the Healers' Chamber." My Pair-bond beat me to it by answering first. "They gave you a sedative, but it's wearing off, and you will regain mobility soon." He kept his tone smooth so as to not frighten her further.

Our mate, though, wasn't one to let go when she wanted to know something. "What happened?" She insisted.

Urien looked at me, silently asking what the best course of action was.

'She needs to know,' I told him. There was no point in hiding the truth from her.

"Your Sabertooth is different, and your body is fighting the Change. We need to complete the union, my love," he said, but she caught on to his hesitation.

"Or?" she asked, and I sensed Urien wasn't willing to explain more.

So I caressed her cheek to draw her attention, but got lost in the sensations filling my body when I trailed my thumb over her lips. *Creator! I want more with her...I want everything.* But for now, I needed to give her an answer that even the thought alone was enough to bring me to my knees. "Otherwise, neither of you will survive."

I'M SORRY
RIVER

After delivering the unpleasant news—I mean who wanted to tell their loved one that there was a distinct possibility they would die—my mates looked so tense and their bodies rigid that I bet if I poked them with my finger, I'd break it. *Did they expect me to deny them?* I wondered.

Silly males. I'd chosen my destiny, and it was with them.

Before I could tell them so, Urien lifted my right hand to his mouth and kissed the inside of my palm—the sweet gesture making me coo.

"River, you shared your worry with us, and we didn't get a chance to put it to rest earlier, but we want to do so now." His eyes were locked on mine, and I could see the vulnerability shining in them. "You said you weren't sure if you could compete with the ghosts in our hearts."

Oh that? I did say those words, but I didn't feel that way anymore. I parted my lips to speak, but Thora's thumb over my mouth stopped me.

"You need to hear this, beloved," he explained as he slid the pad across my flesh.

Great, they've already started ganging up on me. My divided warriors were finally united and I just knew they were going to be trouble with a capital T. Nonetheless, I nodded so they'd continue.

Urien cleared his throat, drawing my attention back to him, then leaned closer. "River, you healed the pain of my loss. You did that with your presence alone." His tone was low and serious. "You," he emphasized, "are the only one in my heart. I never expected to be given a second chance. But now that I'm blessed with Sacred Mates, I won't let a circle pass by without showing you my appreciation and love," he finished, making my heart melt.

Oh my God, I gasped inwardly as tears pooled in my eyes.

He'd just told me he loved me.

Sensation had returned to my body, so I sat up and hugged him tight.

"I've fallen in love with you, too," I said, then turned to Thora before adding shyly, "With both of you."

My blue alien—who now had spots and stripes inter-twined with his other markings—pursed his lips, and I felt the surface beneath me drop from under me, taking my heart with it. *Had I just made a terrible mistake? Would he reject me again?*

"The sight of you stepping out of that vehicle on Earth rocked the foundations of my world. It was terrifying how fast you got under my skin and into my heart without even trying," he growled, and I wasn't sure if his words were meant as a good thing or a bad thing, but he continued, "I let the guilt I'd been carrying for so long dictate my actions...and I hurt you." His eyes drifted downward and his voice shook at the end.

My breath caught in my lungs, and Urien, who sensed my tension, kissed the top of my head softly, silently consoling me.

Thora, though, reached out and pulled me toward him, then cradled my head.

My breath fanned his face in a rush as I realized he wasn't planning to stop.

"I'm going to spend the rest of my life making it up to you," he promised, and the deep smoky timbre of his voice slithered seductively around me, making me shiver. "My hearts...my soul are yours alone, beloved...I love you." He finished and claimed my lips along with everything else that made me who I was.

A door clicked shut.

The sound pierced through the haze of lust clouding my mind and reminded me that we had an audience.

Thora sensed the change in me and ended our public display of affection, but only after he'd covered every inch of my face with kisses. By the time he was done, my skin felt feverish, and I bet it looked it too.

From under my lashes I sneaked a few peaks, checking the room, but it was just the three of us. "Maybe this isn't the right place..." I trailed off, not sure how to ask for what I wanted, which was both of them. Their words had lit a fire in me, and Thora's kiss had managed to stoke it into a blaze.

Urien seemed to sense my internal struggle, he stroked my back, making a catlike purr escape my lips. "There is one more step until our Sacred Union is complete," he said, and got my whole attention. "Our bite will release your saber-tooth, and our bond will be fully established."

His words put deliciously wicked images in my head, and I couldn't wait.

"But first..." my fiery mate hesitated, then frowned and glanced at his Pair-bond as if checking to see what he thought before he continued, "we need to honor the Wravukian customs. Will you let me and Thora bind us closer together?"

"We can't," Thora interjected, sounding utterly devastated. "I destroyed my ceremonial cup and knife a long time ago."

The need to heal the pain I could so clearly hear in his voice was overwhelming. "If it is important to you, we'll find a way," I said, and two sets of eyes rounded in surprise.

Had they been expecting a rejection? I smiled as wide as I could at the absurd thought. Nope, I wasn't going anywhere; they were stuck with me.

A look passed between them—some kind of silent communication going on—then Thora lifted me in his arms, bridal style.

"What are you doing? Put me down, I can walk." I laughed.

He pierced me with his amber eyes. The dark ring surrounding the yellow hue drew me in, made me feel as if I were baring my soul under the bright sun. "And I can carry you," he said—like it was the most logical explanation, and I should have known—and he set toward our room at a brisk pace; his muscles not even straining while hoisting my substantial weight.

My oh my, talk about making a woman feel sexy. I fanned myself, and a sensual, musky scent mixed with notes of dry cedar and sandalwood wafted under my nose. *God, what is that?* I wondered, unable to resist leaning forward and pressing my nose onto the base of Thora's neck before inhaling deeply—making him shiver.

His unique aroma caused a visceral reaction as it entered my lungs; suddenly my breasts felt too heavy, and my core too empty. I ached with the need to be filled, to have my mounds massaged and my nipples teased.

"Are we there yet?" I moaned—the tone breathy and sultry, and one I'd never heard before in my own voice.

Both males stopped in their tracks.

A rumbling, hoarse purr started in Thora's chest, but then the sound went deeper and rougher, changing into a growl.

"Fuck," my Saberian mate cursed. "Not here, get inside our chamber!"

"Urien—" my big, bad, blue alien quivered and passed me on to Urien's waiting arms before turning around and bursting into our room that was not far from where we'd been standing.

Lust was swiftly replaced by fear, and I could think clearly again. "Put me down, I need to check that he's all right."

The warrior rushed after his Pair-bond through doors that were surprisingly still on their hinges, and once we were inside he lowered my feet to the ground.

Frantic, I looked this way and that, searching for my mate, but Thora wasn't there. Instead, someone else stood in his place.

"You have a sabertooth," I gasped, then turned to Urien, "how does he have a sabertooth?" It didn't make sense.

The click of the locking mechanism sounded ominous in

the silence, and a tremor racked my body.

Arms wrapped around me from behind, and my mate's warmth seeped into my cool body. "I'll explain later, psehimou. But don't be afraid, for Reaper, along with Grim, are your protectors, and he couldn't wait to meet you. Are you okay with that?"

The huge sabertooth—with fur the same blue as Thora's skin tone, and dark-green spots and stripes—purred, lowered himself to the ground, and crawled a couple of steps toward me before he stopped, waiting for my permission.

Evidence of his eagerness was clear in the way his muscles twitched, and in the impatient flick of his tail—how could I possibly deny him?

"Yes," I agreed.

Reaper didn't need a second invitation. He stood on his paws and approached me with languid steps, which I was certain were more for my benefit than his.

For the first time, I felt a stirring in my chest—no more than butterfly wings fluttering on a sunny day—that I knew was my own sabertooth reacting to the lethal predator.

When his nose pressed against my chest, the barely there sensation disappeared. She had retreated somewhere I couldn't feel her. Reaper, though, didn't seem perturbed by the fact as he continued sniffing all of me. When he neared my crotch area, I pushed his big head away, and he chuffed.

Turning my head to the one who could answer me, I asked, smiling, "Is he laughing at me?" But Urien wasn't paying attention to me, but to the animal in front of us, and before I had the chance to ask why, I felt the sting that threw me into darkness.

Not again, I groaned, but no sound passed my lips.

"I'm sorry, beloved...I didn't know he was going to do that," Thora whispered, then pressed his lips to my forehead and let them linger there.

Taking stock of my situation, I realized I was naked astride his lap, and we were in the pool because lukewarm water—the perfect temperature really—enveloped our bodies.

"I told you he had to do it. How could he—or you for that matter—deny instincts that are embedded in our DNA?" Urien humphed in frustration. So they must have been discussing this while I was out of it.

Also, I knew the answer to Urien's question. There were things in our nature that we were powerless to deny no matter the species, and Thora needn't berate himself over something that wasn't in his hands. So I managed to open my eyes. "Don't distress, my love. I'm all right."

"River," he cried out, then tipped me backward so he could look in my eyes, and once he saw what he was looking for, he crushed his lips to mine.

The kiss was unlike any I'd gotten before.

It was pure need filled with desperation.

It was savage and voracious.

It was everything I didn't know I needed, and my body was suddenly set alight.

All coherent thoughts fled my head when his hands glided along the length of my body. The rough skin of his palms grazed the sides of my breasts, making my nipples peak, but he didn't linger in one particular spot. He explored every dip and groove on me—tickling me in places, and inflaming all the others.

So lost was I on Thora that I jumped when Urien's front came into contact with my back before his nose touched the shell of my ear, tickling me.

"Are you ready, Mate?" His smoky voice made me shiver. The dark notes full of wicked promises had heat pooling in between my legs. Then his hand snaked around me from behind. It hovered over my belly before it moved lower, grazing the skin above my clit. But it didn't stop there—it went lower still, between my nether lips and into my pussy.

I gasped, then cried out, breaking Thora's kiss, who didn't seem to mind as he lowered his head to my aching breasts and started playing...torturing me softly while he squeezed the mounds, then licked my nipples, and sucked the hard nubs before grazing the tips with his teeth.

Suddenly, the ripples in the water felt like a thousand flaming tongues were licking every inch of my body—adding to the sensations, driving me wild.

One finger became two, then three, steadily moving in and out of me.

The slight burn of being stretched drove me wild, and I let both of them know with my loud moans.

Meanwhile, Thora held a nipple firmly between his teeth as he slowly lifted his head, pulling my flesh taut, and making me arch my back in response.

Encouraged by the sounds coming out of my mouth, the tips of his lips lifted in a wicked smile, and he released my nub with a pop at the same time his finger joined Urien's in my pussy.

The flash of pain, like a stray bolt of electricity, raced from my nipple to my already inflamed core and exploded. My body no longer my own, twitched, then seized as an irresistible spasming spread from my center outward, to the edges of my limbs, and I screamed my pleasure to the world.

"You feel so good, River, and we have so much pleasure to offer you…" Thora's husky voice pulled me back to the ground. "This is only the beginning," he promised as he and Urien pulled their fingers out of me.

I pursed my lips; I might have mewed as well at feeling bereft.

The two males laughed, and I rolled my eyes at them.

They can make my body sing, but they don't have to be cocky about it, I thought and giggled. With the sexual prowess they possessed, they had every right to feel that way. I didn't realize I was retreating inside my mind until Urien, who'd been standing behind me, picked me up and brought me down on Thora's cock—impaling me on the thick girth—then kept me there by his hands, possessively squeezing my hips.

The shock of being filled so unexpectedly caused my upper body to jerk backward, and my head banged on the Saberian's shoulder as my heartbeat went from zero to a hundred in a few seconds. I opened my mouth to scream, but the sound got stuck in my throat. The hunger they'd satisfied only but a few moments ago returned with a vengeance, and staying still wasn't an option anymore.

"Please," I begged, needing them to do something…anything.

A rattling—like the sound of a truck's idling engine—came from Thora's broad chest, and I laid my palms on top of his firm pectorals to get a better feel for it, accidentally grazing the blue alien's nipples. The sexiest groan left his lips, and his cock jerked inside me.

Was I brave enough to do it? I debated for a moment, then leaned forward—slightly lifting off his length—and licked the small, hard tip.

"Fuck," he cried out and thrust upward, making me moan.

My other mate nipped the spot between my shoulder and my neck, and a shiver raced down my spine. "See how good we can make you feel?" he asked, then continued on to peppering every inch of my body that was above the water with kisses before he added, "Don't stop." A command that I wasn't sure was directed at me or Thora, who was surging in and out of me, but either way, I wasn't planning to stop.

Urien's left hand found its way to my breast. His palm enveloped it completely, and he squeezed the mound until he heard my gasp. Then he started playing with my nipple, rolling it, and pinching the elongated nub.

"Her pussy is strangling my cock. Whatever you're doing, Pair-bond, don't stop."

"I won't." My Saberian chuckled, and slid his right hand downward until the rough texture of his pads grazed the skin above my clit. "Are you ready, psehimou?"

Words, must form words, I thought, and even though it took me a second to find the way through the erotic haze in my mind, I managed to murmur, "Ready for what?"

"For the next step," Thora growled, pleasure turning his voice huskier, sexier. "Urien and I will take you together," he said and pulled out of me, while Urien pushed two fingers in my slit. Then my blue mate's words registered, and I opened my mouth to say that wasn't possible, when his cock plunged into me too.

"Oh, God," I stuttered, digging my nails in Thora's flesh. I'd never felt so full in my life. Shivers raced up and down my entire body, making me shake in their arms. I was stretched to the point of pain, but the painful sensation only added to the pleasure coursing through my veins.

My considerate mates, though, remained still, allowing my muscles to adjust to the invasion, but the moment they felt my inner walls relax, all bets were off, and they started moving.

I lost the passage of time, and I didn't know where one started and the other ended; I could only feel the lava that had pooled low in my abdomen rising, threatening to explode and spill all over us. I was standing on the precipice, and the leap was scary. "I'm so close...please," I rasped, trusting they'd know what to do.

Without warning, Urien withdrew his digits and replaced them with his cock.

The volcano inside me erupted, and I exploded.

I hadn't simply fallen over the edge...I'd been catapulted over it.

Then they leaned closer; their mouths latched onto the opposite sides of my shoulders, and delivered the bites that would complete our Union.

Stars, and a galaxy or three formed behind my closed eyes, and the sight took my breath away. I was a meteor myself, flying across the vast space, capable of distraction, but powerless against the gravitational forces of the planets around me, and utterly incapable of stopping the collision course I was on.

And it was glorious.

As I slowly came down from my high, my mates withdrew from inside me, causing sweet aftershocks to rock my body.

What had me snapping my eyes open, though, was their voices in my head.

'*Gently now,*' Urien said.

'*How long do we have before her sabertooth starts emerging?*' Thora asked.

'*Not long, the Line has almost faded.*'

Worry tinged both of their voices.

The same green line that had formed, uniting us the first time I'd spoken in their presence was slowly vanishing.

"I can hear you speak...in my mind," I stuttered, taken aback by the fact that not only could I sense their presence in my brain, but also hear their thoughts, and feel their emotions.

"That's the way it is with Sacred Unions, psehimou," Urien explained, but my focus shifted to the funny sensation on my arms.

I lifted them above the water, and gasped upon seeing something crawling under my skin; fur sprouted from my pores, but then retreated beneath the surface. I whimpered; terror gripping my heart in its painful grasp.

Urien picked me up in his arms and got us out of the pool while Thora went and brought us towels.

They did a thorough job drying my body, but it did nothing to distract me from the paralyzing fear coursing through my veins.

"The fear you are feeling is hers. She wants out, but she's afraid," Urien said, reminding me that I wasn't alone in my head anymore. "You're strong, and we'll help you bring her out." His words wrapped around me like a security blanket, and I felt a little bit braver.

"Ready, beloved?" Thora asked, and I nodded, doubting I could postpone what was happening.

In the blink of an eye, Grim and Reaper appeared in front of me. Two magnificent sabertooths, focused solely on me. They started emitting low-intensity sounds in short, semi loud bursts, then they circled me while rubbing their fur all over my body since both of them reached past my shoulder.

I was surprised to discover I had the same access to the sabertooths' thoughts and emotions as I did my mates'.

'Someone's feeling territorial,' I teased them since their first concern had been to make crystal clear to everyone the fact that I was theirs.

'You're ours,' Grim's guttural voice echoed in my mind, and it was joined by Reaper's raspy one when he added, *'And ours alone.'*

Who gets the possessiveness from whom? I wondered, smiling when my stomach crumbled, distracting me from my train of thought.

At once they returned in front of me, lowered their big heads to my tummy, and roared.

The sound was so loud and unexpected it drove me to my knees.

They kept growling and roaring and pacing in a circle around me.

Even though they weren't speaking in my mind, I somehow knew the meaning of the sounds they produced. Our sabertooth mates were calling out to her, anxious to meet her. They vowed to protect and care for us; to dominate us when no one else would be allowed to do so.

The more they vocalized, the higher the intensity of the pain slicing my insides, and it became impossible to keep my voice down.

I screamed in agony, and my vision turned blurry. I was certain everyone in the palace would have heard us by now.

Please come out, I begged, but she was too far away.

The pain had turned from excruciating to unbearable, and I curled in the fetal position in the forlorn hope of easing the agony. But I knew in my gut that if we didn't shift soon, I would not make it.

Coughs so strong that it felt like I was expelling my guts racked my body.

Blood started dripping from my nose and ears, joining the tears I couldn't hold back anymore, and started a pink liquid stain around my head.

I had failed my mates.

I was dying, and their love for me would cost them their lives.

But before I succumbed, they needed to know. I managed to raise my eyelids high enough so I could look into their eyes. "I'm sorry," I mumbled through the gurgling coming from my chest, and I hoped they understood.

POWERLESS TO CHANGE THE OUTCOME
URIEN

Grim's powerful body was shaking like the leaves of trees during a gale.

He and Reaper had done all they could to draw their mate out, but they'd failed.

And I could sense the invisible tendrils of Lethe slithering toward us, but I wasn't willing to give up yet.

River let out a harrowing sound that would haunt me for the rest of my life and curled in on herself.

I couldn't stand by and watch anymore. *'Shift,'* I growled the command to my Pair-bond, and in a flash, we were kneeling beside her, only to freeze because in the tick that it had taken us to shift, a small puddle of a blood and tears had formed around her head, and strong coughs were tearing her body apart from the inside.

Her eyes fluttered open, and she looked into mine and then into Thora's, "I'm...so...rr...y," she said, her voice barely intelligible.

"No! You don't get to give up on us," Thora yelled and picked her up, jarring her body and wrenching a scream from her lips. He believed the Arch-healer would be able to help her.

I prayed he was right as I raced in front of him to open the doors.

We ran down the corridor, uncaring of the commotion we were creating. It'd be better if the warriors heard us and came to investigate, because if our female died, they'd need to find a way to put us down fast. Lethe had already found a purchase in Grim's terror.

Hang in there, I told my sabertooth as I pushed the doors to the Healers' Chambers out of the way, *there's still hope.*

"Where's the Arch-healer?" Thora barked at Gwyr, who rushed to our side.

"I don't know. Put her in the med-pod. Quickly," he replied while activating the pod's scanner. "What happened to her?" he inquired, but I didn't stay to hear the rest.

I stormed toward my Royals' chamber.

Those few ticks it took me to arrive were the longest of my life, and I barged in their personal space without considering the consequences.

No farther was my foot a step in the chamber than Beast barreled into me, his claws tearing my thigh and shoulder open upon impact, but I felt nothing. Then his muzzle opened wide— the long canines grazing my cheeks—and he roared in my face.

"You can kill me afterward, but right now I need Mes to save my mate," I implored, my voice taut with all the emotions I was trying to keep at bay.

The sabertooth didn't move off me until the Queen came and flicked his nose at the same time she ordered, "Stop it, Beast. Go get Mes."

Just like that, the fearsome predator hopped off me and left.

"Come on, warrior, let's go help your mate," Kali said, and walked as fast as her pregnant belly allowed toward the Healers' chamber with me on her trail.

As we got closer, my Pair-bond and Gwyr's voices echoed in the corridor.

"You fucking do something to save her!"

"There's nothing wro—"

"She's dying!"

"Her body's reject—"

The Queen sped up, and I tried to loop my arm around hers to ensure she didn't trip and fall. If something happened to her or the babies, it would mean the end of the Saberian race. "I'm pregnant, Urien, but I can still kick your furry ass," she growled.

"Arana is going to kill me if something happens to you," I apologized, hoping the name of her mate would make her accept my assistance.

"He might kill you anyway after your little stunt," she laughed, but the sound was cut off abruptly the moment we entered the chamber.

Thora had Gwyr by the neck and was choking the life out of him while River lay nearly lifeless on the med-pod. Her chest was barely rising, and her heartbeat was so erratic—the organ could fail any moment now.

My body went numb, and I fell on my knees. Time slowed down, and I was powerless to change the outcome.

"Shift." The softly spoken command carried so much power that it had an immediate effect on me. Needles pierced my skin and fire licked my flesh as the shift was wrenched from me, and—from the sounds of the roars filling the palace—from many others as well.

But only one mattered to me, and Grim raised his head so we could look at our mate one last time for her raspy breathing was no longer audible.

THE RIGHT CHOICE
RIVER

The pain was unlike any I'd experienced before. That one time I'd broken my leg and ended up in the emergency room with an open fracture, didn't even compare. This agony was paralyzing and never-ending.

I wasn't even sure I was alive until I found myself standing on four shaky paws, every ache gone. The only remainder of the entire ordeal was my lack of energy.

Looking at the strange limbs with the brownish-orange fur and the electric blue spots and stripes adorning it, I felt like I was having an out-of-body experience—I was there and yet I was not.

The scientist in me was thrilled—the Change was complete; she wanted to experiment and study the reactions; she wanted to test out the limits of this new body. But all that would have to wait.

The woman in me was ecstatic—I got to keep my mates and have my happily ever after.

But it was all surreal—I couldn't speak, and I didn't have two legs anymore.

Hi, a soft-spoken voice greeted me at the same time her emotions registered—fear because the new world she was thrust into was terrifying, and desperation because the dominance permeating the air triggered her submissive instincts, and the need to lie flat on her back and reveal her neck was overpowering all others to the point she could barely function.

My sabertooth was panicking, but I was a doctor and could help with that. *Take deep breaths, sweetie...in and out...in and out...* I guided her and air filled our lungs, stopping the room from spinning. *I'm sorry this is a frightening experience for you, but you're not alone, I'm here with you,* I said, keeping my tone gentle, and I felt our heart rate settle. *Thank you for coming out. You saved me, and our mates,* I finished, truly feeling grateful for having her.

Each word of mine drew her a little farther out of her shell, and in the end her happiness radiated as her energy pranced around mine inside my head.

If you need me, my name is Rainbow, she said before she retreated once again farther back, out of the spotlight, where she was more comfortable.

Such a beautiful name, I thought, and I got the impression of a smile.

She wanted me to have full control over this body, but was ready to support us if need be. So it was time to familiarize myself with this body.

In this form our perception was different. It was more complex and astonishingly acute. Sensing, assessing, and cataloging elements didn't require any effort at all. But as we took in our surroundings, the massive influx of scents and sounds all at once made the world spin, and we lost our balance.

Suddenly our new form was sprawled on the floor right in front of two proud sabertooths.

Their sheer size made for a terrifying sight, and they were all ours—worthy of our submission.

I felt her reach for the reins, so I stepped down, curious to see what she would do.

She started purring; the sound resembled that of a sports car's engine idling—elegant and slick—and without missing a beat, she rolled on her back and revealed her neck—accepting their dominance over her.

They chuffed their appreciation, and she jumped back on her paws, eager to feel their silky fur rub against theirs and to show her affection by licking their muzzles.

No one dared interrupt while the sabertooths spend time getting to know one another, but once they settled, King Rorc whisper-shouted at his mate, "Are you fucking crying, little one?"

"Yes," Kali snapped, "and if you tell anyone, be prepared to sleep outside on the balcony."

"Pregnancy was supposed to make you sweeter, Mate, not meaner," he teased, making the other males laugh, but then the purple King grunted because she'd jabbed him in the ribs.

The altercation drew my sabertooth's attention, and now that she'd gotten acquainted with her mates, she urged me to take the next step that would integrate us further into the Saberian society—to pledge our loyalty to the royal family.

This wasn't something she just wanted. It was a compulsion—deep rooted and very powerful.

I don't know the protocol here. Whatever you need, let's do it, I told her, and I meant it.

Her energy shined brightly in my mind's eye—blinding me momentarily with its beauty—before she leaped into action and fused her strength with mine, surprising me with its intensity. She might have been submissive, but weak she was not.

King Arana had his arm around the Queen's waist, and she was leaning her head back against King Mes's front, whereas King Rorc had looped her arm around his elbow. They looked more like a family proud of their children with the way they were watching us, than the Royals ruling this planet.

Having observed them enough, I knew I wanted to be a part of their world. I had my mates, whom I cared a lot for; I had a job that was about to get a whole lot more exciting when I started exploring the planet; and I had my sabertooth, whom I wanted to get to know better.

So I took a couple of steps on paws that were still unsteady before Reaper used his bulk to stop me in my tracks and pushed me backward. A whine left our muzzle, and I wasn't sure if it had come from me or my sabertooth. But I knew that neither of us liked the interruption.

When I tried to sidestep him, he took a swipe at my hind leg with his claws retracted, reprimanding me. My mates were bigger than me by far, and there was no way I could beat them in any form. So with our tail under our legs, we retreated.

Grim growled a warning—cautioning Reaper—that went

unnoticed. Instead, Thora's sabertooth lowered his big head near the ground and prowled toward the Royals before he chose his target in the Queen.

Three massive, angry males formed a wall of protection in front of their mate, but she huffed with indignation and pushed between them until she was standing in front of them once again.

"Kali. Get. Back. He is not in control of his sabertooth," King Arana warned through clenched teeth.

She didn't respond with words, only raised an eyebrow at him.

He scowled in return, and the air became heavier with his displeasure.

It tasted funny on our tongue, and we did not want our mates to feel that way.

"You just earned a punishment, little one," King Rorc growled, and there was nothing in his voice promising pleasure.

Kali, though, wasn't deterred by his words at all. "Promises, promises," she said, and winked at him. Then took a step toward Thora, who was now within jumping distance from her.

King Mes put his arm out over her pregnant belly, effectively stopping her from going farther. His expression was firm and unyielding. She turned and faced him—entirely ignoring the threat that was a leap away—and stared lovingly at his eyes.

It was such an intimate gesture, which made me feel like an intruder, and I had to avert my gaze. My mate, though, didn't share my sentiments and growled—mad by the dismissal.

The Arch-healer released her, but didn't leave her side as Kali turned and gave the sabertooth all of her attention.

The change was subtle when she straightened her posture and lifted her chin slightly, but I felt it to my bones when her voice rang with authority. "Reaper—new warrior and brother to Grim—will you pledge your allegiance to the Kings and Queen of Saber?" she asked, and I held my breath.

Our mate didn't tilt his head, clearly showing his rejection and lack of respect.

Oh no! Couldn't he sense how powerful the Queen was? Why would he challenge her? Rainbow's worry radiated through her voice in my head, but I had no answers to give her.

"You think that you can win the fight against me, when your brother failed?" She sounded incredulous, but when he refused to submit, her tone hardened, and she said, "Challenge accepted."

Her declaration caused an uproar. The warriors that had gathered outside in the wide corridor hooted and jeered. The Kings, though, didn't react.

"Come on, cub," she taunted my mate, "show me what you got."

Reaper's glee bled through our bond to me. He thought a pregnant female was easy prey because she wouldn't risk hurting her cubs. She was smaller than him and he understood she had to put on a show, or none of the males would ever respect her again.

'Mate, please stop. Submit,' Rainbow implored him, but he would not listen.

'*Urien, do something. Stop him, please,*' I begged my other mate.

'*Psehimou, Rainbow submitted instantly because she needed to know where she stood in the hierarchy. Reaper has to find his place too. He needs to do this,*' he explained, and my heart sunk.

I turned to watch my foolish mate, waiting anxiously for the result. '*Did he have to challenge the Queen, though?*' I said, dejected, and Urien laughed. '*I'm glad one of us finds this amusing...*' My voice trailed off as I saw the blue sabertooth's muscles bunch before they released, and he leaped to the spot in front of the Queen.

Fear seized my heart. If he hurt Kali, he could seriously injure the babies, and I'd never be able to forgive him. I wouldn't be able to live with such a monster.

Time froze and I held my breath, waiting to see what was going to happen.

'*How can you be so calm?*' I chastised Urien—it was his Pairbond we were talking about.

His caress over my cheek made me gasp because I felt his touch on my face while we were still in our sabertooth forms. I didn't know he could do something like that. '*I've got so many things to teach you,*' he chuckled, and his eager voice was full of dark promise. '*I'm calm, psehimou, because I know she can handle herself. Do you think her mates would stand by and do nothing if she was truly in danger?*'

My mate had a point, and I couldn't help but wonder how powerful the Queen really was when I noticed Reaper was just standing there, frozen.

Not because he wanted to but because he was unable to

even twitch a muscle, no matter how hard he fought against Kali's hold.

'*Submit, warrior,*' she ordered, and I startled because her lips hadn't moved, yet I'd heard her inside my head. Urien had said it was something only mates were capable of, but apparently so was the Queen.

My headstrong mate denied her request, and she covered the step that separated them—his nose touching her pregnant belly.

She reached out and stroked the top of his head; jealousy flared inside me, but I squished the feeling immediately. She didn't care about my mate romantically—I saw the love for her mates in her eyes—she wanted him to be her warrior because he was strong and worthy.

She dropped her hand as if she were suddenly too tired to keep it lifted.

"Kali, get it over with," King Arana growled, and she obeyed.

"Last chance, warrior. You've already lost the challenge. Do you submit or forfeit your life?"

Black spots distorted my vision, reminding me breathing wasn't optional. Drawing air into my lungs, I waited, when at last Reaper tilted his head, revealing his throat in the universal notion of submission to one of superior strength.

The royal female smiled, and her eyes pooled with tears. "Then welcome, Reaper and Thora, warriors of Saber." The Kings echoed the sentiment, and the warriors watching cheered.

Rainbow wanted us to pledge our allegiance too, and I

agreed. It was time. So we approached the Queen and revealed our neck.

Kali fluffed the fur on top of our head. "Dawn can't wait to go for a run with you," she whispered, and then added louder, "Welcome Rainbow and River, warriors of Saber."

Warmth infused our body, and a tingling surge started in our chest and spread outward when the others echoed the woman's words.

And I knew deep inside I'd made the right choice.

IT'S OVER NOW
RIVER

The energy released from Thora's shift felt like a breeze ruffled our fur, and we turned to look at his glorious male form.

While Rainbow admired the strong build of the other half of her sabertooth mate, I openly gawked—mouth open, tongue lolling to the side and all.

Thora—sensing the thoughts running through my head—smirked and plunged his fingers in our fur behind the ears.

Even though I wasn't in my own body, his touch still made my toes curl, and my sabertooth purred our contentment.

When he bent and touched his forehead to our furry one, Rainbow gave him a wet kiss—by licking him from his chin to his forehead—making him laugh. "Both of your forms are beautiful, beloved."

'Why, thank you, my sweet mate,' I sent through our mind link, and I instantly felt him bristle at my choice of pet name.

I'm not sweet,' he denied, his eyes barely visible through the scowl adorning his face.

'Too late,' Urien butted in, *'you'll be known as the sweet warrior from now on.'*

Talking privately without anyone being privy to the discussion was fun.

I giggled and was about to tease my blue alien some more when his body went rigid.

Is he mad at us? Rainbow asked, and lifted her eyes to him, but he wasn't paying us any attention. He was staring at the crowd of warriors outside the entrance of the Healers' Chamber.

'Challenge him,' Urien urged, and everything clicked in place.

The Saberian he'd been looking for was here. *'Who?'* I said, but my question went unanswered.

"Ivar Al-Jurjani, I challenge you as is my right as a Saberian warrior." His booming voice seemed to rub the other warriors' fur the wrong way, for many growled and snarled at him.

Urien shifted as well and stood by Thora's side, forming a united front.

Shift, I asked my sabertooth, but her protective instincts were in overdrive—even the overwhelming desire to submit to the dominance still permeating the room was overruled by them—and she wouldn't relent.

'Don't shift yet, River. Go to Kali,' Urien ordered, and I obeyed. I wasn't familiar with this world yet, and I didn't want to cause problems.

The Kings watched me approach their mate, without stopping me, and once I was by her side, King Arana turned to my mates. "What is the reason for the challenge, Thora-kin?" He requested, and the crowd quieted.

"Payback for killing my family," Thora growled, and his voice was underlined by Reaper's snarls before he continued, "Did you tell them how you lost your eye, cur?" It was scary how perfectly calm and cold he sounded.

Dread settled in the pit of my stomach as I watched Thora close the distance between them. I tried to use the mental link that gave us access to one another to warn him, but when I tugged the thread that led to my blue mate, I was met with an icy, impenetrable wall.

A low snarl sounded from next to me, and my eyes snapped to Kali's. "This is going to go downhill fast," she warned, voicing my sentiment.

"They deserved it for trying to take my mate away from me," he spat, spittle flying out of his mouth "And the unfaithful female deserved it for having another's scent on her."

Thora stopped in his tracks, standing perfectly still, and I could almost see the tension pulsing throughout his body. "You killed your own...mate?" he stuttered between the breaths sawing in and out of him.

Everybody froze.

"She let another male put his mating marks on her!" he bellowed, and exploded into action.

Ivar's sabertooth burst from his skin and attacked Thora.

My male was a few seconds too late shifting, and the Saberian's claws raked down his leg, tearing the flesh open.

But then Reaper was there, and the two sabertooths tumbled down the corridor.

Roars full of rage, growls full of hate, and grunts full of pain drowned out all other noises as the fight moved farther away from us.

We trotted closer, but our paws slipped on the floor, and a sickeningly dry, sweet, metallic smell assaulted our nose. Looking down at the alarming amount of blood already spilled on the floor, bile burned the back of our throat.

Reaper is strong, Rainbow assured me.

I wanted to believe her, but he was favoring his right hind leg—red liquid staining his blue fur, and he didn't have experience fighting in that form.

The two males were so fast they blurred, but my enhanced vision in this form allowed me to keep track of what was happening.

A vicious slash by Ivar's sabertooth's front claws tore the skin on Reaper's ribs, and the pain blasted through our bond, bringing us to our knees.

How is he still fighting?

His opponent kept scoring hits, and our mate's blue fur had turned maroon. When the knifelike teeth pierced Reaper's shoulder and the other sabertooth's mouth closed over his flesh just a few centimeters away from his spine, our heart stuttered.

Thora! I cried out, and rushed to him without thinking.

Grim blocked my way with his much bigger bulk and growled at me, *'No one is allowed to interfere in a challenge. You will dishonor your mate.'*

'Nobody told us that,' I snapped back at the sabertooth, but

Rainbow immediately lowered our body to the ground, whimpering an apology.

Once satisfied we wouldn't move and put ourselves at risk again, he focused on his Pair-bond. *'Brother, let Reaper take over. He knows how to fight. You're holding him back,'* Urien said, trying to help him the only way he knew how.

'It's my kill. No one else's,' Thora insisted, and my Saberian mate cursed his Pair-bond's stubbornness.

'Our mate needs you. I need you,' Urien pleaded with the Wravukian—no, not just Wravukian any more but Saberian too. *'What if our mating resulted in offspring? Are you willing to give them up too?'*

Momentarily, I was stunned by his words, but then the logic part of my brain kicked in, reminding me that studies showed seventy five percent of women without fertility issues got pregnant after the first six months of trying. So I seriously doubted we were successful with just our second try, but if it'd be enough to make Thora see reason, I was willing to play along.

'Love, please...would you want your son or daughter to grow up without a father?' Silence followed my statement, but then I felt the shift in him.

Reaper, fully in control, dislodged the sabertooth. His movements were no longer stilted but fluid as he went on the offensive.

The two sabertooths lifted on their hind legs, and their bodies slammed against each other, starting a deadly dance.

Unable to look away, I watched as my mate inflicted hit after hit on Ivar until he was just a heaving bloody mass on the floor at Reaper's paws.

The blue predator roared his victory and opened his jaws wide to deliver the final bite.

I knew with certainty that my mates had fought in wars and had killed in the past. But I knew with equal surety that killing out of revenge wasn't the same, and the cost would end up being too high. 'Stop,' I cried out through our bond.

Surprisingly, Reaper did, and I took advantage of the fact. 'Please, don't kill him, not out of revenge...it will change you...it will destroy us,' I rushed to say while he was still listening. 'It's over now. You won. Living with his pain is punishment enough. Please, let him go,' I begged, and as the words traveled to him through our bond, I felt their rightness.

Reaper stepped away from the fallen sabertooth, then the air around him seemed to shimmer before Thora appeared in his place.

Our breath rushed out of our lungs, and we got up to trot to him when movement behind him drew our eyes.

Malice intent sparkled in Ivar's eyes right before his sabertooth leaped toward my mate's back.

'*Nooooo—*' I screamed at the same time Grim jumped over Thora, meeting the dishonorable warrior midair.

A horrendous noise—like a truck backfiring while you're standing right next to it—signified the snap of someone's bone.

My world tilted on its axis, and the ground disappeared under our paws. Terror seized control of our body, and the only thing I could manage was to croak his name, '*Urien?*'

'*It's over now,*' he announced, and the relief flooding my system rendered me incapable of speech.

I shifted, without giving a darn about the fact that I'd be naked, then rushed to Thora and buried my face in his chest.

He wrapped his arms around me and kissed the top of my head. "Shhh, everything is going to be all right, beloved," he cajoled, but I couldn't make the tears stop.

"Psehimou, everything is going to be all right," Urien repeated and pressed his front to my back while his arms wound around my tummy.

Yes, it would be, because we were all here, and we had the rest of our lives to spend together.

WHO NEEDS SLEEP ANYWAY?

RIVER

Two cycles later

"Good news, Kali. Babies A, B, and C, are now fully developed. They are on the smaller side of the scale, but that's normal when it comes to multiples," I reported, like I did each morning.

I, and the other ladies on Saber, had made it a habit to meet after our males left to perform their duties and Kas was off at school. I would examine Kali and the babies, then we would have breakfast before we decided how we wanted to spend our time.

And every day I'd be amazed by what a gift Rainbow was. Because of her, I had an extraordinary ability along with a tingly sixth sense alerting me when something wasn't right. All I had to do was hover my palms over the area I needed to examine. My vision would change, and I'd start receiving the wealth of information I'd normally get from an ultrasound machine—but in so much more detail.

Although, lately, there had been times when I'd called on that power by accident, without having my hands anywhere near a person. Then my eyesight would alter, and instead of seeing their outer forms, I'd see their insides—the unexpected transition was quite a disorienting experience.

It was amazing...but also terrifying, and Kali had assured me similar kinds of changes were happening to her as well due to the development of our gifts.

"I feel like a whale, doc! How long do you think it will be till the babies pop out?" she asked while Tris helped her get up from her bed.

"You're not a whale," the Mardonian was quick to defend her, but then she stopped short. "What is a whale?"

"A huge marine creature, like me," the Queen explained, making me giggle.

She was big, but there were other women carrying one baby who were bigger than her. "I think...something's wrong with the analogy there," I piped in. "But I've been scouring the Athenaeum with Elder Srah for any pregnancy related books. So far, the two that I've read claim that the females' pregnancies last seven cycles—"

"What! One more cycle? I can't, doc," she grumbled.

Mok, who was a tech wiz, had drawn a time comparison chart for me, and I'd learned that one Saberian cycle was equivalent to approximately forty four Earth days. So if the babies had been human, she'd be entering the final month of her pregnancy soon.

Kali had been pregnant for the last six cycles, and it was the first time I'd heard her whine about it.

"Honey, you know I can't give you a certain date. A pregnancy like yours is unprecedented. They don't have any data, but based on what I saw this morning, I don't think you have long left."

Tris tilted her head to the side, and raised her hairless eyebrows. "What's the matter, Kali? Something's weighing heavily on you..." her soft voice trailed off, and we both waited.

Kali lifted a hand and rubbed her neck. Then got up and waddled to the table with the food; but instead of eating what she'd picked, she rolled the food around on her plate.

"We won't be able to help if you don't share the problem, hon," I prompted because I believed every problem had a solution—it was just a matter of whether one could see it or not.

The Queen sighed, and my heart went out to her. "We had a meeting with the territory leaders yesterday...Lethe claimed ten warriors in the last cycle."

Urien had explained to me all about this madness that took over unmated males' minds. It was a horrid thing to happen that only females had the power to stop, and there lay the problem.

"Being unable to help when my warriors are wasting away is killing me," she exclaimed and sat down at the dinner table.

"Why don't you bring more females from your home planet here?" Tris asked as we joined her and put food on our plates.

I had already eaten breakfast with my mates, but looking

at all the delicacies spread in front of me, my stomach rumbled. "Yes! We could make Saber a vacation destination," I added, because Tris's idea was good.

"Hm, that actually might be something we can do," Kali said, and for the next few minutes we were all lost in thought while munching on the local delicacies.

My friends were done before me. These days the biological mechanism that alerted me I was full was malfunctioning. "Oh my God, you need to tell me to stop," I groaned, and both Kali and Tris laughed. "Seriously," I continued, "if I keep eating like this, I'll end up getting bigger than you, Kali, and you're carrying triplets."

"I don't hear your mates complaining." Her swift comeback had me flushing, and I covered my cheeks with my hands to hide my embarrassment.

Indeed, they were overjoyed with my body's new curves— especially now that I was carrying their offspring. But how could I have known that they'd succeed in impregnating me in our first mating? It hadn't even crossed my mind that, besides a sabertooth, I would be getting twins too.

"When the other women arrive on Saber, we must warn them about the potency of the Saberian sperm," I quipped with a straight face, making them laugh.

"Maybe the slogan should be—oh, no..." Kali's voice shook. "I think my water broke."

I looked beneath her chair at the puddle that had been formed. *Yes, water was definitely broken.* "Time to welcome your babies into the world, Kali. Ready?" I asked with a warm smile on my face at the same time three males stormed into the room and rushed straight to their mate.

They were looking a little green around the edges, and it was time I put my foot down before they stressed Kali out more than necessary.

"Everything is all right," I enunciated slowly. "Kali's water broke. We've discussed what happens next—you're all prepared for this moment." My words seemed to calm them a bit, but I noticed Kali was grinding her teeth.

Contractions were becoming stronger. *Good.*

"Mes, we need to move her to the Healers' Chamber," I added because I didn't know how fast she would progress.

Better be safe than sorry, I thought, because when it came to active labor, things rarely went as planned.

And as it turned out, birthing alien babies was a much faster process than we'd anticipated because by the time the disinfectant mist had settled in the room and Kali was on all fours on top of the pod, the contractions had her screaming.

I, on the other hand, was in my element and a familiar calmness spread over me. I could do this. I'd keep them safe. "From zero to ten, how much is the pain, hon?"

"Ni...ne."

"Okay, keep breathing like we learned. You're doing great," I said and timed her contractions—they were coming fast, every four minutes. "We need to check your cervical dilation, Kali. You might feel a little discomfort."

Another contraction had her in its grips, and she was squeezing the life out of King Arana's hand, but he stoically withstood the pain while reminding her to breathe. King Rorc was massaging her back, the way I'd shown him, to help with the pain. And King Mes—with whom I was on a first-name basis, since we spent a lot of hours in the Healers' Chamber working together—was at Kali's feet, checking the progression.

"She's fully dilated," he reported.

"Good, that means it will all be over soon, let me adjust her stance," I said, but my vision changed before I was ready, and a variety of chemical and physical data along with spatial images of Kali's body flooded my sight. I swayed on the spot —dizzy by the sudden influx of information—and someone grabbed my arm to steady me.

"Are you all right?" Mes asked.

"Yes. My gift took me by sur—" I gasped as I turned and looked at him.

Not only was I seeing the pregnant woman and the babies through my ultrasound vision, but all the males as well.

That had never happened before.

"I need to push," Kali screamed, and willed me into action.

Information kept streaming straight into my brain—her elevated heartbeat was in sync with the contractions, and so was the decreasing heartbeat of the babies. They were ready to come out, and the first one was already crowning.

"Wait...wait...now take a deep breath and slowly release it while you bear down," I instructed, and she did as told.

"I see the head of baby A. You're doing good. Ready to push one more time? On my command, Kali...now take a deep breath, release it slowly...and push." The hairy head of a dark-pink colored baby popped out. "The head is out, honey, I need you to push one more time, and then you can take a break, all right? Ready? Push." And just like that, in between Kali's screams and grunts, the pink girl slipped into my hands.

You could have heard a pin drop before the baby's loud cry filled the silence in the room.

She was a bit swollen, but she was breathing, and all the readings I was getting showed she was healthy.

I placed her in Mes's waiting arms, then clamped and cut the umbilical cord that had stopped pulsing.

He took the infant to her mom. "Look at what we made, my love. She's magnificent, just like you," the Arch-healer whispered reverently.

Happy tears rolled down Kali's cheeks as she gasped, "She's beautiful." But before she had time to hold her baby, another strong contraction hit her.

I placed my hand on top of her belly, reading everything my new sight revealed. The second baby was already positioned in the birth canal. She or he would be coming out soon enough.

Once again I guided her breathing through the process, and after a few hard pushes, a lilac colored baby girl entered our world.

King Rorc's body shook, but his hands were steady as I placed his child in them. Then we waited for the cord to stop pulsing before I clamped and cut it too.

While the new parents rejoiced in their little miracle bundles, my gut was screaming at me to check the third baby.

As I hovered my hands above my friend's swollen tummy, detailed information started flowing to me—the baby was already in the birth canal but not in the right position.

"Kali, the third baby will need a little bit of help to come out," I said and saw her square her shoulders in preparation.

"Arana, I need you to place her on her side and hold her leg high." The King complied instantly, but even with the new position the baby wasn't aligned properly.

"Lay her on her back," I demanded, feeling the need to rush.

He did, but it didn't help, and the baby's heart rate had slowed down dangerously.

"Kali, I have to try to turn him. We don't have much time."

Picking up on the urgency in my tone, she ordered, "Do it now."

I could see the top of the baby's hairy head. Carefully, I caught him, and slowly but steadily in very small increments turned him to the right position. By the end, Kali's head was drooping from exhaustion—the contractions having drained her strength.

"Honey, I need you to push again. Are you ready?"

"I'm tired," she murmured, and at once her mates surrounded her, stroking her face while encouraging her with sweet words.

"I know, sweetheart, but I need you to take a deep breath… release it slowly…and now push."

And the brave mama did.

"Very good, Kali. I see the head. Two more times and it's over…breathe for me…now push."

Her screams reverberated in the room, and soon a silver baby boy slipped into my waiting hands.

But he was not breathing.

Mes handed off the baby he was holding to Arana and placed his hands on the little boy's chest. A blinding light emanated from his hands, and the next instant the baby inhaled sharply, then let out a loud cry.

Tears of happiness trailed down my face, and I let them wash away the fear that had seized my heart.

"Mes, can I check him?" I needed to make sure he was all right.

He exhaled a shaky breath and croaked, "Yes."

Not wasting any time, I placed a hand on top of his head and another on his chest. The influx of data was overwhelming, but I paid attention to every single detail because I had to be certain this little one was all right. I was so lost in the process that the moment little fingers grabbed my wrist I yelped.

I focused on his face and my vision returned to normal. "You are a fierce warrior, aren't you, little one?" I cooed.

Upon hearing the sound of my voice, he turned dark colored eyes on me and made a cute baby sound.

The behavior was unnatural for a newborn, but this child was special.

I just knew it.

"He's perfectly healthy," I informed the Kings, and felt their instant relief, like a wave washing over me. "Time to go to your papa, little warrior." I placed him in Arana's waiting arms, and he gently touched the boy's forehead with his.

Kali was busy breastfeeding, and it was the perfect opportunity to take care of the after birth while the happy family was preoccupied, and endorphins were flooding their systems.

Two hours later, I opened the door of the room I shared with my mates and stepped in. What I saw put a smile on my face.

My warriors were outside on the balcony, talking in hushed tones.

What do you think they're scheming? I asked Rainbow.

I got the impression she was curled in on herself and about to go to sleep when I interrupted her.

Something good I hope...maybe a run through the Serenity Gardens, she mumbled, yawned, and fell asleep in a matter of seconds.

Poor kitty, I laughed. We were both exhausted, but I needed a bed to sleep on.

My males must have heard it because, as one, they turned and marched toward me without another word.

A shiver raced down my spine while I watched their sinuous bodies prowl my way. *Yum...my!*

Their steps faltered, and their growls rumbled in their throats.

I knew how the vibration of that sound felt, and it had an immediate effect on my temperature as I suddenly felt feverish.

"Mate." A single word uttered with such hunger—and at the same time reverence—brought tears to my eyes.

They tore my lab robe off me, and, in tandem, knelt in front of me. I giggled—they were so synchronized, even ballet dancers would be jealous.

Then the thought of them in leotard suits had me laughing so hard, I had to hold my swollen belly.

"Oh, sweet mate, that thought just earned you a punishment," Thora casually mentioned with his deep timbre that caused liquid heat to pool in my core every time, without fail.

My warriors must have picked up the visual from my brain because Urien just tsked and laughed.

Then my fiery man placed his huge palm on my belly, covering most of it. "Hello, little cubs, were you good for momma today?"

Swoon! Both males had the ability to turn me into a puddle of goo at their feet with their sweet words and gestures.

Urien placed a sweet kiss on my belly button and moved aside so Thora could rub his cheek on my tummy before peppering it with butterfly kisses.

When they got to their feet, I shivered at the mischievous shiny glints in their eyes.

"Now, Mate..." Thora drawled as he led me toward the couch, "it's time for your punishment."

Mmm.... Decisions...decisions. Their punishments were always accompanied with more pleasure than I could stand.

Oh well, who needs sleep anyway? Not me!

Thank you for reading my book!

Turn the page for an **excerpt** from **BROKEN WARRIORS**, book 4 in The Pyxis System series.

BROKEN WARRIORS—NO PLACE OR PERSON WAS SAFE

LYRA

Lyra—10 years old

"Lyra," my mom called from downstairs, "we're going to the PCP. You'll wait for us here." She sounded way too excited for someone heading to the doctor, and the click of the door sounded before I had a chance to respond.

My parents didn't seem to be ill, yet it was the fourth time this month they'd leave me alone at home to go to one of their checkup appointments.

"Michael, here...here...pass me the ball!" Jordan's voice reached my ears even though I was up in my room in the attic.

I put on the first things I grabbed from my closet and bounced downstairs. The other kids were playing my favorite game—football. Hopefully, Kyle, who was older and for some reason hated me, wouldn't be with them.

Grabbing the lanyard with my key, I wore it around my

neck and under my tee so I wouldn't lose it, and went out the door.

"Hey! That's not fair. I scored," Johny, the youngest of the bunch, yelled.

Mary, Jack, Erik, and Dwight had formed one team whilst Anne, Michael, and Johny another. Great, they had room for one more person but as soon as they saw me running toward them, they stopped talking and started whispering.

The gentle but constant buzzing in my head became louder, but I ignored it this time. I wasn't in danger because there were many people around. While growing up, I'd thought everyone had an internal warning system like mine in their heads, but when I told my friends at school, they started calling me names and making fun of me. I never spoke about it again. "Hi, guys!"

One of the girls whispered something that sounded like 'slug-slimed freak alert,' and the boys snickered.

Slowing down, I furrowed my brows. Anne must have been talking about something else. She was my friend. "Can I play too? That way we'll form two teams of four."

Someone knocked me from behind, and I almost face-planted. "We don't need another player, sack-of-rat-guts-in-cat-vomit," Kyle said, and my heart sank. "Are you going to cry, fartknocker?" he asked and threw the ball at me, hitting me on the head.

I lost my balance and landed on my butt, scraping my hands while trying to break the fall. "Ow." Momentarily, the buzzing in my head drowned out all other noises, and I lifted my palm to rub the sore spot. Instead of making it better, the sting made my eyes water, but I wouldn't let them see me cry.

Defeated and hurt, I got up and turned around to leave, a loud thud, though, made me look over my shoulder.

Surprisingly, someone had tackled Kyle to the ground. He wasn't one of my friends—they stood frozen on the sidewalk as the new boy started hitting my bully. He and his family must have been the neighbors who had just moved in next door.

So many emotions filled me and I didn't know what to do with them.

"Stop," I said, and the boy turned my way while managing to keep a now weeping Kyle still.

His stormy eyes widened as they fell on me, and my cheeks burned with embarrassment, but I had to warn him nonetheless. "You'll get in trouble, and I'm not worth it."

Without waiting to see what he'd do, I fled to my house, smiling the entire way because Kyle was wailing and calling out for his momma.

The rest of the day, I stayed in my room, looking out the window, hoping to see the boy again. It was three o'clock when he went outside to their backyard, holding a small box in his hands. He reverently put it down, then dug a hole.

"What are you doing?" I whispered while I curiously kept watching.

He grabbed two stick-like things and raised them to his eye level. They wiggled suspended from between his fingers, before he lowered them into the box.

He's feeding a birdie! I clapped inwardly with joy. Birds were my favorite animals, and I wished to be like them; they could take to the air and escape. Someday, once I grew up, I would join them in the sky, and...maybe the boy would come with me.

Our front door opened, and shut, then a woman's voice— more lucid than I was used to hearing it after their return from the doctors—slipped through the cracks of my bedroom's door.

"Last week, new people moved in next door, Michael. Maybe we should pay them a visit...to welcome them of course." My mother's laughter covered my father's response, if ever there was one.

My parent's social call would not be a good thing for the new neighbors because they liked to collect things...other people's things.

"I'll bake them a pie," mom said, and my dad added, "we shall go drop it off this evening."

I raced down the stairs, and into our kitchen. I needed to stop them. "You can't go to their house."

"And why not?" my mother sneered.

Suddenly, my throat felt too tight, but I pushed the words out. "Their son was good to me, not like the other children who bully me. I don't want them to go." My voice got lower and lower with each extra word uttered.

They both laughed at me. "Of course the other children bully you. Look at you, whining about everything." Her words hurt more than the worst injury I'd gotten that had needed stitches.

I wouldn't give up, though. "I'll tell on you, so they know not to open the door!" I yelled, angry at both of them.

The sound reached my ears a second before my cheek felt like it was on fire, and I stumbled backward afraid my father wouldn't stop there. Tears wet my fingers as I cradled the side of my face. The pain throbbing along with my heartbeat.

"You will do no such thing, ungrateful little wench. This is how we put food to the table. Maybe it's time you started paying for the things we give you," he bellowed, stunning me with the vehemence in his voice.

"Dad—" My mom interrupted me by pinching my arm hard while pushing me out of the kitchen.

"Go to your room! Nobody wants to hear your ugly cries," she told me, then turned to my father and said, "How on Earth did we end up with a daughter like her? I swear they gave us the wrong child at the hospital."

"Family are those we choose, Judy, not those who carry our blood."

I couldn't take any more of their words. They were even worse than their actions, and they verified that once again I wasn't good enough. Once in my room, I threw myself on my bed and cried until I had no more tears.

Fear of what would happen if my parents found out kept my feet locked in place, but my conscience gnawed at me. I ought to tell them.

The neighbors had done nothing wrong. They seemed to be good people, and I wanted them to stay. Their son was nothing like the other boys. He was nice, my heart insisted, and I had to warn him. He would know what to do because he protected others...although, after I told him about my parents, he wouldn't want to be my friend.

Well, that was okay. Miss Kayleen at school said we should always speak up about acts that were wrong even if it was uncomfortable to do so.

By the time the sun went down, and the stars started twinkling in the sky, I'd made up my mind. Arranging the pillows on my bed to appear like I was sleeping—not that my parents would come to check on me, they never did—I climbed out the window.

The attic of our house was my room. When I was little, my daddy had told me I was his princess and that was why I had the best room in our castle. It was one of my favorite memories, but it'd been a while since he'd spoken to me with warmth in his voice.

I carefully walked across the porch's roof, knowing by now where the creaky parts were and avoiding all of them. The jump off the lowest part of the roof was still a long way down, and I needed to focus on what I was about to do. Taking the leap was the easy part, landing unscathed on the other hand was tricky, but I'd been practicing.

Taking a deep breath, then slowly letting it go, I jumped— eyes open wide. For just a moment I was weightless, flying, and then I landed on my feet, without breaking anything. This time I didn't even feel the jarring in my bones. I was getting good at this. A giggle escaped my lips, and I slapped a hand on my mouth. Standing still—barely breathing—I listened out for sounds from inside the house.

My heart beat fast. *Should I climb back up? If my parents find out I'm gone...* I couldn't even finish that thought, but when no one stirred, I ran stealthily across our yard, making sure to remain hidden in the shadows.

A fence divided our yards, and I leaped over it like a cat before stopping in my tracks.

Do I knock the front door or climb up the wooden strips attached to the side wall? Our houses were exactly the same on the outside, and his room's window was the one above their porch's roof.

I chose the latter. Finding the footholes was easy, and in no time I was knocking on his window. It was shut but the curtain was drawn to the side, and I could see him, sitting at his desk doing something.

The knock didn't startle him; instead, he slowly turned around, then approached me and lifted the pane.

He had the most striking eyes I'd ever seen. They reminded me of the lively color of a clear blue sky.

"Hi," I awkwardly greeted him—the absence of noise in my head, momentarily distracting me from saying anything else. It was never quiet in my world. The buzzing that always warned me when danger was near was quiet. That was how I knew for certain he was a good boy, worthy of my trust.

He smiled, and butterflies took flight right where my heart was, but then furrowed his brows, before wrapping his arms underneath mine, and pulling me inside his room.

Was he was afraid I would fall?

"Don't worry, I'm good at climbing and jumping off the roof." I wanted to reassure him because he hadn't let go yet.

Looking around at his room, I noticed his desk was empty. I wanted to ask him what he'd been doing there, but that wasn't important. My reason for coming over, though, was. "Thank you," I blurted out.

Clouds obscured his eyes as he looked at me, puzzled.

"For earlier with the boys. They were mean to me, but they are my only friends," I stuttered. My chest felt tight, and my tummy felt funny, but my mind was quiet, and it was all because of him.

"They aren't your friends." Anger made him drawl the words out. "I'll be your friend and I'll never be mean to you," he vowed and hugged me tight.

My arms, that had been hanging awkwardly at my sides, wrapped around him. He felt warm and safe. Hopefully, he wouldn't hate me after I told him about my parents. "Do you promise?" I whispered because if he did, then he couldn't take it back.

"Yes." There was no hesitation, and I breathed a little easier.

We let go at the same time and sat across from each other on his bed.

I had to tell him now, quickly, like removing a band-aid so one would only feel pain for a little bit. "I came here to warn you—" But suddenly, I couldn't utter another word.

Even though the boy tensed, he didn't push me. Instead, he folded his hands on his lap and waited patiently.

My eyes followed the movement, and I was able to build my courage. It was easier to talk when not looking at his face, so that was how I confessed. "My parents are going to visit yours. They are bad. They will take things from them and then drive your family out of this house, but you're my new friend and I don't want you to go."

His breath whooshed out of him, and his body shagged. "My parents are bad too," he whispered.

My eyes rounded in surprise, then met his. This time the blue sky was stormy, and I understood—his life was like mine.

302

I threw myself at him—knocking him backward on the bed—and hugged him tight. "I'm sorry."

He pressed his face between my shoulder and neck and shivered.

"My name is Lyra." My voice trembled, and he disentangled himself so we could look at each other while we talked.

"Mine is Hunter. Not every one is bad, you're safe with me." This was his second promise to me, but I didn't want to make him sad by telling him that I was big enough to know no place or person was safe, the same way I knew that Santa wasn't real.

BROKEN WARRIORS—MY GIRL
HUNTER

Hunter—11 years old

"Please, Jack," my mom cried out and grunted in pain, but then silence followed and it was more terrifying than anything else.

No, no. We had moved to this place for a new start; he'd promised he'd change.

I took two steps at a time going down the stairs, nearly tripping over my feet when I stopped abruptly because she was sprawled on the floor, unmoving.

Dark shadowy wisps reached for her defenseless form causing cold chills to race across my skin. "Mom—" I did not get the chance to say anything else because the monster, who I called dad, turned his blood-shot eyes toward me.

Dread, the kind only he could induce, exploded inside me, causing my body to shake.

His lips lifted in a lecherous, sardonic smile, and he pulled his foot back, getting ready to deliver another kick to his own wife.

Get up...get up, I prayed but she didn't even blink. Her chest barely rose and fell.

Terrified, but determined to protect her anyway I could, I threw myself on my father, managing to knock him off her. The action, though, drew his attention on me, and that was never a good thing.

It might have been a couple of minutes, or a few hours, but as I lay on the floor, the monster's fists still raining down on me, I stopped feeling—my body no longer my own but a rag doll in the hands of the person whose mirror image I was.

I could no longer see my mother's still form, just the dust particles rising in the air, then falling all around me, before darkness pulled me under, and I knew no more.

Intense, unbearable pain racked my body as someone shook me. Electricity zinged through my aching muscles at the same time pins and needles dug into my vulnerable flesh, making me cry out.

"Thank God, you're alive! I thought I lost you," my mother cried out while hugging the life out of me.

I wanted to be strong for her, but couldn't stop the tears and the groans that escaped. Then I noticed her black eye and busted lips. "Momma, nana taught me that boys mustn't hit girls, and I'll never hit you...please, let's run away together," I begged hoping that this time the answer would be different.

She pressed her face into the nook of my neck, and I felt

her body tremble. "Nana taught you well, but it was my fault this time, Hunter. Papa loves me very much, and it hurts him when he has to discipline me."

My heart sank inside my chest. Every time it was my mom's fault; she was too friendly with Mr. Harrison, our old neighbor; she smiled too much at the grocery store and the other men would find her too provocative; she didn't cook our food to his liking; there was always a reason.

"You shouldn't have interfered, sweetheart…please, never get in the middle again." A sob burst out of her. "Sometimes, he can't control his strength, and now look at you—" Another sob stole her words, but she swallowed it. "Do you still have nana's medicines?"

My grandma was a Healer, and before she died she taught me as much as I could understand because she insisted I had the gift too. The old suitcase with all the herbs, poultices, and roots that had been passed down to me was my most prized treasure.

"Yes," I replied and braced for the pain that would come when I tried to get up.

With her help, I limped up the stairs to my room and managed to reach my bed. At the last moment, my legs gave up and I fell on the soft mattress.

"I don't want you taking medicine on an empty stomach. I'll bring you some food first," she said and draped a blanket over me.

The cocoon of warmth pulled me under fast, and I wasn't strong enough to resist sleep from claiming me.

For five days, I did little else but slumber. My body needed the rest to recover, and my mom made sure I ate broth and soup, so it had the necessary fuel to speed up the healing process. But on the sixth, the pain had disappeared, so I got up, dressed and was out of my room in no time.

I hesitated on top of the stairs, but the house was overly quiet so I felt safe to descent. A loud growl echoed around me, and I clutched my aching belly. Finding something to devour was a priority, but my father didn't allow us to eat unless we were all siting together at the table.

Maybe if I grabbed something for the back, he wouldn't notice before I told my mom and she replaced it. In the second cupboard behind the dry foods I noticed a single can. I pulled it out but could not tell if it contained meat or fish inside.

I had no choice but eat it because I wanted to get strong enough to defend my mother and stop my dad from hurting us. Sighing I pulled the metal lid backward and practically inhaled the disgusting contents of the can, then gulped two glasses of water to wash down the aftertaste.

The combo did the job in quieting my stomach, and I pushed the evidence of my disobedience to the bottom of the trashcan, wondering what I should do next.

Noise from outside startled me, but it was children's voices, happy voices. Looking out the window and I saw them playing football on the street. We'd already been here for a week but I hadn't met any of them yet.

Well now is a great time.

I put on my shoes as fast as I could and went outside.

Something moving high on my periphery drew my attention. The girl next door was walking on the roof slowly.

My heart beat faster in my chest. A fall could take her life.

I wanted to call out to her, to be careful, but it was like watching an agile cat. Not wanting to frighten her, I remained silent.

She stopped near the edge.

There wasn't a ladder nor a tree nearby that she could climb down from. *How will she get down?* I wondered when she answered my question by jumping.

Oh my God! I ran toward her when a giggle full of delight stopped me short. I expected to see her sprawled on the ground, but she was glowing as she started toward the other children oblivious to my presence. For reasons unknown to me, something about her held my attention and did not let go while I followed at a distance.

I was so focused on her that I missed what the other were doing until a boy knocked her on the ground, then said, "Are you going to cry, fartknocker?" Before he threw the ball he was holding at her.

My reaction was instinctual. Anger bubble exploded inside me, and I released it on the boy. Like my father, he didn't know that we should treat others with respect.

The girl said something, but I couldn't hear it over the boy's cries. Then the other kids run to their houses calling their parents.

Not wanting to get in trouble with my father so soon again, I raced back home, looking for her on the way but she was nowhere to be found.

Disappointment filled me because I didn't get to speak to her, to make sure she was all right and to tell her, what those boys had said didn't matter because they didn't know better. But as I stepped into the safety of our house, a horrific realization hit me. I had become my father. I had used my fists to beat someone. Guilt nearly drowned me, discovering I was just like him.

The front door opened but I stood frozen in the middle of the hallway leading to the entryway.

"Hunter?" my mom asked. "What is it, sweetheart?" Her voice was always gentle. Her touch was always loving, and I recoiled when she lifted her palm to my cheek.

Chin trembling, I blurted my shame, "I'm just like him." The words wobbly and barely audible but somehow my momma knew who I was talking about and she enveloped me in her arms.

"You maybe your father's son, but you'll never be like him." Her vehement tone making me pay attention. "You're a Healer, like your grandma. You're incapable of hurting others."

Wrong. She was so wrong, and she'd never forgive me, but I had to tell her. "I hit a boy earlier...with my fists—" I couldn't keep talking.

I expected to see disgust on her face, instead her eyes softened, and she tightened her embrace.

"Did you hit him for no reason?" she asked and ran her fingers through my hair.

"No. He threw a girl to the ground then hit her with a ball..." my voice trailed off trying to understand where my mother was going with this.

She smiled; her eyes lighting up. "Then you did good. You protected her with the means that you had." She kissed my forehead. "You look like him, my handsome boy, but you'll never be him. Let's go make dinner," she finished and I could breathe again.

Much later, once it was dark out, and the house quieted, I sat at my desk to count the bills I had hidden in my shoe box. Fifty seven bucks—not enough to buy to tickets out of here for me and my mom. Maybe I could help the neighbors with their chores for money. Summer was less than a month away, and I could help with the grass cutting—

A knock interrupted my thoughts. Blocking the view with my body, I slid the shoe box behind my bed and turned to look at who it was.

Hiding my surprise, and tried to act cool. Her almond-shaped eyes looked solemnly at me, watching my every move, as if waiting to be ignored or something. Silly girl, I couldn't pretend she wasn't there...I didn't want to.

"Hi," she stuttered the moment I lifted the sash but didn't try to get in.

I swore this girl loved heights and had no sense of danger. What if she slipped? She'd hurt herself. I wrapped my arms around her torso and pulled her in. She didn't resist.

Instead, as if reading my mind, she said, "Don't worry, I'm good at climbing and jumping off the roof." Despite her reassuring words, I couldn't shake the fear that gripped me, and when I didn't let go, she added, "Thank you."

I furrowed my brows in confusion and was about to ask her why, when she beat me to it.

"For earlier with the boys. They were mean to me, but they are my only friends." Her soft voice was what I imagined an angel would sound like.

The need to protect her rose to the surface along with the

anger I'd felt earlier. "They aren't your friends." I snapped at her, then gentled my voice because that boy's behavior wasn't her fault. "I'll be your friend and I'll never be mean to you," I promised and hugged her tighter because she seemed so lost. When her arms wrapped around my back, my heart fluttered in my chest.

She twisted my t-shirt in her fists, and murmured, "Do you promise?"

"Yes," I replied, knowing already that we would become best of friends.

I couldn't keep her in my arms forever, so I let go and we sat on my bed. She rubbed her palms down her pants legs, then scratched her cheek but flinched and pulled her hand away. Something was bothering her, and I waited patiently for her to tell me as I scanned her face. One side of it was light pink, the other light ivory; and on her right arm, the black outline of a bruise was peeking underneath her sleeve. XX

"I came here to warn you—" She started then stopped abruptly, and I held my breath. "My parents are going to visit yours. They are bad. They will take things from them and then drive your family out of this house, but you're my new friend and I don't want you to go," she confessed, and I exhaled the air I'd been holding in a rush.

Suddenly, I didn't feel alone anymore. And even though fear of being heard kept my tone low, I looked straight into her hazel eyes, so she knew I wasn't lying, when I admitted, "My parents are bad too."

Her reaction caught me by surprise, and I buckled under her weight. We fell backward but she didn't seem to mind.

"I'm sorry," she said and once again hugged me tight.

Three simple words...that meant the world to me. I was sorry, too—for both of us.

"My name is Lyra," she said shyly as she got off me, but something in her voice changed; the tremble betrayed her true emotions of vulnerability, maybe even fear.

Exposed was the last thing I wanted her to feel, so I decided to give her something of myself. "Mine is Hunter. Not every one is bad, you're safe with me."

Ly, it seemed was one of these people who showed everything they felt. I saw the denial of the truth I had shared with her coming, so I took a leap of faith and opened up some more to her.

"I have a secret, only two people know, my mom, and my nana who was like me. I have the gift of healing, and when I get older I'll become a doctor and save as many people as I can."

Both of her cheeks turned a bright pink, and she raised her hand to cover the injured size. She shouldn't be embarrassed, though.

"Does it hurt?" I asked and held my breath. Would she trust me like I did her?

She nodded her assent, but remained silent.

"Can I make it better?"

Another nod.

I pulled out my most treasured possession from under my bed. Reverently, I opened the lid of the small suitcase. It was filled to the brim with notebooks and little tins and bottles with labels, so it wasn't hard to find the ointment that promoted the healing of skin injuries, and would make her bruises disappear in a couple of days.

If I was to protect my girl as well as my momma, I needed to train to become a better Healer sooner rather than later.

If you enjoyed this excerpt from BROKEN WARRIORS, ask for a copy at your favorite bookstore.

GLOSSARY

Astronomical Unit (AU): AU is the distance between Earth and the sun.

Circle: A full circle is the Saberian day and is equivalent to twenty-eight hours.

Cycle: A full cycle is the Saberian month and is equivalent to thirty-eight circles.

Monakrivimou: My precious, my one and only.

Pallium: A rectangular length of cloth, worn around the waist and over one shoulder. The Saberians used it as a cloak.

Pneuma: Soul.

Psehimou: My soul.

Rotation: A full rotation is the Saberian year and is equivalent to eighteen cycles.

Spires: equivalent to one hour.

Stridulate: to produce a shrill, grating sound, as a cricket does, by rubbing together certain parts of the body; shrill.

Tempestuous: tumultuous, turbulent.

Tick: second, moment.

ABOUT THE AUTHOR

Aurora Welkin is a sci-fi and paranormal romance author. She lives in Sydney, Australia. She enjoys reading a little too much, and her loved ones usually find her with her nose in a book. In her free time, you'll find her strolling along the beach with her husband, savoring a cup of cocoa and watching their little prince explore the world.

www.aurorawelkin.com

Aurora loves to hear from readers! The best way to connect with her online is via her newsletter. You can sign up here:
www.aurorawelkin.com/mailing-list